THE ROUGH CUT

Also by Douglas Corleone

The Kevin Corvelli mysteries

ONE MAN'S PARADISE
NIGHT ON FIRE
LAST LAWYER STANDING

The Simon Fisk thrillers

GOOD AS GONE
PAYOFF
GONE COLD
BEYOND GONE *

Novels

ROBERT LUDLUM'S THE JANSON EQUATION

* *available from Severn House*

THE ROUGH CUT

Douglas Corleone

severn House

This first world edition published 2020
in Great Britain and 2021 in the USA by
SEVERN HOUSE PUBLISHERS LTD of
Eardley House, 4 Uxbridge Street, London W8 7SY.
Trade paperback edition first published
in Great Britain and the USA 2021 by
SEVERN HOUSE PUBLISHERS LTD.

British Library Cataloguing in Publication Data
A CIP catalogue record for this title is available from the British Library.

ISBN-13: 978-0-7278-8986-7 (cased)
ISBN-13: 978-1-78029-726-2 (trade paper)
ISBN-13: 978-1-4483-0447-9 (e-book)

All Severn House titles are printed on acid-free paper.

Severn House Publishers support the Forest Stewardship Council™ [FSC™],
the leading international forest certification organisation.
All our titles that are printed on FSC certified paper carry the FSC logo.

MIX
Paper from
responsible sources
FSC
www.fsc.org   FSC® C013056

Typeset by Palimpsest Book Production Ltd.,
Falkirk, Stirlingshire, Scotland.
Printed and bound in Great Britain by
TJ Books Limited, Padstow, Cornwall.

'What the hell did I do? Killed them all, of course.'

Robert Durst, *The Jinx* (2015)

PART I
Viewer Discretion

ONE

I like to watch. Always have. Some of my fondest childhood memories are of sinking into my grandmother's paisley sofa, eyes glued to her thirty-inch Magnavox as witness after witness delineated in excruciating detail the collection, handling and testing of blood evidence in the O.J. trial. Nah, I didn't know what the hell was happening onscreen, just knew the event was momentous, that it had millions of ordinary people riveted to their television sets midday, that a malleable concept called American Justice hung on the outcome.

Frozen, unwilling to risk the sound of repositioning myself on the plastic covering the couch, I viewed the verdict through a haze of my grandmother's cigarette smoke and whooped for joy at the words 'not guilty'. My grandmother huffed, pushed herself off the sofa and stomped out of the room. Remained angry with me for days.

What I didn't know then but know now is that I was on the wrong side of the issue. Not only because the evidence against the Juice was overwhelming, but because of the color of my skin. Because my grandmother and the dozens of talking heads on Court TV told me so.

Twenty-some years later I'm sitting in a hot, cramped editing room on South King Street in downtown Honolulu, logging hundreds of hours of footage from a two-week homicide trial – an enthralling face-off between two of the world's preeminent criminal lawyers – that I recently observed live and in person.

It's a few minutes after midnight and I've been here since four in the morning. My dual role as director and editor of my first full-length film requires me to perform this tedious task, and the partner I chose in both love and labor requires I do it alone. Brody is back at our flat on Tusitala Street in Waikiki, probably smoking a joint and binge-watching the sixth season of *Game of Thrones* without me. He calls it work, says he's studying the visuals, internalizing dialogue, dissecting storylines. Never mind that we're making a true crime documentary, not an epic fantasy with witches and dragons and swordfights.

But then Brody Quinlan has never been a paragon of ambition. Not when we initially stumbled across each other at NYU film school, not when we first moved in together, and certainly not since we moved to Oahu. Brody is chill and phlegmatic, the perfect transplant for Hawaii. Striking to look at, with an underlying intensity, not unlike the islands themselves.

Still, in the six months since the murder he's shown somewhat more initiative: scouting locations, lugging equipment, capturing on camera as much of the unfolding drama as he could. To say I couldn't have taken on this project without Brody would be a drastic understatement, yet I can't help but be irked by his utter lack of interest and participation in the postproduction process. Because every first-year film student knows that post is the period when mere footage actually becomes a film.

Of course, looking at and logging footage sucks. Not only do you learn for the first time that the flawless film you envisaged isn't the one that was actually shot, but that the visual evidence you accumulated over months doesn't necessarily translate into the visual arguments you want to make. But you can't reshoot a unique event, especially one as extraordinary as a murder trial. And you certainly can't alter the ending. You can twist it and shape it, even spin it to some extent, but in the end you have to live with the result and its consequences just like everyone else. As in every other facet of life, you have zero control over the past – and it aches.

As I jot down the time code for the start of the prosecution's opening statement, my eyes fall on the untouched container of chicken and broccoli from Lung Fung. Back at NYU, Professor Leary and I used to sit around the table in the editing room eating Chinese takeout and discussing the types of films I aspired to make. While so many of his other students were intent on saving the world by taking on such weighty subjects as guns and global warming, I never shied away from the fact that my true passion was tabloid justice: sensationalist coverage of criminal cases, with a glaring spotlight on the human drama. Titillating an audience, not by expounding on minutia like the penal code and rules of evidence, but by turning the camera on the players themselves, lifting the veil from their private lives, disseminating their deepest and darkest secrets, laying bare their hidden passions and fears. In other words, telling a story. The bloodier, the sexier, the better.

Professor Leary didn't necessarily encourage this route, of course, but he said I had an eye, that if I applied my talent I could be one of those precious few documentarians who make a living doing what they love. He even offered to mentor me after graduation. Only he died in his sleep less than three months before I bounded up the stage to accept my degree. Incredibly, in his Last Will and Testament, Professor Leary bequeathed to me a sum large enough to fund my first full-length documentary and then some. Having tossed the notion around for nearly a year, Brody and I finally decided to live in the islands until the perfect crime came along.

Of course, never in my wildest dreams did I think the perfect crime would occur on Oahu; never in my most unnerving nightmares did I believe that an act this savage, this callous, this tragic could transpire right here in paradise.

Let alone to someone I knew.

TWO

A ll good films open with an image, Professor Leary told me repeatedly. Following the initial fade, you have four or five minutes, tops, to seize your viewers' interest, so there's no time for fucking around with bland exposition or protracted dialogue. Open with an image, a visual that establishes a sense of place, of mood, of texture, a snapshot your audience has never seen before, something unexpected, something unsettling.

Start with the crime scene.

On the night the weathergirl died I'd forgotten to wear deodorant. Only registered that trivial fact when the dude drooping next to me at the bar commenced asking questions about my tattoos. I elevated my arm to give him an optimal view and was thumped in the face by a blend of Dove soap and body odor; that pungent and distinctive funk that only seems to accompany nights you're sporting your sexiest tank-top. Not sure whether he noticed, but then I cracked wise about it, prompting him to abruptly lift my left arm and deposit his nose in the center of my pit. Already four rum drinks in, I was still trying to calculate the appropriate level of outrage to display when my iPhone began buzzing in my back pocket.

I excused myself and took the call outside.

'Where are you?' Brody said, with an assertiveness that was rare for him.

'Just down the street. Da Big Kahuna on Kuhio. Why don't you come down for a drink?'

'I'm in the Jeep.' There was an urgency in his voice. 'On my way up the mountain.'

'Tantalus? What the shit for?'

'Remember that police scanner I supposedly *wasted* our money on?'

'*My* money on.'

'Either way, the investment just paid off. Big time.'

'How so?'

His tone softened. 'Riley, it's Piper.'

I only knew one Piper on the island. 'Piper Kingsley? What about her?'

Eight, nine, maybe ten seconds passed in silence.

Then: 'She's dead.'

As those two words sunk heavily in my chest, the pit-sniffer from the bar came up behind me, reached under my arms and, with his ten tiny digits, attempted something akin to tickling. Reflexively whirling around, I drove my left elbow straight into his mug, striking him square in the very pug nose that had violated my armpit a few minutes earlier.

'Jethus,' he cried nasally.

Blood streamed freely from both his nostrils. There was blood, too, on my arm.

'You bwoke my fucking noth.'

Instinctively, I parted my lips to apologize, but stopped myself before making a sound. Footage of a young prosecutor named

Nicholas Church rolled in my mind, his voice like an echo as he confronted one of the defense's most critical witnesses on the stand: 'Yet you apologized, didn't you? You said you were sorry? Why would you apologize if, in your mind, you had done nothing wrong?'

A Japanese family stood gawking fifty feet away, so I pointed at the pit-sniffer, hollered to them, 'Self-defense. This man just attempted to sexually assault me.'

Four of the five family members nodded their heads. Good enough; at the very least a hung jury. But then, the pit-sniffer was twice the size of me. No one with eyes would ever convict me of battery.

Doubled over, the pit-sniffer staggered back toward the bar, muttering, 'Thomeone call the poleeth.'

I swiftly turned and started up the street. Held the phone up to my ear.

'You there?' I said. 'What are they calling it?'

'Probable homicide. You remember where Piper lives?'

'It's been a few years, but yeah, I can find it.'

'Hire an Uber. I'll meet you there.'

I first spotted the flashing red and blue lights careening up the mountain from the backseat of a Hyundai Elantra at a stoplight on Ala Wai Boulevard.

'Blow the light,' I told the driver.

He was an older man, mid-sixties I'd have guessed. Bald, with a beard, a beer belly, and an open aloha shirt I recognized from Target.

'You kidding me?' he said in a gruff smoker's voice. 'Not for the dough I make.'

'This light takes forever.'

'Sorry, I'm not risking a ticket.'

I reached into my pocket and offered him a crumpled hundred.

'*And* I'll pay the ticket,' I said.

His eyes fixed on mine in the rearview. 'I would, sweetheart, but I don't want to risk a DUI.'

My buzzing brain must have screwed up my facial muscles in a way that looked to him like I was about to explode.

'I'm *kidding*,' he said, and turned and took the hundred from my hand. Barely scanning a single direction, he then accelerated through the intersection, almost causing a three-car collision.

As we climbed the mountain in the jackass's burgundy coupe, the pressure in my eardrums built to the point I feared they would burst. I pinched my nose and swallowed hard, stretched my jaw in a yawn to no avail.

Drunk and flushed, I pressed my cheek against the chilled window. Watched the psychedelic tropical flowers and greener-than-green hanging vines go by for miles.

Though jolted and jostled from hanging one sharp left turn after another, I couldn't help but think that Tantalus Drive would make a phenomenal setting for my film. Just picture it: the road a ten-mile squiggle through an enchanted jungle that always appears on the verge of coming alive.

The first time I rode up Mount Tantalus was roughly four years earlier, a month after my parents died in a freak kayaking accident back home, off the Oregon coast. I'd been just a couple of years out of college, a couple of years into my career as a lackey for Big Pharma: a sales rep who held her nose and toed the company line, dispensing disinformation about little things like cost, the severity of side effects, and whether the drug actually worked.

I spent my days carting samples around Portland because as any good pharmaceutical sales rep will tell you: samples help doctors decide how well their patients might do on a particular drug; samples provide time cushions for patients to get to their pharmacy; samples make patients more eager to see their physicians because, hey, free drugs.

Of course, we only left samples of the newest, priciest medications. A supply just robust enough to get a promising number of the physician's patients onto the drug. But the drugs were really only half the product I placed on display day to day. The other half consisted of what little cleavage I owned and a generous length of my legs. Not to say there weren't benefits to playing cat and mouse with physicians; there were gifts, there were dates, even all-expenses-paid vacations. Not to mention signed blank prescription slips on demand. I suppose the real downside to the game was that in the two years I hawked pharmaceuticals, I flirted with so many doctors I forgot which ones I genuinely liked.

Ironically, it was my dad who'd pushed me into that job, said I had to get off my ass and find work. Hell, I'd already graduated from college with a bachelor's degree in finance two and a half weeks earlier. What was I sitting around for?

So I got off my ass and found a job, tossing away, at least temporarily, my dreams of becoming a filmmaker. It wasn't the first time my father had taken charge of my life because I 'didn't know how to live'.

At nine, I abandoned art for volleyball. At fourteen, gave up boys for church. At seventeen, I chose Oregon State because, hey, in-state tuition rates, never mind that we could afford UCLA. And, of course, once I got to college, my major was chosen for me because 'the arts are for hippies and hobbyists, but there's a real *future* in finance'.

For twenty-one years I wore what Daddy wanted me to wear, maintained my hair at a length and in a style that was 'ladylike'. I kept the right friends, I drove the right car, I supported the right political candidates. I watched the right shows, read the right books, spent just the right amount of time on the phone.

Sad thing is, it wasn't just me Dad kept under his thumb. It was Mom, too. We ate what he wanted to eat when he wanted to eat it, slept when he wanted to sleep, lived where he wanted to live. My mom simply stood no chance against my dad's despotic personality.

And yeah, sure, sometimes in the dead of night, as I lay naked between the sheets next to Brody, I worry. Because there is simply no more use in ignoring the fact that I am more like Dad than I am Mom.

A couple of weeks after my parents died, I chopped off my hair and launched a mission to ink every last inch of me. Pierced parts of my anatomy my mother never so much as muttered aloud. I wasn't lashing out at life or anything. And I was by no means happy that my parents had perished. I missed them desperately; particularly Mom, I miss her still. But after their deaths, for the first time I felt completely free to be myself, not just because my father had always wanted me to be someone else – the perfect student, the toughest athlete, the most girlish girl

– but because it was only once my parents died *upside down in a fucking kayak* (on their thirtieth anniversary, no less) that I recognized life was absurd.

Mom and Dad didn't leave behind much in the way of money, but it was enough for me to quit hawking hard-on pills and move to New York to earn my MFA in filmmaking. But first, two weeks in Hawaii, where this girl, who was more than an acquaintance but less than a friend, invited me to stay at her house on Tantalus.

Physically, Piper Kingsley and I were polar opposites (as in: her body was perfect), but we'd met in New York while she was auditioning for *Good Day!* and clicked right on the spot. Had one of those nights you can't really remember yet that's why you'll remember it from the nursing home. You just *know* you had a good time.

Piper flew back home to Oahu the next afternoon but we'd friended each other on Facebook, which, for better or worse, can instantly transform a total stranger into an omnipresence in your life. We 'liked' each other's pictures and posts, even commented. And not just when we felt obligated due to a newborn or death.

Piper and I genuinely *liked* each other, I think. So when I remarked one day on the eye-catching tide pools in the background of her latest profile pic, she told me I needed to fly out there. I replied *that'd be awesome*, the way you respond to casual invitations doled out over social media. Later, though, she made clear in a private message that she'd been serious. She'd moved to the States from Australia right after college and, though she got on well with her colleagues, had no real friends in the islands.

Although spontaneously taking a 5,000-mile flight was antithetical to the parented me, since I'd budgeted some of my modest inheritance for travel anyway, off the newly orphaned Riley Vasher went.

I'd had a blast – not just beaching, clubbing and drinking, but conversing – and promised to come back. Then life happened. Studies and boyfriends, Brody and Professor Leary, all competed valiantly for my time. And with a camera or screen constantly in front of me, I quickly lost interest in what 500 'friends' I barely knew were eating for dinner each night. I fell off Facebook entirely, and somewhat sadly, it was as though 495 people suddenly dropped from my life, Piper being one of them. Because who the hell phones or even emails anyone anymore, right? What are we anyway, a bunch of troglodytes?

I'd planned on calling Piper when Brody and I moved to Oahu, of course. I just kept putting it off; there was simply never a good time. And I didn't desperately miss Piper, because she had once again become a substantial part of my life through the magic of television. I saw her on the local news every evening at six – cracking corny jokes, guessing at the weather, predicting the size of the surf up North Shore – and I simply assumed, as we always do before someone dies suddenly, that we both had plenty of time.

When we neared the top of Tantalus the road was cordoned off. Uniformed cops staged a perimeter around your quintessential crime scene. The uniforms were security, there to safeguard the crime scene investigators, who were adorned in baggy white paper suits, nitrile gloves and industrial respirators, but typically wore no bulletproof vests, and carried no guns or Tasers.

The forensics team were scampering around like hell, suggesting an outdoor crime scene susceptible to the elements. Up here at nearly 20,000 feet, a cold, hard rain could materialize at any moment and damage delicate forensic evidence. Already, arbitrary drops had been dotting our windshield all the way up the mountain.

I said *sayonara* to the driver, stepped out of the Elantra, and immediately breathed in the scent of wild ginger, guava and mango, maybe fresh eucalyptus. With just a twinge of guilt, I studied the lush scenery as a potential backdrop for my film. Visitors to Hawaii don't necessarily come for the rain, but some of the wettest areas of these islands are, indisputably, also the most breathtaking.

I plucked my iPhone from my back pocket and started toward the yellow tape, but before I could tap the camera icon I received a text message from Brody:

WALK DOWN MTN TO NEXT HOUSE, X INTO BACKYARD.

I gazed down the road. Residents here valued their privacy, and paid well for it. Rarely could you see your neighbor's house from your own, and Piper's was no exception.

I texted Brody that I was on my way but first paused, waded

through a thin crowd of onlookers, and snapped a few pictures. The best of them were shots of the lead detective, Lance Fukumoto – an elegant septuagenarian who vehemently refused to retire – as he greeted the first responders then entered the house.

Seconds later I snaked my way back through the growing throng and started down the mountain. Walked a little over half a mile to the neighboring two-story which, surprisingly, remained dark. I entered the property through an unlocked iron gate and proceeded past the garden to the rear of the house.

Slinking through the backyard like the world's worst cat burglar, I set off a sensor and suddenly found myself trapped in a glaring shaft of light. For a moment, I froze. Then, finally, I snapped out of it and darted toward the rocks. There, I eventually found Brody waiting anxiously with his Canon 5-something-or-other balanced on his shoulder.

Together we started back up the mountain, this time through the rainforest behind the houses as opposed to the open road. Branches sharp as cat claws tugged at the exposed flesh of my arms and legs, while I slapped willy-nilly at mosquitoes.

Frankly, I was surprised Brody seemed eager to exert so much energy. But his effort only heightened my hopes that he'd found the perfect perch from which to shoot the backyard, where he said a young guy in a T-shirt and boxers was being questioned without handcuffs.

By the time we reached the clearing Brody had chosen, Detective Fukumoto was surveying the backyard too, off to one side, his eyes on the pool, where a nude woman floated facedown, arms spread wide like a high diver's.

It was Piper. With her ginger hair unfurled on the water, she looked like a broken Barbie doll afloat in the bath.

My stomach clenched as Brody filmed.

Focus.

The pool was lip up, there was blood on the surface. Not a massive amount, but when blood dilutes, it doesn't take much.

'Pull her out of the water,' Fukumoto ordered a pair of cops in white paper suits.

My discomfort instantly morphed into exhilaration.

My eyes widened.

My ears finally popped.

'That,' I said quietly to Brody. 'That right there. That is our opening shot.'

THREE

I like to experiment. Like to play with the footage until I'm fully familiar with it; that's what the rough cut is for. Now that I've logged, labeled and organized the video files in a manner that makes sense only to me, I can begin to eliminate the scenes I'm certain won't make the fine cut – like the footage of Nicholas Church elucidating the fifty-year history of Miranda rights while sitting on the toilet in his suite at the Four Seasons.

In the days and nights to come, I'll also be formulating some semblance of a structure and selecting master scenes. And because we recorded on video rather than film, I'm free to bend, twist and flip every image; to try each scene in divergent positions; to alter the pace of the film from fast to slow to fast again.

Coincidentally, video versus film was the first argument of our business partnership. Sure, I get why Brody favors the handwork, the physical act of cutting a scene from its home on the reel and splicing it to another. It makes the film feel more real, more concrete. But it's merely a matter of taste. Not unlike the difference between a physical book and an e-reader, vaping versus smoking a bowl. Just your typical standoff, old against new. And since video is much less expensive, easier to edit, and far more liberating, I remained adamant we shoot in HDTV from the very beginning.

It's an argument I obviously won but one Brody's still sore about, and ostensibly the reason he stayed home tonight.

'You don't need *my* help,' he opined from the couch. 'Video editing is *your* time to shine.'

But then, I win most fights with Brody these days, because our squabbles are typically about money, and last I checked Brody was living off me, not the other way around. Not that Professor Leary *disliked* Brody, but if he'd wanted us to partner up and split the money he would have named Brody in the will.

I don't know, maybe he has a point. I *did* tell Brody before we moved out here that we were going to be equal partners in this, fifty-fifty. But you'd be surprised how fast paradise and filmmaking can join to drain a six-figure windfall.

So we clash.

We're not quick to make up either. No. It's during these battles that we each retreat to our respective corners. Stare one another down, try to outlast the other. Of course, sooner or later he'll show up with a peace offering and the whole thing will go away . . . at least until the next flare-up.

Yet I love Brody to pieces. Love him for his aloofness, for his calm, for his ability to make me feel like I'm someone who matters. Sure, Brody has his faults, we all do. *He* seldom reaches for his wallet; my feet smell. *He* dresses in flannel and corduroy even in the tropics; I occasionally drink orange juice straight from the carton.

He has a good heart, though, and that's what matters. Despite spending an inordinate amount of time melting into the couch ripping bong hits, he is fanatical about getting involved in good causes and local politics.

Sure, given his fervor for the environment and animal rights, Brody's indifference over serious issues in our relationship can be frustrating. But we're also so alike in so many ways. Neither of us, for instance, could ever work a conventional job again. And not just because of the drug tests. We each have a thirst for autonomy that's impossible to quench. We each demand dominance over our own destiny. We each identify as both artist and intellect, both pragmatist and dreamer.

And he's different now, different from the man he was just six months ago. The murder, the investigation, the trial, the verdict have changed him. In ways I never could. Astonishingly, just prior to closing statements, Brody proposed to me, on camera, in front of a crowd. He's even been hinting at wanting children, another full one-eighty from his stance not a year ago.

Ironically, once he finally asked, I realized marriage requires compromise and sacrifice, and it's difficult for me to surrender control. I don't want to become my mother. And, yes, sometimes in the heat of a particularly spirited argument, I worry that Brody will one day become his. Right now he's the reverse of her in every way. But in time . . . it's impossible to tell.

Still, I owe him an answer. I've pushed aside the proposal for too long, using our moviemaking as a pretense, and it's straining our relationship to breaking point. Worse, it's damaging our documentary. We've been together in one way or another for three years now. Brody finally wants a formal commitment and deserves one.

He's been my rock on this project from conception through principal photography.

And the truth is, I've behaved so fucking badly these past several months.

FOUR

E dit the opening last, Professor Leary always told me. Wait until the rest of the documentary is cut. Because during the editing process your film will evolve. So much so that the opening you originally imagined might no longer fit. Since the opening sets the pace, sets the style, sets the tone for the rest of the film, you need to know the film's overall pace, style and tone to discover your opening, *not* the other way around.

But I know my opening already, have known it all along. Of course, you don't *have* to tell your story in chronological order. But where better to start than the night of.

On the night the weathergirl died, Brody arrived on-scene fully equipped. In addition to his video camera, he had packed his black Bionic Ear and Booster set, which could pick up and record a whisper from a hundred yards away. He split apart a pair of earphones and handed one to me.

As Brody panned from Piper's body across the yard to Fukumoto, I crouched beside him, stuffed the single bud into my ear, and watched and listened intently.

Fukumoto hummed the chorus of 'We're Off to See the Wizard' as he approached the man in the T-shirt and boxers, who'd apparently been lorded over by two uniforms from the moment police arrived at the house.

'Ethan Jakes,' Fukumoto said, as though rolling the name around on his tongue. 'Ethan Jakes as in The Two Jakes?'

Ethan nodded. 'Well, I'm solo now, but yeah. My brother Nathan and I used to play under that name.'

'I have to say, you and your brother were very good. *Are* very good, I'm sure.' Fukumoto's voice was crisp and clear and deep, as though he was born for audiobook narration. 'My wife and I used to go down to Da Bleu Sharq to watch you boys play. What was the name of that tune my wife loved? "Don't Wait Up Past . . ."'

'Past Dawn,' Ethan said, clearly flattered he had not only been recognized but had encountered a genuine fan.

We would later learn that Detective Lance Fukumoto had never so much as heard of The Two Jakes before that evening, that on the way to the scene of the homicide he and another officer had researched Ethan Jakes on the web. Had perused his Wikipedia page, scanned his social media history, even downloaded one of his songs.

'"Don't Wait Up Past Dawn",' Fukumoto said wistfully. 'That's the one my wife so loved, God rest her soul.'

Fukumoto never had a wife either. He had a husband who worked downtown as a tax attorney and remained very much alive. But the veteran detective had wanted to relate to Ethan on as many levels as possible before Ethan gained the sense to lawyer up. So this version of Fukumoto knew Ethan's music – was nostalgic for it. Had lost his own wife, so he knew what Ethan was going through. He'd even name-dropped God because Ethan's website mentioned he'd play churches and bar mitzvahs for a discounted fee.

'Should this be a two-shot?' Brody breathed.

'No,' I said softly. 'Go wide. Keep the uniforms in the shot.'

'You sure?'

'Could be important; they're sort of hemming him in.'

Fukumoto turned his head up to Ethan, who stood a few inches taller. 'Let me ask you, Ethan,' he said. 'May I call you Ethan?'

'Yeah. Yeah, sure.' From the sound of his voice, Ethan had not only met a new fan but found a new friend. From the look in Ethan's eyes, maybe even a soulmate.

'Do you live here?' Fukumoto said.

Ethan contemplated the yard as though he needed to double-check.

He crossed his arms, stared down at the tall grass surrounding his feet. 'Yeah, more or less.'

'Good, because I want to help you, Ethan. But we have only one shot at this. And I know you want to help us track down your girlfriend's killer as swiftly as we can.'

Ethan shifted his hands to his hips and looked the detective in the eye. 'Yeah, sure, of course.'

Fukumoto nodded curtly, then spun around as though his next move was a given. 'You don't mind, then, if we look through your truck along with the house,' he said over his shoulder.

Ethan hesitated. His lips parted without sound.

Fukumoto halted his steps and slowly rotated to face Ethan again.

Ethan said, 'I'm sorry, was that a question?'

Fukumoto said the only thing he could: 'Yes.'

Ethan eyed the dark woods for answers, for one split second even stared straight into the camera he wasn't aware of. 'Do I need a lawyer here, or . . .?'

Fukumoto shrugged. 'I don't know. *Do* you?' The implication, of course, being that only the guilty need lawyers.

Ethan visibly wrestled with the decision. The footage shows his lips bent firmly in a frown, his tongue sweeping over his teeth, jaw working as he chewed the inside of his cheeks. His Adam's apple bobbed in his throat, his pupils ping-ponged from the pool to the house to the woods and back. At one point he even looked to the uniformed officers as though asking *their* opinions on the subject.

Finally, he said, 'Nah, I don't need one, I'm all right.'

'Of course you are,' Fukumoto said warmly. 'If you don't mind, we're just going to look around the house for now, see if Piper left behind anything that might help us learn what happened here tonight.' He paused. 'Then we'll search your truck.'

Ethan said something then, something that could later be disputed, possibly something crucial to the criminal case and thus crucial to our movie. The Bionic Ear, however, didn't pick it up and we didn't hear it. Because a mosquito flew into my mouth and hit the back of my throat. Causing me to fall backward against a tree and cough like I'd caught walking pneumonia.

*   *   *

They'd heard something. That much Brody and I concluded right away.

'Stay perfectly still,' he hissed, as a thin ray of light advanced in our direction.

Above the chirping of the coqui frogs and whistling of the crickets, I could hear my own teeth grating, my own gut rumbling. I swallowed down the brick rising in my throat.

The light barely arched over us.

Seconds later, Brody sighed in relief. Thankfully, as so many of my classmates and colleagues have kindly reminded me over the years, my cough sounds less like the human reflex of throat-clearing and more like the yelp of an asthmatic dog.

Following a cursory scan with the flashlight, the foursome unanimously dismissed the sound as Tantalus wildlife and resumed their talk. Fukumoto asked a few questions, Ethan grumbled a few answers, then the detective ordered the two uniforms to assist with the search of the house.

'I'd like to speak to Ethan for a minute or two, alone,' Fukumoto told them.

The story Ethan told Detective Fukumoto that night would evolve over the next few months. But it always started with Craigslist.

That evening, at around six p.m., as the sun started to sink into the Pacific, Ethan began to itch. He became antsy and irritable, couldn't sit still and watch the evening news, even though in all the months they'd been together he'd never once missed Piper doing the weather.

He logged onto his laptop and punched in the address for the popular classified-ad website. On the Craigslist homepage, Hawaii was already pulled up. He clicked on Oahu then browsed the selections; he'd forgotten how he found Guy, who he'd been using the past several months.

Ethan checked the personals first: the strictly platonic, the casual encounters, the missed connections. Although internet hookups weren't really his thing, he knew most of the codes. 'Fun times', for instance, means *looking for a one-nighter*; 'DDF' means *drug and disease free*; 'water works', well, that one sort of speaks for itself.

But Ethan wasn't looking for sex, and he sure as shit wasn't looking to get peed on. So he turned to the For Sale section and clicked on Farm+Garden.

There were plenty of ads for 420, Mary Jane, medicinal and violet. He could score plenty of Molly or Tina, he could even go 'skiing'. But he saw no H, no horse, no dragon, no mud, no junk. No chiva, no scat, no scag, no sack, no skunk. What was that goddamn term he needed to search for? What keywords had Guy used before he got pinched last week for felony distribution of narcotics?

Ethan finally happened on it by accident, happened on it because he still technically shared, with four other guys, a shitty top-floor apartment up North Shore in Waialua, where heavy rains had recently caused the ceiling of the bedroom/closet he sometimes slept in to spring a leak. So, on Craigslist, he dropped into the Materials section and clicked on an ad for 'roofing tar'.

Roofing tar. That was it. He smacked his head, exhaled audibly and typed a brief email in the hopes of setting up a meet.

Then he waited. And waited. Paced around Piper's house for over an hour, refreshing his inbox obsessively.

No word.

Since Piper wasn't hip to the whole heroin scene, at around eight p.m., when he heard her Jag in the driveway, Ethan tucked away his laptop and turned on the TV.

She kissed him on the cheek, went upstairs, changed into her favorite University of Hawaii shorts and T-shirt, then returned to the living room, where she and Ethan sat together, silently, watching the animated adult comedy *Sausage Party* on VUDU.

Hilarious, but Ethan's mind was elsewhere. So when roughly an hour into the movie, Piper hit pause for a bathroom break, Ethan hastily checked the inbox on his laptop again.

Sure enough, the Craigslist guy had replied: *Call me from a pay phone.* That and an 808 telephone number comprised the entire message.

A pay phone? Ethan thought. Where the hell am I going to find a pay phone?

Then he remembered. There was one at the gas station where he bought his Zig Zags. Even closer than that, there was one at the top of Tantalus at Pu'u 'Ualaka'a State Park, where tourists went to gawk at a twenty-five-mile swath of the island, from Barbers Point to Diamond Head.

'I've gotta run out for a minute,' he told Piper as soon as she made it back to the living room.

Depending on when Ethan was asked, Piper either shrugged her shoulders, said 'Coolio,' or asked him to pick up some Tampax while he was out.

Ethan never drove his pickup when he could walk, so he started up the mountain on foot. It took him roughly fifteen minutes to make it to the park at the top. He went straight for the single pay phone nestled between the two restrooms. From about ten feet away he could tell that the silver phone cord was cut. He turned and cursed inwardly, then, without touching the pay phone in any way, started back down the mountain.

Sixteen minutes later, *this*:

911:	[A female voice] Where is your emergency?
JAKES:	My name is Ethan Jakes. Hurry! Please!
911:	OK, what's happened, sir?
JAKES:	[Panicky] My girl, she's had an accident or something!
911:	What kind of accident?
JAKES:	I don't know! Maybe she fell, OD'd, fucking electrocuted herself!
911:	Is she conscious?
JAKES:	Her head is bleeding.
911:	Sir, is she conscious?
JAKES:	What?
911:	Is your girlfriend conscious? Is she awake?
JAKES:	No!
911:	Is she breathing?
JAKES:	Hurry! Just . . . Please, hurry!
911:	Sir, I've already dispatched an ambulance.
JAKES:	[sobbing] Thank you, thank you, thank you.
911:	Again, sir, *is* she breathing?
JAKES:	Thank you.
911:	Sir, is your girlfriend *breathing*?
JAKES:	No, for Christ's sake, she's facedown in the fucking pool!

911:      In the swimming pool?

JAKES: That's what I said!

911:      Have you tried getting her out of the water?

JAKES: What? Oh, God, you've got to hurry.

911:      Sir, I want you to get your girlfriend out of the
          water right away.

JAKES: Shit. Shit, OK.

911:      But do not disconnect this call.
          [PLUNGE]
          [Eleven seconds of silence]

JAKES: [Yelling from a distance] She's not breathing! She's
          not fucking breathing!

911:      Sir?

JAKES: [Barely audible] She's gone, she's fucking gone.
          [WATER MOVING]

911:      [Louder] Sir?
          [WET FEET ON PAVEMENT]

911:      [Louder still] Sir, are you there? Sir, I need to—
          [CALL DISCONNECTS]

FIVE

It's 4:32 in the morning when I hear the key in the lock of the door directly behind me. I stab at the keyboard to prevent the 911 call from repeating itself, although at this moment it's as clear as any song in my head.

I'm sweating, my palms are wet, the surface of the control panel in front of me is slippery. Despite the heat, I've developed chicken skin up and down my arms and legs.

I stand and turn to face the door. It's all I can do in this shoebox of an editing room. There's nowhere to run and hide.

The key stops, without the door opening. Which suddenly unnerves me even more. Is it a stranger trying random locks, is it a burglar with no key at all?

I try to convince myself I'm being paranoid, that being locked alone in a tiny room all day and night, watching footage concerning a violent murder, is making my imagination run amok. But if this trial proved anything, it's that you can never truly know anyone, and that no earthly geographic location is entirely safe.

The key in the lock again, only this time it turns. The door creeps open and a man's hand slithers through the crack. Followed by his canvas sandals, his khaki cargo shorts, and finally his furry face.

'Brought you malasadas,' Brody says.

Deep breaths. 'From Leonard's?' I ask.

Malasadas are Portuguese confections popular here in the islands, and Leonard's are by far the best.

'From the all-night ABC Store down the street.'

With a heavy sigh, I sit and swivel my chair back to the monitor. 'Thought that counts and all, BQ.'

'Come on, Rye, cut me a break.' He glances at the screen. 'You finished logging?'

'*Finally*, yeah. There are hundreds of hours of footage and it takes ten times as long to look at, log and label it. *And* I was doing it all alone.'

'Really? This again?' Beneath his beard an unmistakable smirk. 'Who *found* this case?'

I chuckle. 'Pretty sure I would have heard of it.'

'Yeah, the next morning, once you'd missed the shot of the body in the water.'

'There are plenty of crime scene photos.'

He scoffs. 'You know *damn well* the difference the footage I took that night is going to make in this film.'

'OK, fine!' I throw up my hands. 'When you're right you're right, and you're right.'

'Was that sarcastic?'

'*No*,' I say, sarcastically.

'Riles . . .'

'Ew, don't call me that.'

'Then stop calling me BQ, especially in the script.'

'It's a space saver. Leaves a lot of white paper.'

'I hate that name,' he mutters. 'Have you thought about what we're going to play over that opening shot?'

My turn to scoff. 'From, like, the minute I heard it.'

'Church's opening statement, right?'

'*No*, the nine-one-one call.'

'Why the nine-one-one call?'

'Because it's dramatic, because it's unsettling.'

'Church's *opening* is dramatic,' he says. 'Church's *opening* is unsettling.'

'But this film is about the defendant. *His* struggle, the question of *his* fate.'

Brody shakes his head, steps closer to me. 'I fundamentally disagree. This film is about Nicholas Church.'

Hard for me to believe we're having this conversation at this late stage in the process.

'Nicholas Church has been done to death,' I tell him. 'He's a phenomenal player and he'll nab the lion's share of the lines, but there's already a doc about Nicholas Church.' I pause, then add: 'I am *not* making the sequel to *The Prosecutor*.'

'*I?*'

'*We*, whatever. *We* are not making the sequel to *The Prosecutor*.'

'Why *aren't* we?' Brody cries. 'It was one of the most successful true crime documentaries of all time.'

I raise my voice till it bounces off the walls of the micro-room. 'I'm *not* riding Marissa Linden's coattails, Brody! I made that clear from the start.'

'You're not! You're taking something familiar and adding a twist. That's how all art is created.'

'How am I adding a twist?'

'Because Church is on the *other side*. He's not a prosecutor seeking higher office anymore, he's a seeker of truth, a defender of the rights of the accused.'

'Marissa's done updates on Church before, you know. Why don't you go back to our apartment, spark a bowl, and check them out on Starmax? I have work to do.'

'Marissa hasn't done another trial, has no interest in doing one. She told us that herself.'

I finally rise out of my chair to confront him face to face. 'Do you not *get* how my film will be compared to hers by every viewer, every critic, every *studio* in the goddamn world?'

'So?'

'*So* – what if it doesn't measure up? What if it doesn't even come close?'

Brody takes my upper arms in his hands, gently, and kneads each like a kitten before slowly pulling me toward him. Tenderly, he kisses my lips. Lingers like he did in the early days of our relationship.

'We *have* the footage, Rye,' he says quietly. 'You know we do, you were there. This film could be another *Staircase*, another *Jinx*, another *Making a Murderer*.'

'Maybe,' I say, as I take a step back from him. 'But it's not going to be a documentary about Nicholas Church. It's going to be a film about Ethan Jakes. And it's going to be titled *The Defendant*.'

SIX

I like to film us, Brody and myself, in the act of making a documentary. I like performing for the camera, like flexing my silver tongue. Like any director, I also like bending the players' behavior to fit the film I want to make. Or, as Brody puts it, I like playing God.

Professor Leary forewarned me that the repercussions of this could be calamitous, particularly in this genre of film. 'Erect that invisible wall,' he once told me, 'that unseeable barrier that separates crew from cast. That wall is essential; it has purpose. The less you intrude, the more natural your players will behave. More importantly, the less you influence events, the better your odds of averting a perfect disaster.'

Sometimes abiding by that rule is harder than others. Sometimes temptations are simply too strong. After all, we *do* become part of the story, whether we want to or not. From the very beginning, Brody and I remained on call at all times, prepared to capture unforeseen events on a moment's notice. We attended every court appearance, every press conference, every defense meeting at the Four Seasons. Observed mock trials, listened in on countless conference calls. Over the past several months, Brody and I shared more meals with the defendant and his legal team than most immediate families.

Naturally, the more time we spend with the individuals we're filming, the more we want to know them. A *good* trait, I think. *Indispensable* even. Because if *we* want to know these characters, then our audience will, too. 'Intriguing people are intriguing,' Professor Leary would say. 'If they aren't intriguing, why the fuck are we filming them in the first place?'

Like any temptation, it's all a matter of whether we act on it, right? How well we resist is ultimately how well we will be judged. By our audience, by critics, by the internet. Even by the players themselves.

As editor, sure, I'm given some liberty to polish, to modify, to abridge my own behavior when absolutely necessary. I mean, we all edit our lives to some extent, don't we? When we tell our story, *if* we tell our story, it's limited to the parts we're eager to tell.

Hell, even the final story written of us is only ten lines in a local daily, half the lines spent naming our survivors. About us, hardly anything. Our name, our age, our occupation if we had one. Certainly no mention of the laws we broke, of the people we betrayed.

And in the *very* end, our lives are pruned to a mere pair of lines: one with our name, the other with our dates. *Unless* we do something truly astounding in our lifetime. *Then* we live on, *then* we leave our mark on the world.

That's what this film represents to me. My chance, my fifteen minutes, my moment in the sun. It doesn't have to be picked up by a major studio, doesn't have to win an Oscar or Golden Globe. It doesn't even have to make much money. Just some goddamn form of validation, so that I no longer have to suffer the incessant echo of my father's voice: 'See, Riley? I was right, you were wrong.'

Rational or not, until I've created something I'm genuinely proud of, I'll always feel like I'm no one. With this film, I'm not seeking immortality so much as admission to the human race.

So it's only natural to be passionate about the project. To be so rapt by the players that we yearn to alter their lives in some spectacular fashion. Genuine objectivity in this business is simply an impossibility, a pipe dream, a myth. Getting the players so accustomed to us, so disinterested in us, that they ignore us or forget our presence altogether, runs contrary to every instinct we have as human beings. The compulsion is rather to crawl *inside* these people, to inhabit their skin, to show our audience events through their eyes. Viewing these people as we do – at their rawest, at their frailest, at their most human – isn't the least bit conducive to emotional distance. No, distance in such instances is pain, is torture, it's what I imagine blue balls feels like. Why cast ourselves outside just when we most want to be in?

Is it even possible to resist?

I'm in the editing room, rewatching footage, this time with a more critical eye. Since shooting on video is less expensive than buying and processing film, we were able to record far more footage than we need. The downside of having to go through hundreds of hours of audio and images we won't use is far outweighed by the upside of the dozens of perfect moments – like when Ethan tossed Church and his 6,000-dollar suit into the penthouse suite's infinity pool – that we wouldn't have otherwise caught. Our shooting ratio (minutes of footage shot to minutes of footage in the final film) will be roughly 100:1. Which means that for every sixty seconds of brilliant cross-examination from Nicholas Church, there are ninety-nine minutes of bullshit to sort through.

Because over the length of a criminal case like this one, there is an immense amount of downtime. And that's when temptation hits hardest. That's when we most want to spur our players on, push them to act, to *react* to something, anything. We're scared witless that a long stretch of nothingness will kill the momentum we so skillfully built from the sidelines. So, occasionally, we do what directors do: we direct. Not in the way that reality TV producers feed their casts lines (I abhor any comparison), but in the sense of merely moving things along, of pushing the players forward, of – in Hollywood parlance – cutting to the chase.

And then there are times when we inadvertently fall into a power vacuum. Times when there is a complete collapse in front of the camera, and we behind it feel the need to take charge.

There were several times over the past six months when the defense fell into utter chaos, when communication between Ethan and Church broke down, seemingly beyond repair. During these times, yes, I stepped in. Yes, I broke the rules, consequences be damned.

But then, as Brody constantly reminds me, it was long before the trial even began that I nudged my first pawn on the chessboard. Even before the arrest and indictment. In fact, if I hadn't already made myself a part of the story on the night of, I certainly did so the very next morning, around six a.m., when I turned on the television.

SEVEN

'When you're filming a unique event such as a criminal trial,' Professor Leary once lectured, 'it's vital to remember that it's not airing live, that the outcome will already be known. You're *not* going to exhilarate your audience with the final score of the 86 Super Bowl. Comparably, in a true crime documentary, you *cannot* rely on the intrinsic suspense of a whodunit. You need to dig deeper, you need to help your audience fathom the legal process and the emotional toll that it takes on the players. To accomplish that you need to accumulate as much rock-solid visual evidence as possible. And to get it, you need to be ready, willing and able to do whatever it takes, *especially* these days.'

The morning after the weathergirl died, I could have flipped from one local station to the next to record my Act One montage. Local stations KHON, KITV, KGMB, KHNL all led with Piper's murder. Her home station, however, remained eerily silent, devastated by the sudden loss of one of their own.

I settled on my fallback channel and fell into the couch to watch just as an attractive middle-aged male anchor, who could well be confused for a life-size Ken doll, filled the screen. In the upper left corner, a fingerprint graphic overlaid with police tape displaying the words 'Homicide Investigation'.

'Honolulu detectives are investigating the murder of local weather reporter Piper Kingsley,' the Ken doll said, 'whose body was discovered last night by her boyfriend, unclothed and face-down in the swimming pool of her Tantalus home. Kingsley's boyfriend Ethan Jakes, a local musician who was residing with the victim, dialed nine-one-one and reported the grisly finding. According to police, Mr Jakes is currently cooperating with the investigation. We now go live to correspondent Kalani Webb, in front of Piper Kingsley's home on Tantalus Drive.'

Enter a baby-faced male Pacific Islander in an aloha shirt. Cute. OK, *super* cute. But his delivery, in my opinion, was strangely dry.

'Thanks, Seth. Police say the victim was last seen by her boyfriend, local musician Ethan Jakes, at her home here on Mount Tantalus. Mr Jakes told investigators that he left the home for less than half an hour before returning to find his girlfriend dead in the swimming pool behind the house. Meanwhile, friends and colleagues of Piper Kingsley are in shock at her death.'

Cut to: Neighbor, an upper middle-aged Caucasian female in a boho muumuu, one of those 'rich hippy' chicks so prevalent in yoga studios across the islands.

'I just can't believe it,' she said, shaking her head as though she couldn't find the arugula aisle at Whole Foods. 'I'm still in shock. She was so beautiful, so talented, so *full of life.*'

'Save the poem for spoken-word night, sister,' Brody said to the television as he flopped onto the sofa next to me, a bowl of dry Cinnamon Life cereal in his lap. He immediately reached to his left and retrieved the last half of the blunt he'd started last night. Spent several seconds searching for his Zippo, finally located it between the couch cushions, and blazed up.

Cut to: Random Gal on the Street, a twenty-something in a sports bra and hot pants, either on her way to an early-morning workout or doing the walk of shame following a night with a personal trainer from 24-Hour Fitness.

'Yes, I know Piper Kingston! She's the redhead who does the weather, yeah?' She paused, her words suddenly lodged in her throat, a tear threatening to fall. 'This is just so, so sad.'

The moment they cut back to the Ken doll, something in my stomach capsized and I moved to the edge of the couch to throw up. Behind me, Brody extinguished his blunt. Set his hands gently on my shoulders and soothed me with his voice.

'You're OK, baby,' he said. 'You're going to be just fine.'

I didn't vomit but held that position for fifteen or twenty seconds until the feeling passed.

I suffered them all the time, these goddamn panic attacks.

I pulled my pill case from my pocket and popped a Klonopin. As the pill slowly dissolved under my tongue, I thought: *Piper was a person.*

Piper wasn't just a person, she was someone I knew.

Piper wasn't just someone I knew, she was a friend.

Why couldn't I at least cry?

Even Brody, who'd never met Piper, who had just seen her on the news with me nearly every evening, cried last night when we got home. Not the usual waterworks triggered by 'major life events' such as the death of his beloved fifteen-year-old tabby, but a good, solid cry for the occasion.

'She was just so young,' he said. 'And I know how much you were looking forward to getting together with her.' He leaned his head on my chest and I ran my hand through his soft hair. I could feel his tears through my cotton tank-top. 'I'm so sorry, Rye. I can't imagine losing a friend that way.'

I felt sympathy for him. Then relief that I at least felt sympathy for *someone*. But the defensiveness in my voice was unmistakable. 'I only hung out with her twice.'

'Yeah,' he said, matter-of-factly, 'but wasn't one of those times two weeks as a guest in her house?'

I didn't reply. Tried to nod but my head just kind of fell to the side. I felt Brody's eyes on me. With every awful memory in my head I attempted to summon a tear but ultimately came up dry. 'Dry as a dead dingo's donger,' as Piper used to say at the bar when she was impatient for drinks.

Brody is just so goddamn sensitive, I thought. It was true, too. Brody felt things more intensely than the rest of us, especially painful things. But his sensitivity was always a pro, never a con, particularly after the last asshole I'd seriously dated: an investment banker from the northeast, handpicked by my dear old daddy.

I hadn't realized Brody had paused the television; I'd thought he'd just muted it. So I was startled when I glanced up at the still screen and saw Piper's father, photos of whom had ornamented every room of her house, at least back when I visited.

Daddy's little girl, she liked to call herself.

Brody pressed PLAY on the remote.

Zane Kingsley was an older man, well-built but short, head

shaven bald. With a single duffel slung over his right shoulder, he shot past the luggage carousel like a bullet. The cameras could barely keep up.

'I hope they arrest her killer,' he said curtly, with a deep Australian accent, 'and I hope they string 'im up.' There was a seething in his voice, a ferocity perfectly in line with how Piper described him. ''Cause if they don't, I will.'

I snatched the remote from Brody's lap and paused the TV to consider his words. Zane Kingsley hopes they *arrest* – not *find* or *catch* – the killer. Hopes they string *'im* up, not *'er*.

Piper's dad was insinuating police already knew the identity of the killer; they just hadn't effected an arrest yet. Which could well have been true. Maybe Ethan Jakes was currently under surveillance, maybe detectives were hoping he'd fuck up and take them to the murder weapon, lead them to a lover, say something incriminating over the phone.

It might just be a matter of time until his arrest. At which time Ethan Jakes would become inaccessible to me. If I wanted his side of the story before the indictment, I knew I had to act fast.

I hit PLAY. Onscreen the Ken doll extolled: 'Piper Kingsley was a rising talent in the Hawaii news industry and she will be sorely missed.' He paused for effect. 'Once again, Piper Kingsley, dead, at only twenty-eight years old.'

Everyone was trying to reach Ethan Jakes that day. But only I got through.

The previous night I'd made a few calls from our Waikiki apartment to those of Piper's colleagues and friends I'd met a few years earlier. Unsurprisingly, many of their numbers had changed, and those I managed to reach didn't remember me.

I did, however, catch the weekend weather guy, Kyle Myers, a fabulous gossip who, like me, was in his late twenties. From Kyle, I learned that Ethan and Piper had been together about eight months. However, that Ethan was living with Piper was news to Myers. Maybe staying over a lot, but he didn't think Piper would have made that kind of commitment. She'd given no hint that she and Ethan were that serious. In fact, Myers told me, Piper had planned to move to the mainland in the upcoming months. She'd recently been hired to do morning weather for a CBS affiliate in a large market in southern Wisconsin.

While I made the calls, Brody googled the name Ethan Jakes and found a Wikipedia page, which confirmed Ethan was a local musician but little else. He then moved onto Net Detective, which he'd subscribed to for just such an occasion. He discovered Ethan's date of birth, his cell phone number, and the address in Waialua that appeared on his current driver's license.

I tried Ethan's phone. Got voicemail, and it was full. I sent a text but had no way of knowing whether it was received. (I'd later learn it *was*, not by Ethan but by the police.) I tried an AOL account listed for him but didn't hold out much hope. The only person I'd known who still used an AOL address was Professor Leary, just before his death, and he'd assured me that it was an exclusively sixty-and-over club.

I flipped to Facebook, took to Twitter and Instagram, but Ethan Jakes had been silent since before Piper's murder. I reached out to a few of his friends, sent him a couple of direct messages, but went to bed having failed in my quest to make contact.

But less than two hours after I woke, I succeeded. Once the segment on Piper's murder finally ended, I felt along the couch for the remote, hit the mute button, said, 'How the shit am I going to get in touch with Ethan?'

Brody blew a dense stream of smoke from the side of his mouth. 'How about that address we found for him last night?'

'The one up North Shore?'

'Waialua, right?' He was already toasted. 'There's an apartment number. He probably rents. Find out who owns the property in Waialua. If Jakes has a landlord, the landlord may have an emergency contact or something.'

I said, 'Brody Quinlan, I could blow you.'

He smiled. His eyes were already bloodshot. He was forty-one, and looked every minute of it. He was in the same clothes he'd worn yesterday and the day before that. Three days' growth had accumulated on his face, his hair was a jungle, and he reeked of pot. Probably hadn't showered in a week. Yet I loved every inch of him. Loved him for his heart, loved him for his head. Loved him because he somehow still gave a fuck while so clearly having no fucks left to give.

A Zillow search yielded the name of the landlord. Net Detective imparted his number. When I called, he explained Ethan had four roommates and supplied me with the number for one of them. That one was 'more roommate than friend', but did have the number of one of Ethan's amigos. So I called that cat, told him who I was, what I was doing, how I wanted to help Ethan through this perilous time and would pay a shit-ton to do so. I had him repeat back my cell number, twice.

Thirty minutes later Ethan called my phone from restricted digits.

'I don't have access to anything of hers,' he started. 'Or anything of mine for that matter. It's all considered evidence now, it's crazy.'

'That's why we need to meet,' I told him. 'We need to get your side of the story on record, because if—'

'On record? No, no, nothing on record.'

'Look, Ethan, if the worst happens and you're charged and convicted, *we're* the Court of Last Resort. Appeals go on for years while you rot in prison, *unless* you have the public's attention. And the best – and sometimes the *only* – way to do that these days is to star in a documentary. You think Brendan Dassey's conviction would have been overturned if not for *Making a Murderer*?'

Following some seconds of silence, he said, 'Didn't seem to help that Durst fellow, though.'

'For every Durst, there's an Amanda Knox and a West Memphis Three.'

He changed tack. 'You told my boy Chuck you're Piper's friend. How do I know that's true? Send me a photo of you and Piper together.'

I thought about it. Only a few pictures existed and they were taken before I'd ever heard of such a thing as the cloud. 'That's going to take some time and—'

'Well, that's what it's going to take to speak to me.'

I tried to counter with an offer of alternative evidence of my friendship with Piper, like maybe answering some questions about her favorite color (red), her favorite movie (*Bad Santa*), her favorite song ('Rehab'), but he'd already disconnected the call.

Brody once again swept into action. He scanned Piper's Facebook page, but she hadn't posted very many party pictures, probably as a precaution for prospective employers. Brody then vanished into our bedroom and returned minutes later with a shoebox full of memory sticks.

Before we'd moved from the mainland, Brody had downloaded all our photographs in case our computers were damaged in transit. Which was lucky since I'd scrapped my five-year-old HP laptop less than a month after we arrived in the islands.

Brody plugged in one stick after another and scanned the contents. Sure enough, after a little over an hour, we found the file containing the photos from my last Hawaiian adventure.

To Ethan's friend, Chuck, I texted a picture of me and Piper at a beach bar in Kailua.

Minutes later I received a text message back:
MANOA FALLS 7 P.M. ALONE.
I tried: JUST ME AND THE CAMERA GUY.
Got back: NO CAMERAS. ALONE OR NO DICE.

There would be no B-roll of Manoa Falls, because as far as the documentary is concerned, the first meeting between myself and Ethan Jakes never took place. Although the scenery would have heightened the beauty of my film, given his insistence that I carry no camera, I was less than thrilled with the location he'd chosen.

First, there was the twenty-six-minute drive in the Jeep from Waikiki to Manoa Road. From there, I walked a mile-and-a-half dirt trail to the falls. It was dusk and the mosquitoes were out in full force. I'd gotten a few bites the previous night on Tantalus Drive, but Brody had taken the brunt: dozens of itchy, bright red bumps, up and down his arms and legs, even on his neck.

Like last night, a thin rain fell, just enough to make the trail muddy and slippery, just enough to threaten a downpour, which could result in a flash flood. Not only would I get swept away, but the overflow from the freshwater stream was lousy with *Leptospira*, a corkscrew bacteria that caused the infection leptospirosis, symptoms of which included headaches, muscle pains, fevers, severe bleeding from the lungs, and possibly meningitis.

No, I'm not a hypochondriac, but Brody damn sure is, and he likes to discuss his findings with me. So I knew all about the café waiter on Maui who gradually turned yellow from kidney failure, and the schoolteacher who became infected on her Kauai vacation and died of severe pulmonary hemorrhage six months later.

The idea petrified me even more given the scores of scrapes I'd collected during my sprint through the razor-sharp branches behind Piper's house the previous night.

I tried to keep my mind off the deadly bacteria. Unfortunately, the spores were instantly replaced by Brody's bedtime stories of the Night Marchers, ancient Hawaiian ghost warriors, who just so happened to march at sunrise and dusk.

'You'll hear their drums,' he told me late one night under the covers, 'followed by a foul and musky smell. *Run*, Riley. *Run*. Because once the conch shell sounds, you'll see the glow of dozens of torches, fires that burn brighter and brighter as the Night Marchers near you. Chanting. Carrying crude but effective weapons. And once their eyes are on you, it's over. They take you, Rye. They take you back to their camp and then it's just a matter of time. Until they strap you to a stake and burn you alive.'

Brody had told me how to protect myself, but damned if I remembered that part. It's like listening to flight attendants telling you what to do in the event of a water landing; how can you concentrate on inflating your fucking life jacket when you're suddenly panicking at the possibility of the jet crashing into the ocean?

When I finally reached the falls, I was out of breath, and there was no one in sight. Because of its camera, I'd been strictly forbidden from bringing my cell phone. *Shit*. Maybe Brody was right. We'd argued vociferously on the matter. He'd demanded I not go by myself.

'It's the *only* way he'll meet me,' I shouted in our twenty-third-floor open-air apartment.

'Of course,' he said. 'The guy is very likely a killer of women. Why would he want you to bring someone along?'

I shrugged theatrically.

'Don't make light of this, Rye. This isn't funny.'

'How about, let's just not have this conversation at all.'

From 150 feet above, water gushed over the falls into the fresh-water stream, while all around me the jungle turned to night.

Ethan was nowhere to be seen. I waited five, ten, fifteen, twenty minutes, and still no sign of him.

Then a voice. His voice. The voice I'd heard briefly over the phone, the one now forever seared into my memory.

'Riley,' the voice said.

I turned toward it. Out of the lush greenery stepped the man I'd seen speaking to police in Piper's backyard the previous evening.

He motioned up and down with his finger. 'Lift your shirt.'

'We're a little forward, aren't we?'

Highlighted by moonlight, Ethan Jakes was truly a sight. Movie-star handsome, basketball tall, with a swimmer's body, he appeared equally hard and soft. As I peered into his perfectly symmetrical face with its perpetual five o'clock shadow, I nearly relented and removed my shirt. Then I swiftly reminded myself that no, this wasn't the way love stories started. Not in real life, not even in movies. This, if anything, was the plot to a bad porno.

'I need to know you're not wired,' he said.

'Then take my word for it.'

'Not good enough.' He took a step toward me. 'Get wet, then.'

'Wow, we *are* forward,' I said.

He pointed to the stream.

I grinned and shook my head. 'Leptospirosis. Pat me down instead.'

He did, gently, timidly even, running his fingers over my ribs like a classical pianist. He was sheepish, apologetic, not at all what I had imagined from the looks of him. He performed such a half-assed job, I could have hidden a three-man crew with equipment inside my G-string and Ethan would not have been any the wiser.

'I can't make a move without being watched,' he said. Even in the dark, I could tell his cheeks were burning red following the pat down. 'They took my cell, my tablet, my laptop, everything.'

We both spoke in hushed tones. 'What about that apartment in Waialua?'

'I've got nothing there, really. Some clothes.' He peered into

the black as though he'd heard something, but no. 'Anyway, I
can't get the boys involved.'

'The boys?'

'They're fellow musicians, you know. Scraping by, same as
I've been. Now, though, who knows? The way they've been
talking about me on TV, I might never book another gig again.'

'What can I do to help you?'

'Get in touch with my brother, Nate. Tell him I need a lawyer.
A *good* one, top notch. A criminal lawyer who tries felony cases.
There aren't many in the islands.'

As he said it, I felt weak in the knees. I had always had a
thing for musicians. Depending on your personal experience, that
fact was either repellent or hot. But I wasn't a groupie or anything,
didn't go down on guys on a tour bus or lift my skirt onstage. I
just dug guys who played instruments. Well, *some* instruments.
Not like the tuba or anything. A guitar though? The drums? Even
a piano, tuned right, turned me on. Ethan Jakes, I already knew
from YouTube, played a ukulele. And he played it crazy well.

They say a girl knows within the first half-minute whether she
would, under the right circumstances, sleep with a guy or not. I
knew in one, *maybe* two seconds, and two only because I was
conscious of the fact he could well be a murderer. Yet, tonight,
Ethan Jakes had such a gentleness about him that I'd have doubted
he could step on a slug, let alone kill someone he professed to
love.

Of course, I knew there were such things as sociopaths, knew
that calm, soft-spoken men could lack a conscience. I'd seen
countless documentaries on serial killers like Dahmer, Manson,
Gacy and Bundy. Each could seem perfectly normal on a night
like this.

'Do you know any?' he said.

I'd completely zoned. 'Serial killers?'

'Good lawyers.'

I hesitated, considered whether to make 'the recommendation'.
Would the case instantly become a media circus? Would his
participation help or hinder us in garnering interest in the
movie? What if he refused to take part in another documentary?
Worse, what if he brought in Marissa Linden to film?

As all these thoughts intersected in my head, I considered

Ethan's pale blue eyes, and in that moment, I forgot all about the hidden camera I almost brought with me, the contract I desperately needed him to sign. All I wanted to do in that moment was help him.

'I don't know anyone in the islands,' I finally said, 'but I do know who *I* would call if I were in your situation.'

EIGHT

Size matters.

Knowing the approximate length of your film goes a long way toward helping you structure it. Used to be that documentary filmmakers had forty-something minutes for a commercial hour, fifty for a noncommercial on a premium channel. Maybe an hour and a half to two hours for a theatrical, at most.

True crime docs like Marissa Linden's *The Prosecutor*, a five-hour film broken into six episodes, changed all that.

Before Brody and I started shooting *The Defendant*, I frankly had no idea how I would ultimately structure my first film. But now that I've viewed the massive amount of footage and separated the treasure from the trash, I can finally guesstimate the overall running time I'll have to work with. This story, Ethan's story, is manifestly too large for a single feature; it's a docu-series, maybe eight or nine hours long. Roughly the time it takes to read a bestselling thriller.

I'm in the editing room, trying to determine how to introduce Nicholas Church. There are seventeen empty cans of cola lined up like little enemy soldiers on my right. I don't 'do' coffee, so I rot my insides with soda instead. Shit, I can't even make healthy choices concerning my caffeine intake.

Church. Church, the big coffee-drinker. A coffee aficionado, a coffee *snob* as a matter of fact. The world first learned this, let's call it a quirk, about Church during the first few minutes of *The Prosecutor*, the painfully popular Starmax documentary which sensationalized the trial, appeals, execution and posthumous

exoneration of Roderick Blunt – a Charlotte, North Carolina man
convicted of murdering the mother of his daughter and three
sons.

The film also turned Nicholas Church into a national pariah.
From the *Chicago Sun-Times*:

> Filmed over six years, *The Prosecutor* focuses on rookie
> assistant prosecutor Nicholas Church, who brilliantly takes
> over the State's case against Blunt after his boss and mentor,
> the Mecklenburg District Attorney, suffers a heart attack
> on the eve of trial. Thrust into legal stardom following a
> flawless performance at trial, the film then follows Church
> as he soaks up the spotlight, successfully runs for the office
> of District Attorney, and strenuously defends the conviction
> that propelled his career at every stage of appeal. But the
> most powerful moment of the film comes when D.A.
> Nicholas Church almost gleefully enters Central Prison in
> Raleigh to witness Blunt's execution. Because, concluding
> the film is footage of Nicholas Church on the steps of the
> historic Mecklenburg County courthouse, tearfully
> resigning his position as District Attorney. Just eighty-two
> days after his death by lethal injection, Roderick Blunt's
> latest appellate attorneys discovered physical evidence that
> exonerated their client beyond any whisper of doubt.

Since that time, Church has dedicated his life to defending the
accused in capital cases across the country. Licensed in eleven
states (including Hawaii), with designated local counsel in a
dozen more, Church recently expanded his practice to include
non-death-penalty homicide cases like Ethan's. Why? Because
so terrified were prosecutors in death penalty states like Florida
and Texas of facing off against the former D.A. that they began
dropping the death penalty in death-eligible cases the moment
someone breathed Church's name. In the decade before Piper's
murder, Nicholas Church had tried a dozen high-profile homicide
cases and walked away with an acquittal in every one.

Meanwhile, it's widely known that, despite their tempestuous
beginnings, Church is engaged in a frenetic relationship with filmmaker Marissa Linden, whom he publicly credits with changing

the direction of his life. 'Sometimes you need someone to hold up a mirror,' he said in a recent interview with *Vanity Fair*. 'Preferably, your flaws aren't revealed in HD to twenty-two million viewers. But Marissa has her ways and I have mine.'

The article goes on to cite anonymous sources who say that, between shouting matches and sexual liaisons, Church works madly to prove to Marissa that he is no longer the lawyer who prosecuted an innocent man right up until the moment of his death, but that he is now someone else. Someone stronger, someone better.

Ironically, today, Church is far less vilified for his overzealous prosecutorial past and hand in executing an innocent man than he is for standing as a tireless advocate for the constitutional rights of criminal defendants. To most law-and-order types, Nicholas Church represents a wrench in an otherwise faultless machine designed to efficiently punish lawbreakers. On legal news shows like *Judge Jacqueline*, Church's name is a four-letter word.

OK, admittedly, Church's unorthodox methods, both inside the courtroom and out, have earned him a reputation for skirting the rules. However, when recently asked by reporters whether he'd violated ethics rules in any of the six states in which he was currently under investigation, Church quipped that the system itself is so fucked up, he rarely needs to resort to anything illegal.

I pull up footage of Church standing alone in the dark, empty courtroom at the Circuit Court on Punchbowl Street the night before Ethan's trial. How to introduce Nicholas Church? I know precisely what Professor Leary would say: 'Be brief. Feed the audience just what they need and no more. Focus on the primary story problem. Let the particulars of your players' pasts and personalities trickle in as necessary. No information dumps. Give the audience some credit; they can handle some ambiguity, some uncertainty. Keep exposition to a bare minimum. Because, as any decent storyteller knows, no one likes exposition – it's a product of pure fucking laziness.'

NINE

Three days after the weathergirl died, Nicholas Church arrived in Hawaii. I'd offered to pick him up at the Honolulu airport, but he declined in favor of a stretch-limo ride to the Four Seasons in Ko Olina, where he'd reserved the penthouse suite indefinitely.

I'd then asked if he could at least provide me his flight number so that we could film his arrival at the airport. He said, 'Sorry, no. No cameras on me until you and I have a signed contract.' It sounded like he was walking through one city or another; I heard the wind howling, heard car engines idling, heard the occasional horn.

'I can bring a copy of the contract to the airport,' I said.

'We can't execute any contract until I've been formally retained by the client.'

'Fine, fax over the retainer agreement.'

'The retainer agreement is meaningless; it's the exchange of currency I'm interested in.'

'All right, we can do a wire transfer.'

'The client and I haven't even met.'

'I've assured him I'm fully familiar with your reputation, and he's totally sold.'

'Oh, you sold me?'

'That's not what I meant. I'm just trying to say that Ethan Jakes is one hundred percent certain he wants you as his lawyer.'

'I see. Even without meeting me? That's an awfully big decision to make without so much as a single face to face. Is he aware of how big a decision this is? How our lives will be intertwined for the next several months, maybe years?'

'Believe me, he's intelligent and he's aware.'

'Are *you*?'

'*Excuse* me?'

'Intelligent. Are you aware?'

'I'd like to think so.'

'Well then, surely you comprehend that when I say "*our* lives will be intertwined for the next several months, maybe years", I'm talking about his life *and mine*. When I say it's an awfully big decision to make without so much as a face to face, I'm not only referring to *his* decision, Ms Vasher. Even if *he* is "totally sold", I require a face to face before *I* decide whether I will accept Mr Jakes as a client.'

```
Dissolve to:
Establishing shot of ext. of Four Seasons
at Oahu.
```

Beneath that I scribble: *First add stock footage of Ko Olina resort community. Aerial shot of its two miles of coast; residential condos and villas; Disney's Aulani and Marriott's Beach Club resorts. Close-ups of LPGA golf course; white-sand beaches; four azure manmade lagoons.*

In the editing room, I reach for our legal file. Pull out the location release for the Four Seasons, which still feels like a trophy, like something I fought for, something I won. Even though it was actually Nicholas Church who won it for me.

Following our conversation an hour earlier I'd been reluctant to ring Church again.

'Now what?' he answered.

'We need you to select a different resort,' I said.

'Non-negotiable.'

'Brody and I were just there. They won't allow us to film anywhere on their property, not even in your suite.'

'The reason?'

'He didn't explicitly say, but I got the impression he was afraid filming you would bring negative publicity to the hotel.'

'Because I'm a criminal lawyer?'

'Well, because you're you.'

'Give me the name and number of the person you met with.'

From the background noise and exertion in his voice, it sounded as though he was still walking outside.

'Do you need to, like, "pull over" first and grab a pen?' I asked.

'I'll remember it.'

I gave him the name and number of Oliver Pryce, who was the kind of snooty, stick-up-his-ass hotel manager John Cleese would play in a slapstick comedy. Hurried, formal, condescending, and so goddamn full of himself he probably thought our doc was about him. He was also resolute, so I anticipated bad news.

Church phoned me back ten minutes later. Said, 'Ollie apologizes and says you may drop by with the location release at your convenience.'

'Seriously?' I was incredulous. 'I mean, this Oliver Pryce, he was *adamant.*'

In the background, I heard a set of brakes screech to a sudden stop.

'So was I.'

The penthouse suite was ginormous, a whopping 3,200 square feet of living space and an additional 800 square-foot wraparound lanai with an infinity pool and a panorama of the Pacific. From the seventeenth-floor terrace, we could see the entire coast in either direction.

'What a shot,' I told Brody, while light trade winds brushed our cheeks.

'Great,' he grunted, 'if only Church would let us start filming.'

'There'll be time.'

Inside the suite, I said to Church, 'This place is amaze-balls. It must cost, like . . .'

'Seventeen thousand,' Church said.

'A *week*?'

'A night.'

'A *night*? Each week you're here, that's like—'

'Hundred and nineteen thousand,' Brody said.

'Actually, I'm not paying at all.' Church spoke as he moved from light switch to light switch, testing each multiple times. 'Six years ago, I won a massive verdict against their holding company on behalf of a client.' *Click, click.* Another light switch. 'They appealed, lost. Threatened to appeal again. I let their lawyers think I was scared. Called their office every hour on the hour for eight straight days, hinting I wanted to settle and might be willing to get creative when it came to my forty percent. They called back, started offering me a week here, a month there, began blathering about blackout dates. Within a week, we'd reached a deal I was more than satisfied with.'

I glanced at my Swatch, surprised Ethan and his brother Nathan hadn't yet arrived.

Leaks at the Honolulu Police Department indicated that an arrest was imminent. Church, however, warned us that this news wasn't necessarily true, that HPD could be applying heat on Ethan in the hopes he'd break down, confess to something, run.

'But you might be here on Oahu for a year or longer,' I said.

'What can I say, I'm a hell of a negotiator.' *Click, click.* 'In their defense, however, when they agreed to the deal, they weren't cognizant of the fact that I am technically homeless. They failed to do their due diligence.'

'Homeless, as in . . .?'

'As in, I don't have a home.' *Click, click.*

'You're a drifter?'

He moved on to inspecting the drawers and closets. 'Kind of like Jack Reacher if Reacher stayed at the Four Seasons instead of seedy motels, and didn't travel by bus but private jet, and didn't beat the shit out of bad guys or shoot them, but defended them in a court of law.'

'So you stay in the most expensive Four Seasons suites around the world year-round?'

'Well, it *was* a significant verdict.'

'What the hell did they do to your client?'

He silently counted the number of hangars in the closet, said, 'As part of my agreement with the holding company, I'm not at liberty to discuss that. Especially with documentarians.'

I remained dubious. 'If you stay in this suite for a single year, the cost would be astronom—'

'Six million, two hundred and five thousand,' Brody said.

Church shrugged. 'For the room itself, yes. But I also negotiated complimentary amenities such as daily dry cleaning, spa treatments and valet parking.' He checked the safe, closed the closet door. Evaluated the kitchen.

I gazed around the room, at the custom fixtures, the formal dining room, the fully stocked bar. 'Jeez, you thought of everything.'

'Well, not everything,' he conceded, as he ran the faucet, hot then cold. 'I do have to pay out of pocket for my pornography. That bill, sadly, *will be* astronomical.'

Church walked into the bathroom, to vet the plumbing or appraise the marble, I assumed, since he didn't close the door. But a few seconds later we could plainly hear him urinating.

'I also get a deep, *deep* discount on meals,' he called out mid-stream, 'so feel free to grab a menu and dial up room service.'

The Jakes brothers arrived twenty minutes late but just in time to order room service with the rest of us. Church insisted we splurge, and splurge we did. Tomato bisque, lobster salad, blackened mahi-mahi (to Brody's out-and-out horror), and warm pineapple tart with macadamia nut ice cream – and that was just *my* order.

Once our empty plates were stacked on the cart and set outside the room, we all stretched and sat down to our meeting.

In his lap, Church opened a briefcase and took from it an old-fashioned speaker box. He placed it in the center of the mahogany conference table.

Ethan pointed to it. 'We're not recording this, are we?'

Church shook his head as he jotted the date on his legal pad. 'Of course not. This is Charlie.'

'Charlie?' I said.

'My investigator.' Church's eyes shot to the speaker box. 'Say "hello", Charlie.'

The speaker squawked. 'My name is not Charlie.'

'Holy shit,' Brody said. 'Is that AI?'

Church said, 'Unless AI is an acronym for "teenage shut-in with a severe case of social anxiety disorder", no.'

'My name is Jesse,' the speaker said. 'The *Charlie's Angels* bit is getting old, Nick.'

Church cleared his throat. 'Now that you've all met Charlie, let's the rest of us introduce ourselves. I'm Nick Church, defense lawyer extraordinaire.' He pointed to Ethan.

'Ethan Jakes. Person of interest, according to the media.'

'Suspect,' Church corrected him. 'You were a suspect the moment police arrived at the house.' He pointed to Nate.

'Nathan Jakes. Ethan's brother.' He smiled awkwardly and gave Ethan a jab in the arm. 'And, now, I suppose, his benefactor.'

Nathan was a few years older than Ethan and every bit as attractive. Dressed in a blue Hermès suit, he was thoroughly groomed right down to his manicured fingernails. I knew little else about him, then, other than that he was a partner at a successful personal injury law practice downtown.

'Brody Quinlan. Camera operator.'

'Riley Vasher. Director.'

Church pointed to us one at a time, starting with Ethan's brother. 'You're Nate Dogg, you're BQ, and you're Riles.' He pointed to the speaker. 'And *you're* Charlie.'

'I don't want to be BQ,' Brody said.

'And I don't want to be Riles,' I added.

He waved us off. 'You're gonna thank me someday when your film is a huge success, you're both big stars, and AMC produces the new hit crime drama *BQ & Riles*, starring Shailene Woodley and a very scruffy Joaquin Phoenix.'

'Wait,' Nate Dogg said, smiling, 'what about my brother? What do we call him?'

Church frowned. 'Well, I haven't seen the evidence yet. Once I do, I'll label him somewhere between lucky and motherfucked.' He pointed to Ethan. 'Which leads us to our next topic of discussion: the evidence and just how well it stacks up against your story.'

At that moment, and over our strenuous objection, Brody and I were unceremoniously kicked out of the meeting.

Once we were permitted back into the room and reseated at the table, Church pointed to me. He did a lot of pointing, Church.

'Next order of business is your documentary,' he said.

A fully executed retainer agreement sat in the middle of the table beneath the speaker box.

Jesse of the speaker box said: 'I just want to reiterate for the record that I am opposed to the entire notion of making a documentary of what will likely already become a high-profile homicide case.'

Church bowed his head. 'The paperweight's objection is duly noted.'

I reached into the bag on the back of my chair and carefully pulled out a twelve-page contract.

'Ethan and Nathan have already signed it,' I said, passing the pages over to Church, 'so it just needs your signature and . . .'

Church tore it in half and set the pieces neatly down on the table. Then he reached into his own briefcase and pulled out a bound document six inches thick. Dropped it onto the table with a thud.

'*This* is our contract,' he said.

Brody and I stared at one another for several seconds as Church leisurely nudged the tome in front of us with his fingertips.

Grudgingly, I hefted the thing and started reading.

This agreement by and between Nicholas Church & The Church Law Firm (hereafter 'Church') and Riley Vasher & Brody Quinlan (collectively 'BQ & Riles') dated . . .

I looked up from the page. 'You nicknamed us before you even met us?'

'I knew as much about you then as I do now, Riles.' He motioned toward the speaker box. 'You don't hire an investigator who lives in – and works out of – his mother's basement for his sparkling personality.'

'All lies,' the speaker box said.

I leafed through the weighty tome. Some of it was standard stuff I'd seen in other complex contracts concerning film rights; parts of it were anything but.

'You get *creative input*?' I cried. 'An *ownership* stake? You can take *control* of the production by buying up all the footage and hiring a new production team to finish the film?'

'Only under extraordinary circumstances, for that last one.'

'*You* approve final cut? You've got to be kidding!'

'Now, Riles.' He held up his hands in a calming motion. 'I can't withhold approval *unreasonably*.'

I flipped a page. 'Says here, "Approval may be reasonably withheld if any part of the film includes any single communication which would be subject to exclusion under any relevant evidentiary rules as work product or attorney–client privilege." That encompasses *everything*.'

'Not everything. Not the hearings, not the trial.'

'You want total control over how you *and* Ethan are portrayed. That's outrageous.'

Church leaned back in his seat, said calmly, 'What did you tell my client when you first spoke to him? What, in your opinion, *sold* Ethan on your documentary? What was the primary reason he agreed to do this movie at all? Was it the money you offered for the defense?'

'No,' I said, 'he told me his brother, Nate, would have his back.'

'Did he seem interested in fame? Or notoriety, rather? Is that how you sold him on this?'

'No.' It was all I could do to avoid Ethan's eyes. 'If anything, that was a con for him. He said he didn't want to be known for anything other than his performing.'

'Then what did you say to nudge him?'

I suddenly felt like I was on the stand, felt myself starting to sweat. 'I told him we were the Court of Last Resort.'

'Ah, the Court of Last Resort,' Church said. 'And by that you mean the American public, right? Your viewership? They're the jurors you're tacitly referring to?' He eyeballed me like a hostile witness. 'Tell me, do you plan to wait until all of Ethan's appeals are exhausted before releasing your movie?'

'That could take years.'

'That's right, and that wouldn't help at all, would it? By then it would be too late. Too late for you, too late for Ethan. It's not *literally* the Court of Last Resort, then, is it? That would be the Hawaii Supreme Court and ultimately the United States Supreme Court. So the only way Ethan benefits from this film is if it is: *one*, riveting enough to capture the attention of millions of viewers; and *two*, persuasive enough to convince at least tens of thousands of American citizens to launch a public campaign. Correct?'

I remained silent.

'While the case is still on appeal,' he continued, 'I could not in good conscience allow you to release footage that would be detrimental to my client's odds of winning a new trial. We can agree on that, right? That my paramount duty is to my client? Well, to successfully protect my client's interests, I need to ensure that this movie is both riveting and persuasive, and I can only do that with approval of the final cut.'

'I am *not* making a docuganda,' I said.

'I'm not asking for a hit-piece,' he scoffed. 'Nothing like what Marissa did to me in *The Prosecutor*, OK? And I'm not asking you to lead the audience. I'm not asking for narration here. You don't have to endorse one position or another, in the film or in publicity. I'm merely scrutinizing what gets shown, and in what order.'

'Taking what's on camera and presenting it in a dishonest fashion is no better than—'

'Nothing about it will be dishonest,' he said. 'Take my word; my word is good.'

I studied his eyes but he had a practiced poker face, and I instantly realized that no matter how long I knew Nicholas Church, I'd never be able to read him.

'Well,' I said as casually as I could, 'we're going to have to consult with our lawyers.'

On the way to the parking garage, Brody said, 'We don't have lawyers.'

'No shit,' I said.

TEN

I like to fantasize. Nothing unrealistic, nothing too grandiose. I'm not striving to be the next Werner Herzog, Ken Burns or Morgan Spurlock. I don't need my name to be recognized alongside the modern greats in true crime. I'm not a young Andrew Jarecki or Jean-Xavier de Lestrade. Brody and I aren't the next Moira Demos and Laura Ricciardi.

This is our first film, after all, our maiden voyage. We film-makers learn from experience, just like everyone else. We absorb our bloopers and blunders, we strive to surpass our past projects, we work our entire lives attempting to master an unmasterable craft.

Thing is, I recognize – recognized from the very beginning – that the murder of Piper Kingsley is a once-in-a-lifetime opening. Thanks to Professor Leary, we have the money. Out of sheer luck, we were on location from Day One. The reality is, we might never get another shot like this. Surely not without one or both of us getting a 'real job'. So if our maiden voyage crashes and burns, there might never be a second. In other words, this film could be our *Titanic*. Either the doomed ship, or 1997's Oscar Winner for Best Picture. And, I admit, it's disquieting that we won't know which until the final cut.

I'm shitty at budgeting, just no good with money in general. That much was clear early in my first year of film school at NYU, when I realized I was on pace to blow through my parents' inheritance before earning even half the credits required for my MFA.

With Leary's inheritance, I've been no better. First, the move to Hawaii cost more than I ever expected (and I thought I'd figured high). Then finding a long-term rental in Waikiki turned into a night terror. In the end our rent was nearly double what we were paying *in Manhattan*. Granted, we upgraded from a third-floor studio in a pre-war, red-brick walk-up in the East Village to a twenty-third-floor one-bedroom overlooking the Pacific. But then we also had to eat.

I'd factored in just so much for groceries, with the asinine idea of sitting down with Brody and learning to cook. It never happened. In Waikiki, we rediscovered bar food. Not that bar food itself is ultra-expensive, but the dozen or so mai tais you down with your meal begin to add up. Then there are the Hawaiian necessities I somehow hadn't anticipated: sunscreen, snorkeling gear, cute swimsuits and hats at Ala Moana Center. Payments on a Jeep Wrangler and insurance. All of it on top of rent, electric, cable, Wi-Fi, cell phones. And weed, an ounce between us, each week.

Then there was the film. The equipment, the editing room, the occasional crew members working per diem. Plus we *did*, despite his purported motives for signing with us, contribute heavily to the cost of Ethan's defense. Sure, Nate paid the lion's share; according to his wife Cheyenne, half their life savings. But then,

Nicholas Church is one of the costliest criminal attorneys in the United States. Worth every penny, of course. Ask anyone – from the upper echelon of legal academia right down through the streets of Detroit, St Louis, Miami, New York.

Following *The Prosecutor*, the name Nicholas Church went viral, and his performance earned him several high-profile cases. The media love him. An easy cure for the slow news cycle, he regularly flirts with female anchors live via Skype on all three of the major cable news networks. A recent *USA Today* poll showed that nearly as many Americans are familiar with the name Nicholas Church as they are with the name Johnnie Cochran.

Last year, while Brody and I were shooting a short doc in Los Angeles, we heard it firsthand – unprompted, unsolicited – from a bona fide gangbanger named Still: 'You get hit with a one-eight-seven up in *this* bitch, fuck *Better Call Saul* – you better get yo ass to Church.'

When I showed Church the clip, he raised a single brow and said, 'That quote would look totally bad-ass on a billboard on I-5. If only I advertised.'

As for production costs, we save where we can. We'd intended to hire a scriptwriter; instead, I'm writing the script. We'd intended to hire a location coordinator; instead, Brody took over the position. At home, we've stopped ordering extra cheese on our pizza, because fuck that additional dollar-oh-five. We eat in more too, prepare what food we can, which mainly boils down to pasta, English muffins, cold sandwiches, frozen pizza and blueberry Eggos. When we do eat out these days, we dine casual, limit alcohol consumption and screw servers out of tips. *I'm kidding!* But we *have* started taking home doggy bags, notwithstanding the fact that we have no doggy back home.

At one point Brody even offered to get a job. 'I can bartend,' he said. 'I can wait tables.'

Made me feel terrible. He's just so overqualified. Until we graduated film school, Brody had been a perpetual student and holds several prestigious, if useless, degrees. Bachelors in both philosophy (median salary for recent grads: $30K) and anthropology ($28K), a Masters in social work, a PhD in Comparative Religion. All from good schools, all paid for with student loans, placing him in hundreds of thousands of dollars of debt. Each of these areas of study once held his passion, at least until he felt satiated and abruptly moved onto another.

'I can't seem to find my footing,' he told me soon after we first met. 'I don't know my purpose.'

He did know that he wanted out of the tri-state area in which he grew up, knew he wanted away from Connecticut, away from his mother. Since my two weeks with Piper were the most fun I'd had in years, I joked that after film school we should move to Honolulu.

Brody, who'd traveled alone through Europe but otherwise never left the east coast, fell instantly in love with the idea. For a while it was all he could talk about.

Although I gave lip service to the concept, deep down I wanted to stay in New York. I had no real desire to flee the feverishness of the city, to blow off the Big Apple's opportunities. Above all, though, I didn't want to leave Professor Leary.

When the professor suddenly passed, the decision became that much easier. That week, New York ceased to be my city of dreams and mutated into something else. Something broken, something painful.

The shock of the inheritance sealed the deal. Honolulu suddenly sounded a lot like hope, and on paper, it all appeared doable. But as it turns out, the rumors are true: it's *fucking expensive* to live in Hawaii.

What's so clear only now that we've gone overbudget is that if Piper wasn't murdered when she was, Brody and I wouldn't have lasted another six months, not here in paradise, not without dipping into the money we'd set aside for production of the film. And the film, in many ways, was – is? – the glue that kept us together.

Besides, by accepting such a significant inheritance, I felt as though I'd made an implicit promise to Professor Leary. And that was one promise, in a lifetime of broken ones, that I sure as shit intended to keep.

But then, maybe the greatest price tag we paid over the past six months was the unremitting guilt, lingering like a canker sore still. Although we choose not to discuss it, there were so many times when it appeared Brody was about to throw down the camera and say, 'I'm sorry, Rye, I can't do this. This just isn't right. You *knew* her, for Christ's sake.'

But that's always been a possibility. From the evening we initially agreed to do a film, I questioned whether Brody truly has the stomach for this. And I admit, over the past six months, I questioned whether *I* have the stomach for it as well.

I question it still.

Going into this business, you realize your success must come at the expense of others. But that's true of countless professions: certain doctors, understudies, second-string athletes, personal injury lawyers. But, of course, you never expect your success to come at the expense of a friend.

I've rationalized over and over that no matter what I do – make a movie or go back to Oregon – Piper Kingsley will still be in an urn in her father's hotel room. At times, I've even rationalized that I am helping get at the Truth. Piper deserves as much, I told myself, as does Professor Leary.

But, at the end of the day, I fear that what I'm in this for isn't Piper or Leary or anything as noble as Truth. I fear I'm in this purely for recognition, fear I'm in this for money. I fear I'm only in this because it's *my* dream. Which is why, as I sit here in the editing room, I accomplish little tonight other than rewatching footage and assuaging my guilt.

This is something I didn't learn in film school, something even Professor Leary never taught me. Even if you're born for this shit, as I think I was, this job becomes fucking *hard* once you meet the cast. Becomes fucking *impossible* once you start seeing the players as people.

ELEVEN

S ure enough, a week after the weathergirl died, the police arrested Ethan under circumstances we never could have imagined yet were somehow ready to capture.

Earlier that day Brody and I were engaged in Day Four of negotiations with Nicholas Church over whether we – BQ &

Riles – would formally join the defense team. The contract remained unsigned between us in Church's suite.

'I'm not sacrificing my objectivity,' I shouted across the conference table. 'I intend to act ethically. I intend to be credible. I intend to search for the *truth*.'

Church waited until my echo faded, then used his indoor voice, in an effort, I realized, to make me appear hysterical.

Softly, he said, 'And what makes you think I'm in this for anything different?'

I turned down the volume. A little. '*Your* job is not to search for the truth. *Your* job is to get your client acquitted.'

Dressed meticulously in Brioni, Church gingerly placed his elbows on the table and leaned forward, a pensive look on his face, and like a silent train bolting out of the pitch, it suddenly struck me why he had allowed us to film this part of the negotiation and no other.

Church pursed his lips. 'What if those things are not mutually exclusive?'

I was outraged, more now at myself for allowing us to be so blatantly used. 'What if they *are* mutually exclusive?'

He leaned back, folded his arms, shrugged and said simply, 'Then I wouldn't be here.'

'Yeah, right,' I tried, now more aware of the camera than ever. 'So I'm supposed to believe that each of the men you defended – who walked away scot-free after trial – were innocent?'

'Unless you're on my jury, I don't give an orangutan's ass what you believe, Riles. But to answer what I *think* you meant to be your question: *yes*. Each of the men – and one woman, by the way. Each man and woman I've walked since becoming a criminal defense attorney has been *not guilty* of the crime of which they were accused.'

'You don't know that!' I cried. 'You *couldn't* know it.'

'Listen, Riles.' He shot his cuffs, silent for a moment to allow that goddamn nickname to burrow into my skin. 'As unbelievably talented and humble as I may be, I am *not* a miracle worker. The reason I was able to get all those individuals acquitted is simple. They had a tremendous benefit that, frankly, most criminal defendants lack – they were actually not guilty.'

I looked away from the camera, sighed heavily. 'You know

damn well I'm not talking about whether the prosecution proved their case or not.'

He swiftly rose from his chair. 'Neither. Am. I.'

The tone in his voice startled me, pinched something in the pit of my stomach. It was a tone I would hear frequently over the next six months, but never fully get used to, even when it wasn't directed at me. At the time, it struck me speechless.

Church took a few moments, during which I imagined him counting to ten (probably *en français*) in his head, then he exhaled audibly and sat.

'One case,' he said, with a single finger in the air to clarify. 'In my twelve years in criminal defense, I've never taken on more than one major case at a time. Most private defense lawyers have fifty or sixty felony cases at any given moment, and *still* work bankers' hours. How? As a defense lawyer, how can you zealously protect the lives you hold in your hands and treat your job like a regular nine to five? You *can't*. Because to earn any kind of living at all in this business, you have to speed things along, you have to cut corners, you have to phone it in. Who suffers? The clients. *They're* the ones who are fucked without adequate representation. And I'm talking now about defendants who *paid* for their lawyers. Don't get me started on the poor bastards who have to rely on the public defender system in certain states.'

'How is *this* related to the guilt or innocence of your own clients?'

He smiled. It was a charming, disarming smile, an exceptional knock-off of the genuine thing I'd see over and over the next six months.

'One major case at a time,' he said, again with the finger. 'One case. One client. One fate. So I'd better choose wisely, right? I'd better vet every prospective client. I'd better learn who he is, who loves him, who will cry if he's convicted and sent away to prison, or worse. Who will attend his funeral if he receives a sentence of death.' He paused a beat, took a sip of iced water from a hulking crystal water glass then set the glass neatly back on its coaster. 'But above all, I ask myself, will *I* be at this man's funeral if he's sentenced to die? Will I stand over his grave *knowing* that the State has taken the life of an innocent man?' In his eyes rose a thin mist I wasn't expecting, but his voice didn't waiver. 'If so, I had better be *damn sure* I did everything humanly possible to stop it. Which is why I needed to meet with Ethan face to face before I took him on as a client.'

I swallowed hard, suddenly desperately thirsty. 'You took it even though it's not a death case?'

'Life in prison or lethal injection; same difference for a guy like Ethan.'

I was now less interested in the argument over Church's dozen clients than I was about his belief in Ethan's innocence.

'So you're one hundred percent sure he's innocent?' I asked. 'Absolutely certain that he didn't murder Piper?'

Church leaned back in his chair, carefully folded one leg over the other. Took a deep breath and declared with uncut confidence: 'One. Hundred. Percent.'

Seconds of silence passed, then Church said four words that would echo endlessly in my head, four words that rang out like a warning shot, shrilled like a faulty alarm clock. Four words that would unfailingly deliver me an unspecified dread over the coming half-year.

'Turn off the camera.'

'Of course not,' Church said, once the camera was off. 'How can I be *sure* Ethan Jakes is innocent? I'm not a mind-reader, I wasn't there when it happened. I was in Indianapolis, with Marissa, arguing like hell, with the utmost civility.' He paused, sipped more water. 'But *you*, Riles, *you* I'd like to have on my jury. Together we'd walk the lot of them.'

A deep heat ascended the length of my neck, flooded my cheeks. My heart beat faster, my systems on the verge of an unthinkable panic. Sweat at the hairline, a sensation like ice in my veins, shortness of breath, then . . .

No, not in front of this fucking guy.

'In all seriousness, though?' he said. 'I absolutely factor in my belief in my client's innocence. And I set that bar extremely high. Much higher a standard than reasonable doubt. I need to truly *believe* a man who tells me he's innocent to even consider taking on his case.'

I realized then what made Nicholas Church such a superb trial lawyer. First, he lures you in with his gifts – his eloquence, his magnetism, that smile – then, once he has your ear, he casually lets you in on a little-known secret: that he's a bullshitter; you can't believe a word he says. By conceding as much, he conversely appears sincere, unaffected. Just a guy who speaks his mind, sometimes crass, sometimes vulgar, but frequently to humorous effect. Harmless, right? Meanwhile, he pockets that credibility, that faux integrity he's built, for moments like this, when – true or not – he wants you, he *needs* you, to believe him.

I was again witnessing that sorcery I'd first seen him perform all those years ago in *The Prosecutor*, only this time live and in person. This was the true Nicholas Church. He was handsome, he was charismatic, he was articulate as fuck. He was sitting here across the table from me, and the magic in his eyes was alive. How could I be anything but mesmerized?

Moreover, I was elated. Because I *was* convinced he genuinely believed in Ethan's innocence. And I so wanted Ethan to be innocent. I so wanted him to be the man I met at Manoa Falls, the man I watched performing 'While my Ukulele Gently Weeps' on YouTube. I so wanted Ethan to be innocent for reasons I didn't yet comprehend. But more than anything else, I so wanted him to be innocent for my movie.

Two hours later, the phone rang in Church's suite. Brody began filming again.

Church placed the call on speaker. 'This is Nick Church.'

'Mr Church, this is Detective Lance Fukumoto, HPD.'

'What can I do for you, Detective?'

I noted Church didn't dignify Fukumoto with a nickname.

'I'm giving Mr Jakes one final invitation to come down to the station and explain what happened last Thursday night.'

Church didn't hesitate. '*Mahalo*, but no *mahalo*.'

Fukumoto chuckled. Said, 'Mr Church, what you are trying to say is "*Hoomaikai aka, aole hoomaiki*". Thanks, but no thanks, yeah?'

'Sorry, I haven't had time to brush up on my Hawaiian. It was a brief twelve-hour flight from Indianapolis International.'

'Mr Church, I think you and I would get along just fine.' There was a smile in the way he said it. 'Why don't you bring your client on down to the station and we'll hash this out together, you and me. We just want to confirm your client's version of the events that night.'

In front of me sat Church's linen business card. On the front, just his name and email address. On the back, three lines, his instructions to clients on what to tell police:

I AIN'T GOT SHIT TO HIDE,
BUT I AIN'T GOT SHIT TO SAY EITHER.
LAWYER MY ASS UP.

Below that, some boilerplate about how neither Nicholas Church nor The Church Law Firm was responsible for any resultant police ass-beatings, though he *would* represent you in the subsequent civil suit. 'USE DISCRETION', it read.

'As much fun as that does sound,' Church said, 'my client and I are going to have to decline. We're previously engaged.'

'Nothing that can't be changed, I hope. Because in the case of your refusal, I'm afraid a warrant will be issued for your client's arrest.'

Church sat up straighter. 'If you have enough to charge him, why are you sitting around on the phone playing grab-ass with me? Why haven't you charged him?'

'Mr Church, you will find that I am a very *thorough* man.'

Church scrawled those last few words on his legal pad.

'Mr Church, I am also a reasonable man. So I am extending you the courtesy of surrendering your client.'

Church glanced at his Rolex. 'Tomorrow morning, ten a.m.?'

'Today. Four p.m.'

Church opened his mouth to negotiate further but the line had gone dead.

'Well, this just got interesting,' he said. 'Turn off the camera.'

'Wait,' I shouted to Brody. 'Don't.'

Church said, 'No more filming until you sign the contract.'

'I can't give you approval over the final cut.'

'Listen, Riles. You and I both know damn well that if Ethan did this and there's concrete evidence to prove it, you and Shaggy over there have no movie, right? If he's found guilty but it's not as clear-cut, there will be as much interest in the appeal as in the trial itself. As a filmmaker, you know that *some* belief, some hope, that Ethan is, in fact, innocent of this crime is what drives your audience to follow this story. Nothing else. Not me, not Detective Fuck-your-mother, and certainly not the victim. If Ethan's found guilty, your film's *only* chance is the very same chance I'm trying to protect in this contract. If he's convicted, your only hope is that one day justice is done and Ethan's set free. Either way, it behooves you to allow me final-cut approval so that we can show our case – *Ethan's* case – in a light most favorable to the defense.'

'And if he's found not guilty?'

'Once double jeopardy attaches, you can edit the film any way you like. You can make it NC-17 for all I care. Just note Paragraph thirty-two, Section six-B assures me considerable compensation for any full-frontal nudity.'

I turned to Brody. 'Did you get those words on film?'

'About the full-frontal?'

'That I can make whatever the hell film I want to make if Ethan is acquitted.'

Brody gave me a thumbs-up.

'All right,' I said to Church, 'we have a deal.'

But Church had already moved on to his next task. Phoning Nate from his mobile as he paced the room, telling him in a voicemail to have Ethan call him back as soon as possible, without giving a reason.

Then Church set the speaker box on the table and said, 'Sheena, call Charlie.'

A Siri-like voice, only sexier, said, 'Calling Charlie.'

'Charlie,' Church said to the speaker box when Jesse picked up, 'I'm with my angels, BQ and Riles.'

As he wore out the plush carpet around the table, he filled Jesse in on his phone call with Fukumoto.

'They're going to charge him based on nothing but circumstantial evidence?' Jesse said. 'Well, at least you have a strong argument for bail.'

Church appeared skeptical. 'Let's run through what they have again. Trace evidence – hairs, fibers – but he practically lived there, so that's relatively meaningless, right? Fingerprints on the beer bottles out by the pool. That's certainly no crime, unless . . .' Church stopped mid-step. 'Unless she was struck in the head with one that night.'

Jesse said, 'To charge him based on that, they'd need the autopsy report, and we know that hasn't been completed yet. It's not in the system; I've been in their system all week.'

Church's hands clenched into fists. '*That's* what he meant.'

'Who?' Jesse said.

'Fukumoto. About him being a thorough man.'

'Nick, I checked the medical examiner's files, too. Everything's on the same network. There's nothing there.'

'When he said that he was thorough, he wasn't referring to the murder investigation at all. He was referring to *me*.'

'What do you mean?'

'Get out of their system, Jesse. Get out of their system *now*.'

'Why?'

'Because they know you're there.'

Just as Fukumoto had researched Ethan on his way to the crime scene, he'd done his homework on Nicholas Church. As Church explained it (off camera, of course), Jesse had hacked into HPD's system from the moment Church was retained (though I suspect even sooner), to monitor whatever evidence was discovered in real time.

'I'm eventually entitled to it anyway,' he said. 'It's called the Brady Rule.'

Every courtroom junkie was familiar with the Brady Rule. It held that the prosecution has an ongoing duty to turn over any exculpatory evidence they discover to the defense.

'If I remember correctly,' I said, 'the Brady Rule does not entitle the defense to hack into the government's servers to extract the information themselves.'

'Not explicitly, no. But I need to go on the offensive. There are too many shady prosecutors out there.'

'Says a member of the *defense* bar?'

Church's brows shot up. 'Would you agree that there are a great many shady defense attorneys, then?'

'In my experience, yes.'

'Well, there you have it. Half of the defense bar is comprised of former prosecutors.'

Nate finally called Church back at around one p.m.

Church put him on speakerphone, said, 'Tell your brother to pack a toothbrush and meet me at my suite at the Four Seasons no later than three this afternoon.'

'What's happening?'

'Great show, but let's get serious for a minute. Ethan's going to be charged. Tell him not to worry. We may have a strong shot at bail.'

'That doesn't sound very reassuring.'

'Is your brother with you now?'

'He just went for a walk around the neighborhood.'

'Which neighborhood?'

'Hawaii Kai.'

'That's on the east side of the island, we're on the west. You'd better get moving. If we're late, the penalty is a perp walk, and the last thing we want is for our prospective jurors to see Ethan on the cover of the *Star-Advertiser* in handcuffs.' He glanced in the direction of Brody and the camera. 'Not to mention, local TV will have a field day with it.'

Three o'clock came and went. So did four. Ethan hadn't shown and Church was pacing the room, vocally beleaguered by his client's stupidity. He repeatedly called Nate's phone, but all calls went straight to voicemail.

At 4:15 in the afternoon, Fukumoto phoned Church, who put the call on speaker for the benefit of the camera.

'Mr Church, why do I not see anyone standing in front of my desk?'

'I don't know, are your eyes open? That often helps.'

'Mr Church, this is no time for jokes.'

Church smiled; this time it was the real deal. 'Oh, you're gonna love me in court, then.'

'Mr Church, are you, or are you not, going to produce your client?'

Just as swiftly, Church wiped the smile from his face and cleared his throat. 'Yes, Detective, I apologize, for both my tardiness and my flippancy. The goodbyes are taking a bit longer than expected. But we'll be walking out the door at any minute.'

Church disconnected the call and eyed Brody, then me.

'Well, don't just fucking stand there,' he said. 'You're part of the defense team now. Help me find our client.'

TWELVE

I hate sleeping alone. Maybe because I'm an only child who never shared a room with someone – never shared a bed until my third year at college. My father didn't believe in sleepovers: 'What are you going to do there that you can't do here?' Didn't tolerate overnights after prom: 'You think I'm stupid, Riley?' Didn't even allow me to sleep on campus during my first two years at Oregon State: 'If I'm paying the bills, I'm making the rules.' I knew all his rules had a singular purpose, even if left unsaid. It was all about *sex* – his hang-ups, his double standards, his innate possessiveness. It was about protecting his daughter's virginity, her purity. So intent was he on safeguarding my cherry that he continued to safeguard it several years after it popped.

Because, despite Dad's obsession, despite years of Sunday School, and quite possibly *because of* the purity vows so popular at the time, I had sex at sixteen. Sex with a guy just home from his first semester at UPenn. Shagged him in his father's Camry's backseat, twice in one evening. Because, believe it or not, Pops, you needn't be out of the house the entire night to get laid. You needn't wear provocative clothes. You can do it with a purity ring around every finger, with a rosary in your pocket, and a crucifix at your throat. You can do it stone-cold sober, with the lights on or off, with the door open or closed. You needn't have any makeup or piercings or lingerie. Needn't have easy access to condoms or sex education or birth control. You needn't have parental permission, needn't have explicit images or vulgar language on television. You needn't watch X-rated movies or listen to dirty song lyrics. You needn't even have a bed.

There's a rap on the editing room door. Then a key turns in the lock.

'I have Leonard's tonight,' Brody chimes as he steps inside.

His face is clean shaven, he's gotten a haircut. He's dressed in a new Tommy Bahama T-shirt and cargo shorts and smells like coconuts.

'Why did you knock?' I say, though I'm still processing the image before me. Brody looks the way he looked when we first met in film school, when I still thought he was a bit of a dork.

He says, 'Because I don't want to, you know, just walk in on you.'

'What the hell did you think I'd be doing in this shitty little editing room? Throwing an orgy?'

'Nah, you know.'

Yeah, I know, but I suddenly have a potent desire to bring color to Brody's cheeks, finally liberated as they are from his two-and-a-half-year winter beard.

Placing my weight on my toes, I lean in toward him. Kiss his bottom lip long and slow.

'For the malasadas,' I say.

'I shiver to think what would have happened had I bought the full dozen.'

'What made you shave?'

He takes a step back and grins, his right hand stroking his chin as if he's experiencing the texture of human skin for the first time.

'I just feel like we've reached a new chapter, you know? I feel hopeful again.'

I'm so thrilled to see him happy, and know I should just let it go, but I'm curious. When you know someone as well as I know Brody, you think you can interpret his every expression, you think you can decipher his every thought, you think you can read between the lines of any page he writes. You regularly take the power for granted, yet on the rare occasions you can't read him at all, you suddenly need to know his every thought.

'What about the past half-year, all the while we were filming?' I say. 'What's changed?'

'I don't know. I guess I feel like we've just lived through the climax after holding our breath the past six months.' He grips me by the waist and pulls me to him. 'Now that we know the ending, we can finally turn to the epilogue. The happily ever after part.'

I should keep quiet, I should just shut up. 'There were losers in this too, though.'

'I get that, and I'm not trying to discount them. I'm talking specifically about you and me and our film. We can finally move on to the next phase of our lives.'

He wants an answer.

Truth is, I don't know yet if I'm ready to move on. But I don't say so. Instead I lean in and kiss his neck, feel the shiver run through his body.

His eyes fall on my monitor.

'What are you working on?' he asks, in a tone carefully measured to preserve the mood.

I put my lips to his left ear, whisper, 'The night Ethan ran.'

He presses his body against mine. He's excited.

Softly, he says, 'That footage is so dark and shaky.'

I take his earlobe on my tongue, run my lips over it and feel him shiver again. In the center-left of his cargo shorts rises Little Perry Mason, the name we jocularly bestowed upon his sizable member during trial.

Through the linen, I take him in my left hand.

'I don't need all of it,' I say. 'Just Ethan's words when he first saw me on the rocks at Kaena Point.'

'The audio's grainy.' His voice suggests his mind is far off. 'How about Church's performance on the phone?'

'The Great Stall?' I ask, slowly working my fingers up and down. 'I've turned it into a montage.'

He grips the back of my head, presses his lips to mine, probes my mouth with a renewed passion.

The conversation is over.

As we kiss, I eye the box of malasadas with a shameful twinge of hunger.

I move my hand faster.

I think about the rough cut.

Think about Kaena Point.

Think about that night.

Think about Ethan's voice as Brody moans.

I think about Ethan's touch, even as Brody comes.

THIRTEEN

On H-1, at the cusp of dusk, I sat in the passenger seat of the white Jeep Wrangler we'd nicknamed the Yeti, gnawing my nails. Brody remained silent, the radio off, the soft top down, as it had been for a week. Tonight, though, I thought it might rain. Even on a cool, clear evening like this, weather in the islands could restyle itself without notice, especially where we were heading: Oahu's westernmost point.

Back at Church's suite, there had been as much commotion as one human being could generate. Brody and I had shrunk back against the sliding glass door, ready to bolt, while Church paraded back and forth past an invisible jury rail, spewing expletives like legal arguments.

Every five minutes, the phone rang.

Every fifteen minutes, Church answered.

'*I understand, Detective, he's just getting his affairs in order . . .*'

'*Any minute now, Detective. He's just, uh, cleaning himself up . . .*'

'*To be frank, we are photographing him, Detective – all of him – in case your boys decide to beat him silly with billy clubs in his sleep . . .*'

'*Here's the thing, Detective. We've decided to go in another direction with the whole ass-beating thing. Now we're doing what they did to Ed Norton in* 25th *Hour: kicking his ass before he goes inside so that he looks too tough to fuck with, too ugly to rape . . .*'

'*He – and this is embarrassing, Detective – he has the runs . . .*'

'*IBS, Detective, he's still in there, and God help* us *out here once he opens the door . . .*'

'*Damnedest thing, Detective . . .*'

Amid Church's tennis match with Fukumoto, Nate finally called back, only *not* with information, *not* with Ethan's whereabouts; he had no idea where his brother might be.

'You guys grew up together,' Church said over speakerphone,

'you had to have your private spots. Like that tree in the woods where you stashed your first *Playboy*? Or that pond all the kids went skinny dipping in after dark? Maybe that cave where you joined in your first circle jerk?'

Church had already phoned a local private investigator named (I shit you not) Tahoma Kaihanaikukauahkahihuliheekahaunaele to check Manoa Falls, the spot where Ethan and I initially met last week.

Following some thought, Nate said, 'We grew up in Waianae but haven't been there in years. As for hanging outside of our town, we went to spots all over the island.'

Church rolled his eyes. 'Examples?'

'We were friends with some military kids who lived out by Barbers Point.'

Church pulled up a map of Oahu on his phone. 'That's right near here, I'll take that one. What else you got?'

'There's a park over by Koko Head we used to play ball at.'

'That's near you, Nate. You check that spot. Give me another.'

'Uh, I guess we went out to Kaena Point a few times.'

'That's all the way at the westernmost tip of the island.' Church zoomed in on his map. 'Looks a little rocky around there.'

'Yeah, you need a four-by-four.'

'BQ and Riles have a Wrangler. They're here, they're listening. Head them in the right direction and give them a sense of this place.'

'All right,' Nate said, as Church headed for the kitchen, 'you guys are going to take Farrington Highway all the way out to the very end of the road. There's a chain across the road, with a sign that says, "Authorized Vehicles Only". Take the chain down, put your Jeep in four-wheel drive, and take the unpaved path as far as you can. Wear your seatbelts; it's a bumpy ride. After a few miles, you'll reach a point where even the unpaved road is washed out, so you'll have to park there and go the rest of the way on foot. Bring flashlights. It's *very* dark and *very* rocky. You can break an ankle, or worse. Anyway, hike that to the very end, and stop once you hit ocean.'

'How far is that exactly?' I asked.

'About three miles.'

My jaw fell.

'All right,' Church said, a Stella Artois in hand, 'BQ and Riles are on it. Updates as necessary.'

Once Church disconnected the call, I said, 'Kaena Point sounds like a shot in the dark.'

Church grinned. Set down his beer. Slapped his palms together. 'Which is why it will make *spectacular* footage if you find him there.'

Forty-five minutes later, Brody and I reached the end of the road. The *paved* road at least. Raindrops dotted our windshield as Brody put the Wrangler in park, removed the chain with the 'Authorized Vehicles Only' sign, put the Wrangler in four-wheel, and stepped lightly on the accelerator.

Seconds later I felt like Matt Damon in his rover traversing the terrain of Mars. To his credit, Brody proceeded as heedfully as possible. Still, every other inch of the ride was either a steep ascent or steeper descent, the tires seldom agreeing on a single direction. I grabbed the oh-shit bar and held tight.

'This isn't going to help my herniated cervical disc,' Brody muttered.

The anti-road went on for just a few miles but took us twenty-six minutes. By the time we reached the spot where a vehicle could travel no further, it was full dark and raining hard.

'Stay in the Jeep, babe,' Brody said. 'I can do this.'

I'd already opened my door. 'I have to speak to him,' I said. 'You and he haven't really exchanged two words.'

'I'll get the camera. You going to mic up?'

I hesitated. 'Yeah, of course I am.'

Our odds of finding Ethan at Kaena Point had increased some-what substantially since Church, Nate and Tahoma had all come up empty in their own searches. Last I spoke to Nate, he intended to phone all friends and family. Last I spoke to Church, he declared he'd be at the hotel bar.

As Brody and I clambered over a mile of rocks, trudged through another of wet sand, and finally landed on something resembling a hiking path, I pondered what Ethan's running said about his guilt or innocence. Conventional wisdom held that the guilty run, the innocent stay and fight to clear their name. But then, as Brody wisely pointed out, 'If you were innocent, would you want to leave *your* fate up to twelve people who are able to take months off work without being missed?'

Slogging through foot-deep mud, three miles felt like the length of the island. To make things more interesting, my iPhone's flashlight kept blinking out. Brody couldn't use his camera to light the way because he'd forgotten to charge his spare battery and didn't want to risk us missing the scene if we located Ethan.

As we neared the water, Brody stopped short, froze his phone's flashlight, and gripped me by the arm. 'Shit, Rye. There's someone over there.'

I tried to focus on Brody's beam of light. 'I don't see anyone.'

'Over there,' he said, lowering the beam a little. 'Splayed out on the ground.'

In the editing room, Brody and I bite into our malasadas. Into the fattening filling, into the fattening fried dough. I don't give a shit, I've earned this. I want to pig out, want to devour the malasadas then hit that Moroccan and Lebanese eatery on Nuuanu Avenue. I'd start with some baba ghanoush then move on to the kofta sandwich. As I chew the malasada and nearly orgasm just *thinking* about Middle Eastern food, I glimpse Brody's newly shaven face and those dimples I'd all but forgotten.

'I love you,' I tell him.

He turns to me, surprised. 'You never say that.'

It's true; never first, anyway. There are people who say, 'I love you' and people who say, 'Love you, too.' I'm neither.

'Are you done working for the night?' he asks.

'Not even close. I want to at least edit Ethan's audio and play it over the B-roll of Kaena Point at night. I'm eager to see how it all comes together.'

'Church may want us to cut that, you know. He thinks it's too self-serving and looks staged.'

'Church tried the case he wanted to try. I'm going to make the movie I want to make.'

Brody takes a bite of his malasada and doesn't reply. He has a fondness for Church that's irritated me this whole time. So desperate is he for a father figure that he would literally take in the homeless if I let him. The homeless in Honolulu move Brody to tears some nights. Growing up with no father and a borderline mother, he knows that it might have been *him* setting up a tent, begging for spare change, waiting to get shooed away by police. It's something he's feared his entire life. As he jumped from job to job, from school to school, he never felt safe, never felt settled, not until we moved to Hawaii.

Here, thousands of miles away from his mother, Brody can kick back and enjoy life in a way he never could back east. Days after we arrived, he discovered his 'perfect spot' on Waikiki Beach. Spent time there every morning, smoking his bowl, absorbing crime novels. As I prepared for the movie we as yet knew nothing about, Brody learned to surf, drank oversized beers at Lulu's, and listened to music 'to support the arts'. It was a happy time for both of us. I enjoyed the work and it was nice seeing Brody having the time of his life. Especially nice that he was having it with me.

Brody aimed the flashlight at his target, still some distance away. 'Right there, see?'

'I see a few boulders.'

'Well, that boulder just moved. That boulder is a human being.'

'Shoot from here,' I said, as soon as I observed motion myself. 'I'll go over and talk to him.'

Brody placed a gentle hand on my shoulder. 'Wait, we don't know that it's him.'

'Look, the tide splashes right up near those rocks. No one who isn't suicidal would sleep there. It's got to be him.'

I started down the rocks, focusing the flashlight on my feet. Rain was falling harder, water accumulating in my sneakers. My drenched clothes made me cold, colder than I've ever been in Hawaii. Brody had at least had the sense to wear his weathered black Mets cap, the frayed brim protecting him from all but the most aggressive rain. Meanwhile, every drop from sea and sky slapped me straight in the eyes. Me, with all those fancy fucking hats at home in my closet.

'Ethan,' I called, when I thought I might be close enough. But I could barely even hear myself over the winds, over the tide, over the teeming rain. Onward I went into a blackness that seemed to be waiting for me, until finally I froze like a child at the top of the basement steps.

'Ethan,' I yelled again in the direction of the boulders.

A soft sound returned from roughly that direction. I placed my hands in front of me and hurried down the slippery rocks. Maybe Ethan was injured, I thought, maybe he tried to hurt himself. After a few seconds of my standard worst-case-scenario thinking, I was terrified at what I'd find when I reached him.

When a flash of lightning lit the sky, I saw him lying in the sand with his back to me. I took several brisk steps then stopped dead at the crack of an incredible thunder I could feel in my stomach. Then my iPhone's flashlight blew out, stranding me in the ink.

Slowly, blindly, I started again and, as I neared him, his presence became palpable. Even over the smell of the ocean, the rain on the rocks, I could tell he hadn't bathed. When I finally reached his prone body, I stopped, petrified for a moment, then went slowly to one knee. Gently placed a hand on his bare back. Said, 'Ethan?'

The moment I did, he swung his head in my direction and growled – '*wuuahahhhaaaaa*' – like fucking Chewbacca.

I screamed some obscenity as I fell backward into the mud.

Flat on my back but uninjured, I was thinking Ethan's breath was for shit, when a second 'boulder' suddenly awoke from its slumber and sneezed in my face.

There were four in all. Humongous (maybe 400 pounds each) but harmless – Hawaiian monk seals. An endangered species with only 1100 left in existence. Suffice it to say, I'd never encountered one before. Certainly never had one sneeze in my face. I pushed myself to my feet, promised the seals I'd donate a thousand bucks to the Marine Mammal Center if I sold my film, and was about to move on when from far off I heard: 'Riley!'

Although the voice rose from the darkness it didn't sound like it was emanating from where I'd left Brody. For a moment I thought I'd gotten turned around, but how turned around can you get on a piece of land jutting into the sea? There was ocean on three sides of me.

Then I felt his touch. Ethan's.

'Riley, what are you doing out here?'

'I don't know, sight-seeing? What the hell do you *think* I'm doing out here?'

'It's a downpour, though.'

'Then you shouldn't have picked tonight to run.'

'You don't understand. I can't do time, Riley. I'd rather fucking die.'

'I get that, I do. But if you're going to kill yourself, at least wait until after trial.'

'I might never have the opportunity again, and you know that. I go inside tonight, get denied bail in the morning, get convicted, that's it, that's the end. My window is closing fast.'

'What's the plan here, Ethan? Just to throw yourself into the ocean?'

He looked out at the sea as though he hadn't really thought it through. 'You don't think I'd die in *that* water?'

'I think you'd *eventually* die. But I also think you'd have a hell of a rotten last half-hour. Didn't you used to be a professional surfer?'

'How did you know that?'

'Don't you think your instinct to swim will take over once you're in the water? Were you at least going to pack rocks in your pockets?'

He smiled. In the darkness, in the downpour, it lit the night.

If I got him to smile, I thought, maybe I can talk him back.

I said, 'People get away with murder all the time. You never know what will happen at trial. You never know what a jury will do. And let's face the ugly truth about American jurisprudence. It doesn't hurt that you're Caucasian. Doesn't hurt that you're so attractive. We get a few women on that jury—'

'You think I'm attractive?'

I was suddenly very aware of the fact that my nipples were fully visible through my sopping white shirt.

'Come back with me,' I said. 'Church thinks we have a really strong shot at bail.'

As I said it, I noticed the chest Ethan's own shirt clung to, my eyes lingering longer than proper under the circumstances.

Emboldened, Ethan stepped toward me, placed his hands either side of my waist.

'I'm scared,' he said.

'I know.'

'It's like you said, though. About anything being possible at trial? About the jury being a bunch of random idiots.'

'I don't think I said that exactly.'

'Well, that's what's scaring me,' he said. 'The evidence looks bad, makes it look like I did it. And I didn't, Riley.' He gazed deeply into my eyes. 'I didn't kill Piper. I never laid a finger on her in violence, ever.'

'I believe you,' I said.

And I did.

Kinda.

Sorta.

Maybe.

The ride back to Ko Olina was silent. Brody drove, Ethan in the front seat, me in the center-back with the wind pummeling my saturated head and clothes. Yet I felt good, I felt alive. Felt like everything was falling into place. We'd avoided returning to the mainland bankrupt. We'd discovered an extraordinary case which, no matter what else, contained all the essential elements of a good true-crime story: sex, drugs, violence. A stunning young upscale white woman dead, a dashing Caucasian defendant with talent. Awful, true, to think in those terms. But, as Professor Leary said the day I first revealed my passion for tabloid justice: 'Well, I suppose someone's going to give the people what they want. Might as well be someone capable of reshaping the genre. Maybe even reshaping the justice system.'

During the drive, though shivering, I studied Ethan's profile, his features like cut glass. Despite his significant build, he didn't strike me as a tough guy. His music certainly didn't suggest it either. If anything, soft rock and acoustic indicated he was sensitive. Maybe as sensitive as Brody. If true, then Ethan was right; he couldn't do any significant amount of time in prison. Frankly, I wouldn't expect Brody to last a night.

Shame suddenly turned my blue face crimson. Everything falling into place? An old friend of mine was dead. The man in the passenger seat of my Wrangler was about to be charged with her murder. His life was on the line and he appeared as paralyzed with shock, as delirious with fear, as anyone I'd ever seen. Did it matter whether I believed in his innocence? I didn't think so, not at the time. Because Church was right: unless I could portray Ethan Jakes as a sympathetic character, wrongly accused of a heinous crime, I had no movie at all. Fuck objectivity. I was part of the defense team, and I decided then and there to buy all in.

A half-hour later, we pulled off H-1 into Ko Olina. As we approached the gatehouse to the resort, I studied Ethan's face again. He looked somehow different after this ride. Like a child who'd just comprehended death for the first time. Tears formed in the corners of my eyes as we pulled into the Four Seasons garage.

I wanted to comfort him but couldn't.

I wanted to kiss him but couldn't.

I wanted to film him.

So I removed my iPhone from my back pocket and shot.

PART II
Visual Evidence

FOURTEEN

I like getting lucky. Like winning the jackpot, hitting Blackjack, rolling the dice just right. Like getting my favorite table at Buzz's, my favorite stool at Da Big Kahuna. I like close parking, open roads, green lights. I like having been born into America's middle class while there still was one. I like that I met a man I love, that I landed a professor like George Leary. I like that Brody and I moved to Hawaii and lived it up those first few months.

But I also like that I knew Piper Kingsley when she was alive, that I got in touch with Ethan when I did. I like that Church had just wrapped up a major case when I called, that the defense encountered such a twisting and turbulent investigation. I like that there was such a compelling trial, a riveting showdown between two world-class lawyers. I already like the movie this tragedy will become. I hate only that I feel fucking terrible for it.

We got lucky. There's no other way to say it, no sentence that will soothe the sentiment that we experienced good fortune as far as our documentary went. Although I don't dwell on it now, I knew that Ethan's story could end at any time. There were so many unknowns, so many possible outcomes that could have sunk my film. Had Ethan suicided, had he been found incompetent to stand trial, had he accepted a plea deal – in all those scenarios I could have kissed my film goodbye.

Church knew our respective objectives didn't necessarily coincide, knew he was creating a *de facto* conflict of interest when, under the pretext of expanding Ethan's attorney–client privilege, he placed us on the defense team. I think I knew it too. Knew that Brody and I were nothing more than Church's Plan B, that one day, if Ethan were convicted, he'd turn the case over to another lawyer who'd use our presence, our words and actions, our movie, as a basis for appeal. In the meantime, Church would have us cheering from the sidelines, documenting the events he wanted documented, while simultaneously arguing his case before Judge Hightower *and* the Court of Last Resort. I knew it at the time, but I didn't much care. All I cared about was my movie.

In the editing room, I suck up the remnants of another Diet Coke. I've been here all day, all night, trying to decide how to show the arraignment. On the wall to my right are fifty-six three-by-five index cards, twenty-eight for Acts One and Three, twenty-eight for Act Two, each with a brief overview of events. The card marked 'Arraignment' is highlighted yellow, meaning I've deemed it a master scene. But now I'm not so sure.

'If you're going to work in an established genre like true crime,' Professor Leary told me during my first year, 'you've got to set your movie apart from the rest. Don't make your film a straight procedural. We've seen all that shit before. Show people the shit they *haven't* seen.'

The arraignment lasted all of twenty minutes and was about as dull as a visit to the DMV. The evidence against Ethan, which I'd learned about from Church the previous evening, was laid out in lackluster fashion by a young male assistant prosecutor, rather than the dynamic Naomi Lau herself. Church, too, merely rambled off the standard arraignment spiel – 'no prior record . . . not a stranger-to-stranger incident . . . confident my client will be vindicated . . .' etc. etc. – then waxed poetic on the logistical difficulties of fleeing a jurisdiction that also happened to be the most remote archipelago on the planet.

When Church finished speaking, a surge of panic ran through me like an electrical current. This was Ethan's only genuine opportunity at bail, and I'd recommended this shyster who had arrived in court this morning reeking of cigars and Wild Turkey. Ethan couldn't do time, I knew, certainly not months – it would decimate him. To the local population (i.e. every potential juror), it would also assign Ethan a presumption of guilt. His imprisonment would hinder his defense, complicate the investigation, make communication with his attorney onerous at best. Worst of all, Ethan's being inside through the trial would be absolute *shit* for my film.

As Judge Hightower ruminated over the prosecution's recommendation of remanding the defendant without bail and Church's endorsement of releasing Ethan on his own recognizance, it appeared His Honor was leaning toward the former, and would either deny bail altogether (for which Ethan's tardy surrender made a *powerful* argument) or set bail so high he might as well deny bail altogether. As the judge cleared his throat to issue his decision, Church popped up from his seat.

'May we approach, Your Honor?'

Hightower, a bear of a man with a thick beard and rich baritone, lifted his eyes from his paperwork and eyed Church like a piece of gum stuck to the bottom of his sandal. He motioned Church and the assistant prosecutor forward.

From my vantage point, Church delivered what appeared to be a humdrum argument, certainly not the emotional appeal I'd hoped for and expected.

With Church away from the defense table, I was better able to observe Ethan, who was still dressed in the tangerine jumpsuit issued to him the previous night at the station. I sighed heavily. If the dark rucksacks under his eyes were any indication, Ethan hadn't caught a single Z since I last saw him. He looked as though he might slump over at any second.

Next to me, I could almost *hear* Brody's blood pressure rising. Hightower had prohibited us from recording audio during sidebars, a restriction that would become increasingly irritating later, over the course of the trial, as Church requested sidebars more and more often. On the rosy side, we *did* capture the images, and the court stenographer *did* take down the discussion, the transcript for which is sitting on the console in front of me, dotted with soy sauce.

CHURCH: As an officer of the Court, Your Honor, I would be remiss not to mention that in my extensive experience with high-profile cases – which this case certainly has the potential to become – an incarcerated defendant will dramatically reduce the public's interest in the case.

| JUDGE: | I'm not quite sure where you're heading with this, counselor. |
| CHURCH: | I'm merely saying, Judge, as a friend of the Court, that in my experience, a free defendant only adds to the mystique and intrigue. I think that when making this decision, Your Honor, it's only fair that you take into consideration the fact that my client's release will very likely turn this island into a media circus, with Your Honor the ringleader. We wouldn't want that now, would we? |

Hightower glanced at the assistant prosecutor, perhaps expecting some objection, some rebuttal, some retort. But the assistant remained silent, so Hightower shooed the lawyers back to their tables, marked up a page in front of him, and again cleared his throat.

'Bail is set at one hundred thousand dollars or ten percent bond.'

In other words, a meager ten thousand, less than a tenth of what Church had told Nate to set aside for a bail bond.

Hightower slapped his gavel.

Brody swung his head in my direction. 'What the hell just happened here?'

For the first time that morning, I smiled. Said, 'Hightower just got taken to church.'

It would become a familiar scene: the five of us – Ethan, Nate, Church, Brody and myself – sitting around the conference table in the penthouse suite. Today, a trio of cameras stood at painstakingly adjusted angles to record the first postarraignment meeting of the defense team.

'Before we start,' I said for the benefit of the camera, 'mind filling us in on what transpired at the arraignment this morning?'

'Jesse?' Church said.

'Yes, Nick.'

The voice startled me. I'd forgotten all about the speaker in the center of the table, as I would consistently over the next few weeks.

'Jesse, do you want to tell Riles here what happened at this morning's arraignment?'

'We simply did our homework.'

'And what did we learn?' Church said, as though speaking to a child.

'That Barry Hightower has stars in his eyes and an ego nearly as big as Nick's.'

'Just provide the play-by-play, Jesse. I'll handle the color.'

'So we decided on simple reverse psychology. *Blatant* reverse psychology, because we knew it'd be too tempting for Hightower not to take the bait.'

'Plus,' Church said, 'we feared subtlety might be lost on Big Barry.'

'Just what did you glean about him?' I asked.

Jesse said, 'With the aid of the internet and some very basic social engineering, we learned that Big Barry Hightower is, among other things, an aspiring novelist.'

Church said, 'He cites as his inspiration that judge who wrote *Carlito's Way.*'

Jesse added, 'So we knew he'd want maximum media coverage.'

I said, 'I don't see the connection. Maybe he just enjoys writing. Not all novelists write to become rich and famous.'

Church smirked. 'Seriously, Riles? What if I were to produce a good, honest, custom hat-maker who will testify under penalty of perjury that, on average, compared to us normals, novelists' heads are *literally* three times the size?'

'What are you even talk—'

'Money and fame drive *everything*, Riles. Certainly, the Arts. Hell, it's why you and BQ are making this film in the first place.'

Brody said, 'I beg to differ,' but went ignored.

Church said, 'What else did we learn about Hightower, Jesse?'

'We learned that nearly eighty-five percent of the photographs posted to his social media accounts are of himself.'

'Average Facebook user's much closer to eighty percent,' Church threw in.

'We also learned that Barry somehow stuffs himself into a Porsche nine-eleven every morning to drive to the courthouse. And that he's the second-most thin-skinned person on Twitter.'

I said, 'And all that told you . . .'

'All classic symptoms of egotism,' Jesse said. 'The photos demonstrate he's a narcissist. The Porsche is clearly attention-seeking behavior. And his thin skin, well . . .'

'Well, what?'

Church winced.

'Hightower's thin skin is a double-edged sword,' Jesse said. 'It's kind of Nick's Achilles heel. Thin skin is a narcissistic trait, but in a judge like Hightower, it also means he's quick to pull the trigger on holding lawyers in contempt.'

Church nodded in concession. 'Contempt citations make up ninety-five percent of my overhead.'

'But the assistant prosecutor,' I said, 'what if he'd called you out on all this? It would have hurt your position, right?'

'The assistant prosecutor wasn't going to call me out on anything,' Church said flatly. 'First, the kid looked like he'd just run over from his swearing-in ceremony. He couldn't so much as look me in the eye. Second, even assuming he had the balls to object to my aside, he wouldn't have. Because the prosecution wants Ethan out nearly as badly as we do.'

I said, 'What? Why? How do you know?'

'We did our homework on Naomi Lau too,' Jesse said over the speaker. 'She has her sights set on the governor's office. Based on our information, she's already decided to run. She thinks she has a slam-dunk conviction here, and she's well aware that this case only stays in the news statewide if Ethan is out on bail. If he's locked up, the story dies, at least until trial.'

'Wait,' I said, 'that's why she didn't handle the arraignment herself?'

'Bingo.' Church touched his nose. 'She can't throw it, that

would be bad politics. So she figured she could get what she wants just as easily by sending in that humu-nuku fish against a Great White like myself.'

'Humuhumunukunukuapua'a,' Jesse corrected.

'Thanks, but when I want the opinion of the centerpiece, I'll ask for it.'

'So,' I said, 'you guys did a lot of homework on the judge's personality traits. How is he *professionally*?'

'Depends on your perspective,' Church said. 'His knowledge and application of the law are lousy. But for our purposes . . .'

'For our purposes?' I said. 'Do we not want a *good* judge?'

Church rose from his chair, buttoning his suit jacket in one fluid motion. He said, 'I believe it was Homer who once opined, "If judges were any good, they would be lawyers."'

As he turned from the table, I asked, 'Homer the poet?'

'Better,' he said, unzipping his fly on the way to the bathroom. 'Homer the Simpson.'

FIFTEEN

It's roughly two a.m. when Brody and I step out of the editing room and start the three-block walk to the garage where we park the Jeep for an exorbitant monthly fee. As I'm reminded daily, there's no free parking in paradise.

While we walk, even in the anemic glow of the streetlamps, I can't help staring at Brody's clean-shaven cheeks. The beard never really bothered me; much to Brody's delight, facial hair is even in style these days. But recently it's as if Brody, for the first time since the early weeks of film school, is suddenly making an effort again. Making an effort for me.

As I gaze at the stars, I say, 'Sometimes everything seems preordained, doesn't it? I mean, when you look at time as just another dimension. Everything has already happened and we're all just waiting to find out what it is.'

Brody shakes his head. 'Time's not the fourth dimension, not in the way you're thinking of it. Not in the way Einstein thought of it. Time is simply a numerical order of change that exists in our third dimensional space.'

'In English?'

'Time itself has no physical existence; it has only a mathematical value.'

As we walk, I pull out my vaporizer and power it up again. 'So there's really no future to travel to, then? No timeline for Captain Picard to explore?'

'Why, had you planned on going somewhen?'

I suck in a lungful. 'How do you know all this random shit?'

'It's not random, it's physics.' He holds out his palm. 'Mind if I take a hit?' He stops, pulls on the vape pen and blows out a cloud of . . . A cloud of what? Vapor, I guess? 'I like physics,' he says. 'You know that.'

'Yes,' I say, as we move on, 'I see the books lined up next to the toilet. You like physics – quantum *and* Newtonian. But you also like law, politics, history, mathematics, medicine, computers . . .'

'What are you saying, Rye?'

The words jump from my mouth before I think them. 'Is filmmaking even in there anymore?'

He looks genuinely shocked. 'How can you ask me that?'

'It's just . . .' In for a penny and shit. 'Your lack of interest in postproduction concerns me.'

Following several seconds of thoughtful silence that make me feel like utter shit, he says, 'You're right. I'm sorry. I think I just needed some time to unwind after the trial. In the morning, we'll come down to the editing room together. I'll stay as long as you'd like.'

Could it be that I'm *the asshole in this relationship?*

'I would appreciate that,' I say curtly. 'You know—'

From out of the recesses of a dark building on South King leaps a tall, slender figure who halts directly in front of us, impeding our progress. I eye his long, bony fingers in an attempt to ascertain whether he's holding a gun or a knife or both. He has this Jack-O-Lantern grin on his face and he reeks of cheap alcohol, urine and body odor – not necessarily in that order.

He points to the sky behind us. 'Look!' he shouts. 'It's a bird! It's a plane! It's . . . *Homeless Man!*' He swings his ratty trench coat around like a cape. 'Fighting off starvation, addiction, mental illness, and all that rotten shit in the streets!'

Brody claps his hands together, a wide smile across his face. While I mentally try to determine the extent of damage to my underwear, the homeless-man-slash-performer takes a theatrical bow. I don't need to look to know Brody's hands are in his pockets following the enthusiastic applause. He hands the man two twenties. Says without the slightest hint of irony, 'Thanks, man. We needed that tonight. We're *also* trying to break into the entertainment industry.'

After receiving terrifically awkward hugs and some, let's say, *unconventional* blessings from our new friend, Brody and I continue to the garage in silence. I didn't say anything when Brody made good friends with a mentally ill homeless man named Roy near our apartment building in Waikiki. Didn't say anything when he started giving Roy our unfinished joints and blunts. I didn't even say anything when he started inviting Roy upstairs for a weekly shower. Now, however, I want to say something, *need* to say something. Yet any way that I try to put it, I'll come off like the asshole.

Thing is, we don't have much left, Brody.

Don't have much left? Rye, that man has nothing.

Maybe I *am* the asshole in this relationship.

'Let's run through the evidence again,' Church said as he approached the table, 'most of which remains circumstantial.'

'Yeah,' Jesse said through the speaker, 'if you don't count the DNA, fibers and fingerprints both inside the house and in the pool area outside, where the victim's body was found.'

'We're not denying he ever stepped foot in her house. He practically lived there, right?'

Ethan nodded. He looked tired, exhausted really. We all did. We'd already been here for several hours, ordered room service six times. I never dreamed I'd yearn for escape from a $17,000-a-night penthouse suite overlooking the Pacific, but you can only suffer so much Church and still maintain your sanity – which was why I knew from the start that he could never play the protagonist in my film.

Church said, 'Ethan could have sprayed every nook and

cranny of that house with his own semen, and that doesn't hurt us, got it?'

'The blood does,' Jesse said.

'Yes, the blood does.'

'Tests show that it's not menstrual and that it was fresh.'

'But its *location* isn't terrible for us. Ultimately, I think it'll be something the *prosecution* will have to explain. Because they're going to have a hell of a time convincing the jury that Piper was killed in the upstairs bathroom.' Church paused. 'In the meantime, research whether hemorrhoidal blood is distinguishable from other blood.'

'No more news on the footprint near the back fence,' Jesse said. 'Only that it's too small to be Ethan's. Unfortunately, we can't prove that it was left that night.'

'We're not in the business of proof. We're in the business of doubt. We know it rains like a bitch up there on the mountain and that it was raining most of the week. We argue that it would've been washed away had it not been left that very night.'

Jesse said, 'We still haven't received anything on digital forensics.'

Church turned to Ethan. 'You're absolutely *certain* there's nothing on your laptop, tablet or phone that can hurt us? No Google searches for "Top Ten Suffocation Techniques" that I should know about? No porn downloads depicting erotic asphyxiation? No arguments with the victim via text or email?'

'Nothing,' Ethan said, irritably.

'The fingerprints on the beer bottles in the pool area,' Jesse said. 'They pulled shards out of the victim's scalp, and Ethan's prints are all over the broken bottles.'

'Shitty, yes, but Ethan could have drunk the beers and left the bottles around, and someone else used one of them to hit Piper over the head. The killer just didn't leave a print.' He pointed to Ethan. 'You sure you didn't have any beers that night?'

'Absolutely positive. We ran out.'

'You'd run out the previous day, correct?'

'Yup, and I put out the recyclables that morning.'

'So there shouldn't have been a single beer bottle in that house?'

'There wasn't, not when I left for my meet.'

'But you do drink Budweiser?'

'I do drink Bud, yeah.'

Jesse said, 'We don't know yet if any shards from the bottles were found inside the house, do we?'

'No,' Church said. 'But that will be key in deciding our strategy. If Lau can prove the murder occurred *inside* the house, we can't go with an unknown intruder.'

'Wait,' Ethan said, 'why not?'

'Because as of now, there's no evidence of anyone but you being at the scene and there's no sign of forced entry.'

'But we *know* someone else did this, right? How can we go with anything *but* an unknown intruder?'

'We leave all our options on the table, E-male. *If* the murder occurred inside the house, no forced entry simply means Piper had to have known her killer. If so, we're going to have to give the jury a reasonable alternative to that killer being you.'

'But who?'

'Well, that's what we need to figure out, Eazy-E. But Jesse and I didn't know Piper, you did. Did she have any enemies?'

'Enemies? No, she did weather forecasts, she wasn't Scarface.'

'Women can have enemies, right, Riles?'

'Oh, yeah.'

'See, Ethan? Riles has enemies.' He turned and started pacing again. Somehow Church appeared as fresh and alert as when we arrived that morning. If anything, he spoke even more rapidly the later the hour became. 'The autopsy is ambiguous,' he said, 'which is both good and bad. Good, because the jury is going to want to know *precisely* how the murder was committed before they convict. Bad, because it gives the prosecution tremendous freedom in *speculating* how the murder was committed.'

'Manner of death is asphyxia,' Jesse said. 'There are bruises on her throat but no injury that appears severe enough to be fatal. In any event, we can rule out accidental death, suicide and natural causes. Unless we can point at another tangible suspect, what we're left with is insanity, diminished capacity or self-defense.'

'Wait,' Ethan said, his face filling with color, 'all those mean I'm guilty, right? That I did it?'

Church held up a palm. 'We're just going through our options, E-mo.'

'Well, then, strike those *out*,' Ethan shouted, as he practically ejected himself from his chair and slammed his hand against the table, 'because they're not options. I did *not* do this. I did *not* kill Piper.'

Ironically, that moment marked the first time I genuinely thought him capable of it.

When we stepped into our dark apartment in Waikiki following the defense meeting, my thoughts were racing. At the arraignment, I'd agonized over the possibility that I'd sabotaged Ethan's defense. Now I thought maybe my interference had had just the opposite effect, that maybe Church was a little *too* good at what he did, that I was helping put not only a killer, but my *friend's* killer, back on the street. A tornado of anxiety ripped through my center. I immediately went to the medicine cabinet for a Klonopin.

'Got an extra one?' Brody called from the hallway.

Brody knew how badly I needed my benzos, so he rarely asked.

I held out a pair of yellows. 'The indica not doing it for you tonight?'

He popped the tranqs under his tongue. 'Real world's more stressful than I imagined. No wonder I avoided it so long.'

I followed him into the living room. 'What's stressing you?'

'You kidding?' He ran his hand through his beard as he collapsed onto the couch. 'You were there.'

I detoured to the fridge, popped open a Diet Coke. 'You mean the pineapple?'

The autopsy report revealed that Piper's last meal had been pineapple, which creeped me the hell out because pineapple was also what they found in JonBenét's stomach. But then, as Church said, 'We're in Hawaii, Riles. If you sliced open the island's entire population, I bet you'd find pineapple in the stomachs of at least half.'

Brody's eyes widened as I stepped back into the living room.

'Riley,' he said, as though I were a stranger, 'the fact that Piper was *pregnant*.'

'Only six to eight weeks,' I said as I sat and searched for the remote. 'She wasn't even out of her first trimester.'

'So?'

'So . . .'

'She didn't *choose* this, Rye.'

I leapt to my feet. 'I *know*!'

While the frosty aluminum bit into my fingers, the air stilled the way it does immediately following a good shouting match. My mind, fogged with a few glasses of wine and exhaustion, searched for some way to flip this conversation in a different direction but went blank.

A few seconds later, as my breathing slowed, I noticed the remote in my hand and wondered how long it had been there. I pointed it at the television and hit the power button. When the television didn't blink on, I recalled the batteries dying this morning during California's afternoon shows.

I sank back into the couch with a huff. Jimmy Kimmel wasn't going to save us tonight; if anyone was going to salvage this evening, it was me. So I dug deep for some words and spewed the first that I found.

'I just think we need to distance ourselves emotionally from the case,' I said. 'We need to look at every aspect, including the pregnancy, from a single standpoint: how do we present this visual evidence so that it has the maximum emotional impact on our audience?'

Brody remained silent.

'On the one hand, the pregnancy adds intrigue,' I said. 'On the other hand, after Scott Peterson, it feels kind of clichéd, don't you think?'

Brody pushed himself off the couch. 'Would you listen to yourself, Rye?'

I tried to replay the quarrel in my head, but I was so fucking tired and had been so fucking laser-focused on my movie all day that I felt like the only subject on which I could concentrate, the only topic about which I could coherently converse, was what we'd learned in the past twenty-four hours and its implications for Ethan's defense.

The pregnancy, for instance, would likely play a small role since Ethan claimed to have known nothing about it. There was frankly no time to debate whether Piper's potential offspring should be treated as a second victim or the embryo that it was. Such extraneous details could be decided in post.

Brody headed toward the bedroom, closed the door behind him. In that moment, the world seemed intensely surreal, though I wasn't sure whether it was a symptom of sleep deprivation, or whether the world simply was surreal these days.

While I stared into the black flatscreen, I finally rewound the footage of today's meeting in my head and stopped at the point where Church had broken the news about Piper's being pregnant. I scanned the penthouse suite in my memory and noted each of the players' faces.

Nate immediately turned green, Brody blue ice.

On Ethan's face, though, nothingness. Not a whiff of surprise. The same reaction he had when we broke the news that Piper was planning to leave him.

Even though he adamantly denied knowledge about either.

Was he telling the truth?

Church bluntly laid out the consequences of lying: 'If the prosecutor discovers evidence to the contrary, E-trade, knowledge of either fact constitutes motive.'

SIXTEEN

I like being on my back. On the beach, next to Brody, watching the toned, bronzed bodies wade into the surf. We deserve this, don't we? Brody stayed true to his word and worked with me in the editing room all day every day last week. Today, we need some light, we need some air, we need some ocean. This morning is for straight-up relaxation, tonight for drunk-high-sexy fun. Because we're now at that pivotal stage of postproduction where we're working with the best footage we shot. This is the period of post when I warn friends and family not to phone the police if I don't emerge from the editing room for a few months.

This is when I switch from Diet Cokes to Monster Energy Drinks.

'I think we should avoid villainizing Lau and Fukumoto,' Brody says out of nowhere as we lie atop a pair of matching SpongeBob beach blankets on one of the less crowded patches of Waikiki Beach.

'I have no intention of villainizing them,' I say, 'but where they were wrong, I'm sure as shit going to point it out.'

'Fine,' he says, rolling onto his side to face me, 'but obviously, there has to be a villain. There has to be an antagonist in this film, don't you think?'

I inhale, exhale, adjust my oversized sunglasses but refuse to face him. 'I know what you're going to say—'

'You don't, though.' In his voice, there's a verve I haven't heard since he phoned me on his way to the crime scene six months ago. 'What if our villain is . . .' He pauses for effect, just one of many maddening attributes he picked up from Church during trial. 'What if our villain is the Truth?'

I literally bite my tongue, yet still say, 'Maybe you should limit the mornings you wake and bake, Brody.'

Undeterred, he goes on: 'You know that powerful scene where Church turns to you and says, "That's the trouble with seeking the truth – sometimes, you find it." *That* – that should be the overall theme of our movie.'

'This is *your* idea,' I ask, 'or Church's?'

'We all want the same thing, don't we? To make a movie every bit as absorbing, as provocative, as *intoxicating* as the murder case itself.'

Beneath my sunglasses, I close my eyes, I stay silent.

'Rye, don't you want to make something we can truly be proud of, something we can show our kids in twenty years?'

Our kids again. The first time he mentioned children I was more shocked than if he'd started belting out the lyrics to 'Bohemian Rhapsody' backward in German. Now he can't seem to gab about them enough.

It's what I wanted, though. I'd written so in my damned journal soon after we moved to Oahu, when Brody, the quintessential homebody, started spending most of his days and nights out and about in Waikiki, and exploring the island. The life Brody describes these days is exactly the one I wanted then, the same one I dreamed of achieving when I first fell in love with him in New York.

'Why aren't you saying anything?' he asks. 'Seems every time I mention kids you go silent.'

I'm going to eventually say yes, why not just say it?

'Sorry,' I tell him, 'I was just thinking about what you said, about Lau and Fukumoto.'

We endure several seconds of unquiet silence while Brody determines whether to accept the swing in subject or further escalate the ongoing argument.

Ultimately, he says, 'Fukumoto's finally retiring, I hear. The Jakes case was his swan song.'

I'm unmoved. 'He jumped to conclusions from that very first night, never had any intention of looking past Ethan. Church basically elicited as much from him on the stand.'

'See, this is *precisely* what I'm talking about, Rye. We can't twist the detective's words or take them out of context in the film. What Fukumoto said at trial was that he went where the evidence led him, just as he's done the past thirty-five years of his—'

'*Listen*, Brody.'

The rise in my voice occurs unexpectedly. I prop myself on my elbows and scour the immediate area to ensure no one's listening – a practice inevitably ingrained in you during a high-stakes criminal trial. 'Jurors could be lurking anywhere,' Church cautioned me one day at the courthouse. He pointed down the second-floor hallway. 'Juror Number Seven could be right around that corner, masturbating or scarfing down a Buffalo chicken sandwich, we just don't know.'

I say, 'Fukumoto decided he liked Ethan for Piper's murder *on his way* to the crime scene, we know that. Then he searched for evidence that fit his theory of the crime.'

'And found what? Ethan's prints on the beer bottle used to smash the victim over the head.'

'Her name was *Piper*,' I say (yes, with feigned indignation).

'*You* were the one in the early days who suggested we remain emotionally unattached to the case.'

Brody's so fucking good at throwing my own words back at me, and I so fucking hate it.

'And we failed badly on that front,' I remind him.

'Whose fault is that? I'm not the one who became attached to—'

'You didn't become attached to *Nicholas Church*?'

Brody sighs, shakes his head, exasperated in a way only I can make him. 'Why have you turned on him?' he says. 'What happened between the two of you?'

I loathe what I look like when I scoff but can't help myself. 'Church and I weren't exactly besties through the investigation and trial, you realize.'

'No, but since the verdict – or since we entered post, I suppose, depending on your perspective – you've been throwing a whole new level of shade in his direction.'

'We'll discuss it once he's back on the mainland, all right?'

'He's not returning to the mainland anytime soon. He's heading over to Maui until he finds his next case, or his next case finds him. There's a super-posh Four Seasons in Wailea.'

My jaw muscles tighten. 'Is Marissa going with?'

'Is *she* who this is about?'

'Is she going?'

'Yeah, I think they're going over together. They had this trip planned. They were supposed to go months ago, but the case kept them from it.'

I roll onto my stomach, unhook my bikini top. I've recently been pondering a move back to the mainland but until now had been afraid to say so. 'We can edit this anywhere, you realize. Why don't we finish postproduction in LA? That'll also give us a shot at making some connections before we shop the film.'

As anticipated, Brody deflates. 'We've got another few months left on the apartment lease.'

'We can sublet,' I say, as the Hawaiian sun massages my sore shoulders in a way no masseuse could. 'The apartment's in the heart of Waikiki with a million-dollar view. If we Craigslist it tonight, we'll have a tenant or serial killer in there by next Thursday.'

'What about the lease for the editing room? To say nothing of the fact that we may need to shoot additional B-roll before we finish the final cut.'

'I just want to move on,' I say, shifting, inadvertently providing the awkward twelve-year-old to our left his first glimpse of side boob.

As I bury my face in my arms, I can feel Brody's eyes on me, scanning my body for language, an incredulous look on his still-naked face.

'Suddenly you're not happy here in paradise?'

'It's not that,' I tell him. 'I just have island fever. I need to get on a freeway and drive somewhere for more than an hour without simply circling back to my point of origin.'

'You *hate* road trips, Rye.'

'I hate a lot of things, Brody. That's the whole fucking point, OK?'

SEVENTEEN

Two weeks after the weathergirl died, I returned to Tantalus for the first time since the night of the murder. The mountain looked different in the daylight, of course. The houses less towering, the jungle less intimidating.

It was a picture postcard day – the entire backdrop in perfect contrast to the evening of. We parked across the street from the house I'd scrambled past that night to locate Brody, and stepped out of the Jeep.

Brody said, 'I'm going to grab some establishing shots before you guys put the Fear into everybody.'

Tahoma, whom we'd picked up in Hawaii Kai this morning, shrugged limply then turned to me and said, 'You mind if I smoke a cigarette before we get rolling?'

Tahoma looked to be around fifty but moved as though he were a hundred and six. But *so* nice, it was difficult to deny him any request; and yet, over the next few months, Church would unabashedly turn it into an artform.

The previous evening, while we sat around the table in his suite, Church had pointed at the speaker box I'd come to refer to as Jesse, and said, 'Since Sam Spade here is allergic to sunlight, fresh air and physical human contact, we're going to need a flesh-and-blood investigator.'

'You don't have one you use regularly?' Nate said.

'I always bring in a local. Every state, every county, has its own mores and customs, and most of them can smell a stranger a mile away. Islands can be particularly difficult to navigate.'

'There's a guy my firm works with—'

'No offense, Nate Dogg. But it needs to be someone *I* know, someone *I* trust. We're going with Tahoma out in Hawaii Kai. Same guy I sent to Manoa Falls to look for Ethan the night of his arrest. Jesse, care to do the honors of pronouncing Tahoma's surname?'

'Ky-han-eye-koo-kow-ah-ka-hy-hu-lee-ha-ak-hu-lee-heh-eh-ka-hau-na-ay-lay. Kaihanaikukauahkahihuliheekahaunaele.'

Nate's face evinced deep skepticism. 'He's a good investigator?'

'He's a solid guy.'

'Meaning?'

'Meaning he won't play both sides. Won't run to the prosecution with information he gleaned from us.'

'That doesn't happen,' I challenged.

Church said, 'No? Well, that's what my friend Jimmy Honka said. That's why, in one West Texas case I was sure I would otherwise lose, I fed a private investigator I suspected of working with the cops disinformation that would fuck up the prosecutor's entire theory of the case. What happens next? First, after twelve months of "Go to hell, Church, no plea bargain," I get a call from said prosecutor with an offer. A *good* offer, a *phenomenal* offer. I tell him to go fuck himself. Then at trial, this prosecutor tosses up some Hail Mary bullshit theory instead of the one-yard run he would have been facing had he not been such a scumbag. Following twenty minutes of jury deliberation, I win an acquittal. Needless to say, I never used that investigator again and neither did the cops.' He paused, took a sip of iced water. 'Or anyone else for that matter. Because a month later, I wrote a feature article highlighting his shenanigans for *PI Magazine* and sent a copy to damn near every criminal defense attorney in the state.'

'Tahoma isn't a Hawaiian name,' Brody pointed out. '*T* isn't even in the Hawaiian alphabet.'

'He's actually only half-Hawaiian. His mother was native American. His ancestors got screwed every which way, which may well account for his being a tad pessimistic.'

'Can we see his CV?' Nate asked.

'You can see his C*R*-V. He drives a beige 2009 with three hubcaps.'

Nate's lips formed a single straight line as he shook his head. 'The decision's up to us, isn't it? Ethan's the one with his life on the line and I'm the one shelling out for all this.'

Church leaned into the table and looked Nate in the eye. 'As benevolent as your gesture may be, Nate Dogg, bottom line is: your brother is my client, not you.'

Ethan sat stock-still, silent and visibly uncomfortable, his eyes nailed to the surface of the table.

'Although,' Church said as he leaned back and folded one leg over the other, 'I would remind my client that he retained me for my expertise in conducting criminal trials and investigations, not for my looks, as Michelangelo-esque as they may be. I would also remind my client that as per our retainer agreement, I may withdraw as his attorney at any time prior to the start of trial.'

Nate turned to Ethan. 'Maybe we should consider other counsel.'

As Ethan lifted his head, Church rose from his seat, took a deep breath and said, 'BQ, turn off the camera.'

Once Tahoma stubbed out his cigarette, he and I walked across the street, where Brody was waiting with the camera. Together we climbed a half-dozen concrete steps to the front entrance of Piper's neighbor's house.

When we reached the red front door I suddenly realized I had butterflies, that they were rapidly multiplying, that I could suffer a hideous panic attack at any moment. I turned away from Brody and Tahoma and tried deep breaths, just a few, before finally dipping into my pocket and popping a Klonopin.

As Brody filmed Tahoma ringing the bell, I stared at the landscaping surrounding the house, until something caught my attention: the iron gate I'd entered through on the night of the murder was locked up tight, not just with a latch, but a heavy chain that looked like it should have been protecting something important, like a bank vault or a medical marijuana dispensary.

When the door opened, I turned and recognized the baby-faced reporter Kalani Webb straight off, despite his being dressed in a *Star Wars* tank-top and Chicago Bulls basketball shorts. He was even better-looking in person and built like a Polynesian god.

'I help you?' he said, already somewhat annoyed.

Tahoma introduced himself, then his filmographers, who he said were making a documentary about *his* investigation into the Piper Kingsley murder. 'Mind if we come inside for a few minutes?'

Kalani eyed the camera in Brody's hand and said, 'Are you people serious right now? I'm a reporter. Everything I know about the case comes from protected sources.' He looked across the street at our Jeep. 'Besides, I don't know anything more than what I've reported in the *Star-Ad*.'

'You're a print journalist too?' I asked.

His face softened somewhat. 'I freelance. My part-time job at the station doesn't pay so well.'

I took a step back, made a show of taking in the elaborateness of his house.

When my gaze returned to Kalani, his Adam's apple bobbed in his throat, his mocha skin turned instantly cherry. He parted his lips to speak, but by then he didn't need to say anything. Because behind him, his dad was waddling by, scratching his ass in his underwear, and his mom was yowling his name, bitching about finding dogshit in the kitchen again.

That evening, Church held an 'emergency meeting' in his suite at the Four Seasons.

'You guys see the fucking press conference Lau gave this afternoon?' he said the moment we stepped inside.

Ethan and Nate had yet to arrive. Considering the fireworks the previous evening, I worried they wouldn't show at all.

When I told Church we hadn't seen the presser, that the three of us – Brody, Tahoma and I – had been pounding the pavement on Mount Tantalus all day, he drew the TV remote from his fancy-dancy Four Seasons bathrobe like a gunfighter, punched on the power and rewound the DVR.

It occurred to me then that I hadn't had a decent, blow-all-your-dough, pamper-yourself-silly vacation in years – and a stay in a $17K-a-night penthouse suite in, like, ever.

Seconds later, there she was onscreen: the indefatigable Naomi Lau, a forty-eight-year-old with a thirty-eight's face, a twenty-eight's body, an eighteen's energy, and all the sagacity of Gandalf the Grey.

'Thank you all for coming,' she said with perfect cadence from her podium, the great seal of the Honolulu Prosecuting Attorney at her back. 'I'm holding today's press conference because I know so many of you are still in mourning over the loss of rising Hawaii television talent Piper Kingsley.'

Off to her right stood Zane Kingsley. Slightly shorter than Lau, his head remained clean shaven, his coffee-colored linen suit impeccably tailored and maintained.

Lau continued: 'But I would like to talk *less* this morning about this senseless killing – and the cowardly man who committed this despicable act – and *more* about Piper herself: who she was, what she stood for, things you can't find in police and autopsy reports, things you don't usually learn about victims of violent crimes, until years later when the family finally feels sufficient time has passed to talk about their lost loved one.'

Lau took a step back and, like a practiced politician, snaked her arm around Zane Kingsley's lean, muscular frame. 'But today, I stand with the victim's father, who has so generously shared with me his lovely daughter's life story, a story so needlessly ripped to shreds by a man whose name I refuse to so much as mention here today. Because today, he is utterly irrelevant to our conversation, and an anathema to our celebration of the life of Piper Kingsley.'

Tahoma pointed to the television. 'I think she's talking about Ethan.'

'Piper Kingsley,' Lau said into the microphone, 'was born just twenty-eight years ago in Sydney, Australia, to Zane and his late wife Willow—'

Church muted the television.

'What are you doing?' I said. 'Don't we all need to see this?'

'You saw enough, you saw her strategy.'

Brody nodded, Tahoma remained silent.

I said, 'Which is?'

Church's lips played with the idea of a grin, as though there was a feverishness bubbling to the surface and it was all he could do to tamp it down.

He said, 'Over the next few months, instead of poisoning the jury pool by shattering *Ethan's* image, Lau intends to lionize

Piper's, plans to amplify *her* voice, to turn *her* into a goddamn island folk hero by the start of trial.'

'So we go out and do the same,' I said.

'It doesn't exactly work that way, Riles. See, Lau's only coming out today because it's the earliest she could, and there's meaning in that.'

'Meaning?'

'Meaning Lau has already done the digging. She knows Piper Kingsley isn't just clean, she's pristine.'

'So . . .'

'So,' he said, lowering his voice a few octaves with every word, 'Piper's the perfect victim. A prosecutor's pot of gold.'

'And it's a winning strategy?' I said, befuddled because I'd never seen it done before. 'How do you know?'

Church's lids fell over his eyes as he drew a breath that seemed to last an eternity.

He said, 'I know because it's how I convinced an all-black Charlotte jury to execute an innocent black man named Roderick Blunt.'

Very few aspects of *North Carolina v Roderick J. Blunt* remained unknown to the public. This, Church said as we took our seats around the conference table, was one of them.

Ethan and Nate still hadn't materialized.

'It didn't make it into *The Prosecutor* because it happened long before Marissa became involved in the story. In fact, were it not for this, she might never have heard of the case in the first place.'

Tahoma placed an unlit cigarette between his lips, asked Church: 'You mind?'

Church's reply practically overlapped Tahoma's request. 'Light it and I'll personally burn you alive.'

Tahoma delicately placed the cigarette back into its crumpled package.

They had a weak case against Blunt, Church went on, every word an effort. District Attorney Ray McGinty was reluctant to even move forward with the indictment. Church talked him into it, packed his proverbial bags and sent him on a racial guilt trip. Cried, 'Ray, blacks deserve justice too, Toya Blunt deserves justice, her *children* deserve justice. We can't turn our backs just because no one else cares. If Toya were a blonde from Foxcroft rather than a black from Oaklawn, you'd *insist* we try the bastard who did it, no matter how fucking difficult it'd be to build a case.'

The facts of the case we already knew from Marissa's movie, but, according to Church, the case was won long before she began filming. No one remembers this occurred, he told us. Journalists certainly had no interest, just more black-on-black violence, domestic of all things. No break-in, no gun involved, happened inside their own home, not on a street your average viewer might have just traversed.

'*No one* would have heard about the murder of Toya Blunt if I hadn't done what I did.'

The trade winds that had been consistently cooling us off seemed to vanish right then, just as a tear descended Church's left cheek. I instinctively glanced at the red light on the camera capturing this moment and, I swear, felt something analogous to an orgasm.

Counter to McGinty's instructions, Church contacted some obscure Charlotte blogger with maybe three followers, and leaked anonymously that the Mecklenburg County Prosecutor's Office was declining to pursue charges against Toya's killer because of her race and the fact that the murder happened in a poor neighborhood. A week later Church had almost forgotten what he'd done, when one morning he jumped out of bed and saw Toya's face splashed across the front page of *The Charlotte Observer*.

The piece was so moving, so incredibly powerful that it went viral. So Church called the reporter who wrote the piece and continued the anonymous leaks. Not a peep about Roderick Blunt, certainly not about the evidence, which was shit, only about Toya Blunt. Toya the daughter, Toya the sister, Toya the auntie, Toya the mother of four.

'It left Ray with no choice but to prosecute, and by the time trial rolled around, the entire city had become so enraged that Toya had been cut down in her prime – that she'd been torn from her babies – they would have convicted *me* if I'd been seated at the defense table.'

Church couldn't deny that he tried the case brilliantly, but only because he was a brilliant lawyer and because he *so* believed in what he was doing, was *so* fucking certain that Toya's husband had killed her. But by trial, Church didn't need brilliance, or even competence. He could have simply pointed at Roderick J. Blunt – who was big, scarred and heavily inked, i.e. someone who *looked* like he did it, whatever *it* was – and said, 'He killed Toya,' and that jury's first ballot would have been twelve-zip to convict.

A wall of water built gradually in Church's eyes until the dam finally burst and the tears flowed freely down his otherwise expressionless face, dampening his bathrobe, which had opened significantly without his knowledge.

'Ironic thing is,' he said, 'in *The Prosecutor*, Marissa makes so much of my relationship with McGinty, my boss, the mentor whom I so gallantly stood in for when he nearly died the night before opening statements. Ironic, because I'd gone against his wishes in this case at every turn. Because he was ashamed of what I'd done to get the case to trial. Ironic, because news of Ray's heart attack provided me with the happiest, most thrilling night of my professional life.'

By the end of the night, I wanted to comfort Church, not quite in the way I'd wanted to comfort Ethan on the night of his arrest, but I wanted to cradle his head in my lap and stroke his hair. I wanted to tell him he was forgiven.

As I stepped past him through the doorway into the lavish hall that led only to the elevator, I spun on my heels and pecked his still wet cheek, asked if there was anything I could do for him, anything at all.

Staring deeply, thoughtfully into my eyes, he quietly said, yes, as a matter of fact there was. He needed to throw back a few bottles of bourbon tonight, so would I drive to the airport and pick someone up in the morning.

'Sure,' I told him with negative gusto, 'not a problem.' Then I asked him whom I was picking up.

'Marissa,' he said, as he started closing the door in my face. Then he paused. 'Which reminds me: there's going to be a lot of drinking, yelling and fucking in this suite over the next few weeks. Be forewarned.'

EIGHTEEN

like it on the couch. Like that I can say whatever is on my mind, short of suicidal ideations.

I've been seeing Dr Yasmin Farrockh on and off since we arrived in Hawaii. More 'on' in the beginning, more 'off' during the investigation and trial.

'How are you doing?' she says with a faint Persian accent.

How are you doing is her opening line every time I visit, and every time she says it I can't help but think of my shitty first job at a Salem McDonald's drive-thru, brainlessly repeating the words, *May I take your order?*

'I'm doing well,' I say, because *well* is proper English, as my father constantly reminded me. 'Doing *well*,' he'd say, his voice full of frustration and deep disappointment, 'means you're fine; doing *good* means you're doing a good deed. How long's it going to take to get that through your thick goddamn skull, Riley Rebecca.'

Following the *How are you doing?*, I always yearn to hold out, to say nothing, to see what Dr Farrockh will say next, whether she even *has* a follow-up question. But not once have I been able to restrain myself from filling the nerve-racking silence. I mean, what if my stomach grumbles? What if *hers* does?

'Trial's over,' I throw out as casually as possible.

'I saw.'

'So Brody and I are in postproduction.'

'And how is your relationship with him?'

'Personal or professional?' I ask.

'Are you able to separate the two now?'

How is it that I'm the one seeking answers, yet she's the one asking all the questions?

'No,' I say bluntly, 'I don't think I'm even capable of separating them.'

'Why do you not think so?'

'Because I'm happy with him when he contributes, and I'm pissed at him when he slacks off.'

Her dark eyebrows do a little dance, a sure sign I've said something I'm going to want back.

'Interesting word choice,' she says.

I run through the sentence in my head once again and narrow the suspect words down to *happy* and *pissed*. Yet, somehow, I know it is neither.

'What is it that you hate being called?' she says. 'What's – as you put it – "the worst effing word to ever disease the American lexicon"?'

Shit. 'Did I just call Brody a slacker?'

She lifts a shoulder. 'More or less.'

Traveling too far down Slacker Road leads back home, and I want to move forward.

'I need to make a decision,' I tell her. 'Can we not leave this room until a decision is made?'

Straight-faced, she says, 'That depends on the options and how decisive you are.'

I allow a half-smile. 'That was rhetorical.'

'It makes what I said no less true. You still haven't decided whether to accept his proposal, am I right?'

'I don't know, it's odd. When I'm outdoors, I *know* I want to marry him, then once I get in the editing room and my mind starts going . . .' A tear surfaces in the corner of my left eye; they always come on so unexpectedly here. 'I don't know why I can't make a decision.'

'I can offer some reasons,' she says. 'First, you're still grieving over your mentor – you had a very powerful relationship with him, the kind of closeness you were deprived of as a child. You want to move on from that grief but it's particularly difficult with Brody around, because Brody is a link back to that world.'

I shake my head vigorously, as vigorously as a head can be shaken so that she receives my signal. '*Everything* reminds me of Professor Leary,' I say. 'Chinese food, my tattoos, the books on my shelves – hell, my entire *profession*. Brody, if anything, takes my mind *off* Professor Leary, because Brody always felt he and the professor were in competition for my time, and he hated being left alone in our shitty Bleeker Street apartment, and who can blame him?'

'If it's not your grief, maybe it's that you love someone else?'

Since I hurt my neck shaking my head, this time I simply say, 'No,' sternly. Because I never told her. Why *would* I tell her? What good can come of the whole truth in here?

'Then it must be Brody himself, right? What are his faults? Is he still running out day and night?'

'No, no – that ended months ago. Once we started filming the movie he became all business and, off-hours, went right back to being a couch potato.'

'Has he been depressed?'

'No more than usual.'

'Is he still – how did you put it? – "a hot mess"?'

'I've *literally* never uttered those two words consecutively in my life. Those words make me want to vom—'

'Must be another patient,' she says over me. 'I apologize.'

I wave her off. 'You don't need to apologize.'

'You looked angry.'

'Just a knee-jerk reaction, because those words—'

'Those words what? How did you feel when I attributed them to you?'

'Angry, I guess?' When she doesn't say anything, I know she's going to make me delve deeper, when all I want to do in this minute is stand up and walk out that door. 'Offended, I guess, that you'd think I spoke like that.'

'What else did you feel?'

Fear.

'I was afraid?'

'Of what?'

I scrunch up my face in a way I once thought was flirty. 'I don't know.'

'You do know.'

'My father's *dead*,' I say, trying to keep my voice steady. 'Gone. He's ashes in an urn collecting dust on a shelf at one of the bars he owned, thousands of miles from here.'

'Death doesn't mean you stop fearing him.'

Tears well, yet I'm chuckling. 'I don't think he's going to come back and haunt me, if that's what you mean.'

She smiles. I constantly wonder whether she smiles because I genuinely amuse her or out of sheer politeness, maybe out of some unwritten obligation shrinks have to boost your self-confidence.

She says, 'The fear you feel is a defense mechanism, Riley. It may be one you haven't needed for a long time, not since you moved out of your parents' home and certainly not since your parents' accident. But the part of your brain that controls this defense mechanism doesn't know that it can lay down its arms. You can't simply turn it on and off with a switch. Your childhood experiences shape the way your brain functions – those experiences largely determine how you will later view the world.'

'Wait, what? How is it that every time we spin the wheel, we land on my father? We were talking about Brody.'

'We still are.'

NINETEEN

Fifteen days after the weathergirl died, Marissa Linden arrived in Hawaii. As promised, I traveled to the Daniel K. Inouye International Airport first thing in the morning. Appeared precisely on time and pulled the Jeep to the curb near Hawaiian Air's arrivals terminal. According to the airline's app, Marissa's plane had arrived on time, but she was nowhere in sight. I put the transmission in park a few feet in front of a *no stopping, no standing* sign.

While I idled and listened to Iz take me somewhere over the rainbow, a teenage airport security guard (one of those unfortunate adolescents more pimple than person) repeatedly ogled me from his position at the terminal entrance. For once in my life, I thought I might finally enjoy some of the privileges of girls with perfectly symmetrical faces and large breasts. When he finally approached my Jeep, I blushed some, flashed my sweetest smile, and waited for the sad yet flattering come-on. But as he neared my vehicle I realized he was one of those rare individuals who looked better up close, and was somewhat older than I'd first thought, early to mid-twenties at least. That tingle that accompanies instant attraction traveled up my spine, and I was actually (but not really) considering giving this guy my number. So when he rapped several times hard on my passenger side door and ordered me in a flinty voice to 'move on, lady, you can't stay parked here', I panicked, stepped on the accelerator, and nearly mowed down a family of four on the crosswalk.

Despite my screeching brakes, mercifully, no one seemed to notice (except for the family of four, of course, who would undoubtedly recount the incident for years in countless nightmares and therapy sessions back home).

In the wrong lane and unable to get over (*thanks, assholes*), I passed the entrance to every last lot and had to circle the airport – a discombobulating ten-minute ride with more stoplights and taxis than midtown Manhattan. I then missed the exit for Hawaiian Air's arrivals terminal and had to circle around yet again.

This time, when I finally pulled to the curb, the security guy (who looked better with every pass) wasted no time in approaching. I raised my windows until they were sealed shut then pulled my iPhone from my rear pocket. Marissa was supposed to ring me as soon as she landed. But now my calls to her cell were going straight to voicemail. As the security guy tapped incessantly on my passenger side glass, I tried Church, but got nothing.

I lowered the window just enough to hear: 'You're going to have to move, ma'am. I can't have you parked here.'

'I'm just picking someone up,' I tried. 'Can't I please just have five minutes?'

'You might as well ask if you can have my job, lady. And my answer would be no, not in this economy.' He smacked my hardtop hard enough to startle me. 'Let's *go*.'

Of course, I interpreted his antagonism as a referendum on my looks and charm, and his repeated use of the word *lady* as a jab at my age. *I'm not even thirty*, I wanted to shout, but instead flipped him off and peeled away, this time only after checking the crosswalk.

After another fifteen minutes, I finally found the entrance to short-term parking. I pulled up to the machine, reached out my window, stretched for a ticket, and with only several minor muscle tears, the gate at long last rose for me.

I sat baking (and not in a good way) in the parking lot for another hour, trying Marissa's phone every five minutes, Church's every ten. Maybe Marissa had missed her flight, I kept thinking. Maybe she'd gotten another and would be arriving any moment. Without word from her or Church, how the hell could I leave?

I was glad I hadn't brought Brody. He didn't do well with car rides in general, but something like this would have killed him. Hell, it was killing *me*. Me, the living fucking embodiment of patience.

I stepped up my calls to Marissa and Church to no avail.

Finally, twenty-five minutes later, as I hung my head out the window for air, I received a text message from Church:

NO NEED TO PICK UP MARISSA. SHE TOOK A LIMO. MY BAD.

Flying into a rage even I didn't recognize, I poked and jabbed in my reply, the first draft of which was pure gibberish, the second not much better. Third time was the charm, but before I could hit SEND, I received a second text message from Church:

BE HERE ASAP. WE HAVE A RISING DEVELOPMENT.

They at least had caffeinated beverages when I finally arrived at Church's penthouse suite with Brody, who I'd picked up in Waikiki. I popped a can of Red Bull, Brody poured himself some coffee, then swiftly set up the cameras around the conference table for the fifth or sixth time this week.

Marissa Linden, somehow just out of the shower yet disheveled, stepped out of Church's bedroom, asking whether the suite had a cappuccino machine. (It did.)

'Riles and BQ,' Church said, once we were all standing in one room, 'Marissa Linden. Marissa, Riles and BQ.'

As I'd suspected, Marissa was even better-looking in person than she was on television. She had long black hair, curled in just the right places, and a face that hadn't aged since she shot *The Prosecutor*. The rather sheer black dress she'd slipped into left little to the imagination, not that the imagination, in this case, could do much better than the genuine article.

Brody, I could tell, was immediately infatuated.

'Shall we get started?' Church said, moving toward the conference table.

'Ethan and Nate aren't here,' I reminded him.

'What time are they supposed to arrive?'

'What? I don't know. What time did you call them this morning?'

'I didn't call them.'

'Sorry, texted them?'

Church frowned. 'Are you saying this isn't a meeting we scheduled last night?'

'*No*,' I said, trying not to lose my shit. 'We're here because you texted me.'

'I texted you that you didn't need to pick up Marissa at the airport because she'd taken a limo.'

Marissa leaned her head to the side in apology. 'A text Nick was *supposed* to send you last night, right after I told him I made other arrangements.'

I shot Church a look.

'In my defense,' he said, raising his palms, 'I was blackout drunk on Old Grand-Dad last night; woke up on the beach with a dozen sand crabs playing King of the Hill on my face.'

'Not *that* text,' I said, 'the second one.'

'What second one?'

I took my iPhone out of my back pocket and read from the screen. 'The one that said, "Be here ASAP. We have a rising development."'

A light finally blinked on in Church's head. 'Oh, I see what happened. I'm sorry, Riles, my bad again. That text wasn't meant for you, it was meant for Marissa.'

'Why would you . . .' As I read the text again, scarlet rose like lava from the bottom of my neck to the top of my ears. 'Ew, ew, ew,' I said.

That night I told Brody I was heading to Breakers up North Shore. I asked if he'd like to come with, knowing he fully intended on ripping a few bong hits and watching *Pineapple Express* on DVD for the 109th time since we arrived in Hawaii.

The drive to Haleiwa took me clear across the island, southeast to northwest, and ate up fifty-eight of your Earth minutes. When I pulled into the lot I nearly ran over a rooster and had to stop for a breath. He'd told me to look for 'a piece of shit pickup', but the parking lot could have passed for a sales floor of them. Up North Shore, country meant *country*.

I parked and went inside, where the noise rivaled Autzen Stadium (take my word for it). I zigzagged my way through a tangle of young bodies then stood on my tiptoes to search the booths in the back. Last table, all the way in the rear, I spotted the dirty blue Dodger baseball cap.

As I made my way back to him, I gazed at the hundreds of one-dollar bills papering the walls and ceiling, each with a pithy message from some blitzed guest who thought a buck a good price for immortality – or at least for impressing a hot bartender.

I slid into the booth next to him. His head remained down so that I couldn't see his face. A pitcher of beer and two pint glasses stood on the table before us. I poured myself a glass, then asked Ethan if he was all right.

'I'm getting nervous,' he said. 'I really don't know whether Church is right for this case. I mean, he's a bit of an asshole, don't you think?'

'To us, yes. But in the courtroom, he turns into something else entirely.'

'He's not an asshole?'

'Oh, no. He's still an asshole. But he's *your* asshole, and everything he has in him will be directed at Prosecuting Attorney Lau and Detective Fukumoto.' I paused, wished like hell I could take that analogy back. 'Juries are putty in his hands. His record speaks for itself.'

'Nate's not so sure.'

'Is this over Tahoma again?'

'Not just Tahoma.' Ethan took a long pull off his pint. 'Nate thinks Church may be a great choice for a jury trial in New York, Chicago or LA. But people are different here. Nate and I grew up here. That personality, the flashiness, it doesn't impress people here the way it does on the mainland.'

'Ethan, he adapts. He's tried cases everywhere from South Beach to Boise, and he's like a goddamn chameleon he blends in so well.'

He hesitated, then said, 'Don't be offended, but are you saying that because you think Nick Church is best for me, or because he's best for your movie?'

I didn't hesitate. 'I can't believe you'd ask me that,' I said, and loved the look in his eyes when I said it.

So, of course, I immediately stepped on those words with: 'Ethan, I don't even *have* a movie unless you're acquitted.'

* * *

For the next hour and a half, the beer went down fast. With the excitement of a seven-year-old elucidating on the limitless particulars of Minecraft, Ethan educated me on the rich and varying history of Hawaiian music and its numberless influences on American culture. I could hear none of it, of course, because the place was too damn loud, but I smiled and nodded and drank and got away with it for over an hour. Eventually, however, talk returned to the case.

'I can't do prison, Riley. I'd rather die.'

'Don't say that, please.'

'I'm serious. I've already talked to someone. I'm going to have a cyanide pill in my mouth when the verdict is read.'

I placed my hand atop his and felt an instant heat come off him. 'Ethan, there are appeals. That's part of the reason you agreed to do this movie, remember?'

'Nate said appeals can take years, sometimes five or ten. I can't do years inside, especially without knowing whether I'll ever get out.'

'Is this what you brought me here to tell me?' I said, suddenly irritated, though not quite sure why. 'Maybe in the hopes what you say to me gets back to Church, so that he knows the true stakes in this case? He already *knows* the stakes, Ethan. I'm pretty sure I have him on camera saying that for someone like you, a life sentence *means* death.'

'Someone like me?'

'Not in a bad way. Because you're . . . sensitive.'

Like Brody. What the hell am I doing here right now?

'How can you say that? Except for Nate, none of you even know me.'

'Your songs give us an insight into your soul,' I *actually* said, slurring every other word. 'They're all gentle and peaceful and about weighty subjects like saving the earth, avoiding war, love and loss, legalizing marijuana.'

The left side of his lips lifted in a half-grin, an image similar to those the bars and nightclubs used to promote him in what now surely seemed like another lifetime. Tonight, though, Ethan Jakes looked nothing like his mugshot, especially the one news outlets doctored to make him appear more menacing. Tonight, he looked like a musician.

'You've listened to some of my music, then?'

I hated that the bar had such great lighting; I was sure he could see me blush. 'I've heard some . . . well, most . . . OK, all of it, yeah. At least everything available on Amazon and iTunes.'

The opposite side of his lips turned up, and I flashed on his conversation with Fukumoto in Piper's backyard.

'People don't seem to like my original stuff at live gigs,' he said. 'They just want to hear covers.'

'Is that so surprising?' I said. 'They're not looking for the next Jack Johnson; they're a bunch of drunks who want to sing the lyrics along with you without looking too stupid.'

'Nah,' he said, with a smile, '*they* make up my entire fan base. They've kept bread on my table and booze in my stomach since high school.'

'No help from your parents, huh?'

'Zero. The week I turned eighteen, they moved to some bumbleshit town in Montana because it was cheaper. They never had much. My mom's a schoolteacher, my father's a gambler and con man.'

'Do they know about . . .'

'Nate's been keeping our mom up to date. God knows where our father is.'

That little voice inside me told me to get out of Parent Territory before it was too late.

'So you played music through college?'

'All the way through UH. Wouldn't have been able to go to college otherwise. Me *and* Nate, we were a team back then.'

'You broke up after UH?'

I took comfort in the fact that he seemed slightly drunker than I did.

'Nah,' he said, 'that's the thing. Nate and I made a pact after college. We were going to keep after our dreams no matter what it took, no matter how long.'

'What happened?' The music was so loud, I practically had to yell it in his ear.

'We did it a couple of years, then one night, right after our set, Nate said he couldn't do it anymore, that he needed some stability in his life.' Ethan threw back the last of another pint. 'No surprise that was around the time he met Cheyenne. Few weeks later, they packed their bags one night, took off for Vegas to elope. Never even told me. Whole time he was gone, I didn't know whether he was ever coming back.'

'Happens to a lot of artists,' I said. 'Their friends start making money, getting married, buying houses, they get scared and bail.'

His eyes locked on mine. 'Is it going to happen to you?'

Probably.

'Never,' I said.

Two pitchers later, I reached for a napkin and our arms touched and I felt the same shock I'd felt when I intentionally stuck my pinky finger into an open electrical socket in the bio lab, sophomore year of high school.

I thought about Brody back home, by now bingeing *BoJack Horseman* on Netflix.

'I think it's time for me to head back to Waikiki,' I said.

'Why don't you come back with me, get some coffee in you first. My place is right down the street.'

'I can't . . .' I started.

He immediately went to: 'You think I did it, don't you?'

'Nooo,' I said, with no small amount of indignation.

'You do. You believe the police. You think I killed Piper.'

'I dooon't,' I said.

All right, now I just sound downright ridiculous.

'You're afraid to even be alone with me.'

'The hell I am.'

'Then why not just come back for coffee.'

'Fine,' I tell him, 'but only for coffee, and I can't stay long. And I don't drink coffee.'

The moment we stepped outside into a light rain, I hiccupped, because, hey, I'm a human being, OK? And because I was sort of a bit really stupid drunk.

We were staggering down the wooden steps when Ethan said, 'Whoa, neither of us are driving right now. We'll Uber it over to my place.'

As we walked he took out his new phone. A few seconds later, he said, '"Randy" is on his way in his white Civic. Should be here in nine minutes. While we wait, mind if we run to my truck? I have a radio in there I don't want stolen.'

Ethan's blue pickup was parked away from the others at the far end of the lot. In the dark and from a distance, a group of people appeared to be boogying around his truck.

'Who are they?' I said.

'I don't know. Let's hope we don't have to find out.'

The light pole over this part of the lot was dark.

'Excuse me,' Ethan said when we reached them, 'we just need to get through to my truck.'

One of the five stepped up to him, looked up at the sky, and held out his large arms as though embracing the soft but steady rain. 'Know why I didn't bring an umbrella tonight?'

'I asked you once nicely,' Ethan said.

'Because I didn't know the fucking weather.'

'I'm asking you again,' Ethan said. 'Don't make me ask you a third time.'

I couldn't help but think Brody would have flashed the guys a peace sign by now, maybe offered them a few bucks in exchange for safe passage through the lot.

'What? You gonna do to us what you done to that poor redheaded girl?'

I grabbed Ethan's arm, said, 'Let's go back inside.'

He pulled away from me.

The next sixty seconds seemed to play in slow motion, but only because Ethan moved so fast. I watched as he took the first out with a straight left to the jaw, the second with an elbow to the throat. The third earned a devastating side kick to the chest, the fourth a disciplined right hook to the ear. The fifth, the biggest of the bunch, actually got off a haymaker, but Ethan wasn't fazed. He jabbed him in the eyes, struck him with an uppercut, swept his leg as he tried to scramble away. He then grabbed him by a fistful of hair and was about to smash his head to the ground when I screamed, 'No! Don't!'

He didn't.

But by then I had learned a few things.

One, Ethan had a temper.

Two, he knew how to fight.

And three, he could become violent. Especially when drinking.

'Come on, let's go,' he said. 'We can hoof it. I'm right down the road.'

'I'm sorry,' I said, 'but I can't go with you.'

He looked genuinely hurt. 'You saw it, Riley. *They* attacked *me.*'

'It's not that,' I said. And it wasn't.

It was that part of me had decided I couldn't betray Brody.

Another part of me was too sick with regret for not capturing the graphic violence on film.

But mostly I couldn't go with him because I was wholly and unreservedly turned on – and I truly hated myself for it.

When 'Randy' finally arrived in his white Civic, Ethan ushered me into the backseat.

'Take her to Waikiki,' he told the driver, then kissed me on the cheek. 'Goodnight, Riley.'

'My Jeep!' I cried.

'Give me the keys. I'll have my friend Chuck drive it back before dawn.'

I tossed him the keys and told him the address was saved as 'Home' on my GPS.

He kissed me on the cheek again.

'But this is your Uber acc—' I started, before he stepped back and closed the door.

Randy slowly pulled out of the parking lot and made a right. In his rearview I could see an HPD squad car speeding toward Breakers, all red and blue lights.

Oh shit, oh shit, oh shit, I thought. *Brody is going to find out who I was with tonight.*

TWENTY

I like the rough stuff. *Love* it, in fact. Leaning back in my seat in the editing room, I lace my fingers behind my head, cross one leg over the other, and sigh in pure satisfaction. Because Brody has accomplished a brilliant feat, truly outperformed all expectations. The footage is even more thrilling than the events as I remember them – and yeah, that's saying a lot.

From the 911 call to the crime scene through the next-day news footage and introduction of Church, this material, if edited right, will make as dramatic an opening as any recent documentary I've seen. Ethan's run and subsequent surrender, the revelation of Piper's pregnancy, the sparks between Nate and Church – all of it was captured with such magnificent precision, it's difficult – yet wildly exciting – to imagine what Brody might be capable of with a full-time four-man crew.

Tonight, I primarily played with Church's tearful tale about the prosecution of Roderick Blunt, because it's one of my favorite scenes. Even though it so flagrantly links this film to *The Prosecutor*, the Church character is just too broad and dickish without his backstory. That scene, along with Church's bullshit description of how he selects his clients, creates a magnificent incongruity that I intend to thread throughout the movie.

Brody, amazingly, is still of the opinion that Church should be the focal point of our film. 'An anti-hero for the ages,' as he put it this morning. 'This tragic character who *knows* he's on a futile quest for redemption, yet, no matter how arduous the search, somehow carries on.'

'He also tried to have the courtroom cleared because a young member of the prosecution team farted during Fukumoto's testimony,' I reminded him.

I can only hope it's his subconscious or his endless search for a father figure that's fueling Brody's drive to continue this fight. I'd even accept it if this were Brody's bona fide professional opinion. Yet somehow I think it's none of these things; somehow I know it's nothing but primal, unadulterated jealousy, the fear of losing me, the kind of domestic discontent that eventually took center stage at the Jakes trial in the strangest and ugliest possible fashion.

Stop it. I'm doing it again, overthinking everything because I'm confined to this five-by-eight editing room that positively reeks of dumplings, eggrolls and sweet-and-sour pork. Trapped in here and, thereby, trapped in my own head. Sure, Brody says, 'There's nothing keeping you from stepping outside, getting some fresh air,' but he knows that's pants-on-fire false, that the Riley in me who always pays utility bills at least one week ahead of their due date, and freaks when she sees dirty dishes in the sink, won't permit me five minutes for fresh air. Because those are five additional minutes that could instead be used for the editing of this film, and in those five minutes I may well see something, hear something, come to some profound realization about the investigation, about the trial, about the movie, that I may never have come to had I stepped outside and *taken five*.

Deep breaths. Disregard the tightening in your chest; it's nothing and will only make the anxiety attack worse. Forget the sweat streaming down your forehead, stinging your eyes – it's just that the thermostat hasn't been working right since, I don't know, like, *ever*?

Never mind the nausea, there's a waste bucket if you need it, two feet to your left.

Palpitations is such a weird word.

No, your left arm isn't hurting, you don't smell copper or burnt toast, and yes, Brody will find your body before the rats get to it, should worst come to worst.

Stop it! I glance at my Swatch; it's still early. Too early to even think of heading home and focusing on the script. Besides, Brody's supposed to be back in an hour. Maybe he'll bring malasadas.

I sit still for a few minutes, breathing in and out (not that I don't *always*, I'm just concentrating on it now), conjuring ways to procrastinate but come up dry. Unfortunately, I've rid the editing room of all distractions for moments such as this.

I turn my attention back to editing the movie.

True, I was part of the story from the very beginning; there's no denying that fact. But now I'm at the point in the film where I inadvertently enter the case itself. In more ways than just one. How do you, as editor, handle the scenes where the director clumsily stumbles in front of the camera? What do you do? Honestly, I don't know the answer to this. My presence as a player is crucial to the story, yet completely contrary to my role as director, whose most critical job is to search for the Truth. All I wanted to do at the time was hide it.

If only I could go back and cut around these parts in real life. If only I hadn't gone to Breakers that night, if only I hadn't had blood on me the night Piper was murdered. There are a million *if onlys* but only one Truth, and it's not the Truth I want in the film.

I pop open a Monster Energy Drink.

If I was going to cut myself out of the footage, I would have done so during my first pass, right? Certainly, by the second.

Only a few minutes of grainy footage exists of that evening at Breakers, but it's pivotal to the film, and subsequent events only make sense in full context. Besides, leaving out visual evidence would be tantamount to fraud. That night was, after all, the night things truly took a turn for the worse – at least the worst turn until trial.

And, quite frankly, it's stunning to watch; it makes a great visual. I'll use it to introduce not just myself but the other side of Ethan, the darker side the audience will have only seen hints of before. I take another gulp of Monster and truck onward. No time for panic attacks tonight, no time for crying or self-pity. No time even for malasadas. Time to take on the scenes dealing with Ethan's second arrest – this time for aggravated assault and attempted murder.

TWENTY-ONE

The day after Breakers began like any other, which was to say I was hungover and in a horrible mood, when Brody began poking and prodding me to get out of bed. How I fell in love with a morning person, I would never understand, but it had been a source of tension ever since we started sleeping together, and would be a source of tension until we broke up, or one of us was dead. Frankly, had Brody not so consistently turned so dour during the day, I don't think I could have stomached him, even as a friend.

My experience of waking up and forgetting what the hell had happened the previous evening was far more vast than I'd like to admit. My record time for euphorically forgetting what I'd done was just shy of ninety seconds. This time, remembering took only half that. But by then, Brody had stripped off my pajama bottoms, heaved me onto his shoulder, and carried me into the shower.

'What's going on?' I shouted, as I was blasted by cold water. I adjusted the temperature as best I could, but this was one of those showers that would remain a mystery long after all the apartment's occupants were worm food.

'Ethan's been arrested again,' Brody said.

I just barely prevented myself from throwing up. A million half-thoughts staggered through my mind. Does Brody know I was with him? Could Ethan have avoided arrest had I stayed and talked to police instead of hopping into Randy's Civic and going home? Was it already time to trim down there again – didn't I just trim that fucking thing last month?

It goes without saying, these thoughts were all sufficiently lofty at the time.

'What was he charged with?' I ask incredulously.

I didn't want to start lying right out of the box. And I really wanted, OK *needed*, to know. I swallowed hard and steeled myself for his answer, but the moment Brody told me 'aggravated assault and attempted murder', the dam that had been keeping down last night's super-crispy and delicious French fries – and yeah, four pitchers of beer – finally let go.

Hours later, the usual suspects – Ethan, Nate, Brody and yours truly – were all seated around the conference table in Church's suite. That's right – even Ethan. Because by the time Brody and I arrived at the courthouse that morning, Church and Nate had already bailed him out. Poor surveillance footage appeared to corroborate Ethan's story of self-defense, but the prosecution wasn't letting this one go entirely, not with stakes this high. The arrest and arraignment of Piper Kingsley's accused killer would make the front page for two days straight, maybe more, with headlines further linking his name to terms like 'aggravated assault' and 'attempted murder'.

Despite the seriousness of the charges, both Naomi Lau and Judge Hightower wanted Ethan out of jail. So with nominal haggling between Church and the same sacrificial lamb Lau sent to the first arraignment, it was only a matter of time before Ethan was liberated, albeit with a new ankle bracelet and additional restrictions.

Church circled us now in the way he did when he was pissed. 'Do I really need to tell you, Ethan, how monumentally *stupid* it was to get into a fight?'

'They start—'

'*Shut up.* I don't care if they come at you with that shit Cersei used to wipe out the entire fucking House of Baratheon.'

'Wildfire,' Brody said.

'*Shut up*, BQ. Ethan, you have one option and one option only in that situation and that is to bend over and permit Hodor to have his goddamn way with you.'

'That makes zero sense,' Brody said, 'in any fathomable context.'

'Agh.' Church waved off the critique. 'I only saw three episodes in a hotel room in Cleveland; what the hell do you want from me?'

I was suddenly so nervous that it felt as though something was lodged in my throat, which made me even more nervous; and wondering whether I was visibly nervous made me even *more* nervous, and on and on until I thought I was about to suffer one of the worst panic attacks of my life.

Then, just as quickly as he'd risen, Church took a seat.

'That's the last I'm going to say on the matter.' He took a long drink of iced water. Said, 'Unless I think of something else to say.'

'Cigarette?' Marissa asked, as I stepped onto the wraparound terrace.

Jesus, Marissa even looked hot smoking, and *no one* looked hot smoking these days. Not tobacco at least.

'No thanks,' I told her.

She held it out to me anyway, in a way that made me wonder whether she owned stock in Big Tobacco.

'It's not a *cigarette* cigarette,' she finally said. 'It's a joint.'

'In that case . . .'

I still hadn't grown accustomed to the spectacular vista, to the gentle breezes, to the soothing sound of the tide seventeen stories below. Hadn't gotten the least bit used to turning to my left and seeing an infinity pool straight off the cover of *Condé Nast Traveler* magazine. I mean, here I was, sponging this phenomenal view, smoking a J with the single most influential true crime documentarian of our time, while inside I was in the midst of directing my own masterpiece. This was as close to a perfect moment as I could have at this point in my life.

Whale songs played in my head.

Four puffs and two passes later, Marissa made conversation. 'So what do you think of Nick? Is he what you expected?'

'Only more so.'

Marissa laughed. She had a cute laugh, too; Christ, I could have killed her there and then.

Quietly, she said, 'If ever there was someone seeking redemption, it's him.'

I turned my head to locate Brody and noticed a slight shift in the position of one of the cameras so that it was facing out the sliding glass door.

Briefly, I wondered whether I was being set up, whether it even mattered so long as it made good footage. I took the joint from Marissa, took a toke, and said, 'You think he'll find it in this case?'

I was surprised by her answer: 'No.' And then: 'He won't find it in his lifetime. Not in the form he's looking for.'

'What form is that?'

'He wants to resurrect the dead.'

I took another puff, almost giggled and replied, 'Well, maybe he should get his feet wet by walking on water.' Mercifully, however, I blew smoke out and kept the bad joke in.

'Blunt?' I said, and yes, as awful as it was, I so hoped she'd say, 'No, the joint will do just fine.'

Instead she said, 'I'm sure Nick didn't tell you this, but maybe you did your homework.' She paused just long enough to make me feel stupid. 'Since that day he resigned on the steps of the county courthouse, Nick has considered himself responsible for four children: three teenage sons and a twelve-year-old daughter.'

The Blunt family had received a significant settlement from the county. Seven figures, I'd heard. The county had had no choice *but* to settle for boku bucks. By then, Church was completely off the rails, and no one had any idea what he'd say at trial. Whatever it was, though, county officials were fairly certain they didn't want it said in such a public forum. Reportedly, there was even pressure from the governor to 'clean up this chicken-shitting mess'. The story hadn't caught fire nationally – and wouldn't until *The Prosecutor* came out. Because quite frankly, an innocent black man dying at the hands of a southern state simply wasn't national news in the world ours had become.

'Has he seen the family since then?' I said.

'Two of the boys have forgiven him, and he spends time with them.' She looked away, muttered, 'More time than I spent with my son.'

'And the other two?'

'The other two children – the younger two – swear they will never forgive him. But that hasn't stopped him from trying. Half of every dollar Nick earns in the law goes to the Roderick J. Blunt Foundation, a charity aimed at stamping out the death penalty and eradicating racial injustice in the American judicial system.'

'He might have picked a more reasonable goal,' I said, 'like maybe putting the first man on Jupiter.'

That one earned me a chuckle, and I liked Marissa Linden for a moment.

Just a moment.

Then her face became cold and she spoke again.

'What were you doing at Breakers last night?' she said.

I'd been thinking about how I would handle this very subject all day, yet somehow had no reply ready, at least not for Marissa, because I never thought I'd get hit with that question from this direction.

'Ethan told you?' I said.

'Nick and I saw the surveillance footage this morning before the arraignment.'

'Shit,' I tried not to say aloud.

She said, 'You do realize that if prosecutors can demonstrate you had a relationship with the defendant outside of attorney–client, they can call you to testify, don't you? That they can most likely get their hands on half of the footage you've shot? Even if they can't introduce it in their case-in-chief at trial, they'll be able to use the footage to impeach our witnesses.

What are you going to do then, when you're called to testify, Riley? Are you going to sink Nick's client, or are you going to perjure yourself and risk prison?'

'I won't see him like that again.'

I knew from her look that my word meant less than nothing.

'Nick was fuming when he saw it,' she said. 'You're lucky you're even getting a second chance.'

She turned toward the sliding glass door.

'Thank you,' I called after her as she was walking away.

At that moment, she turned on her heel but only halfway, and raised her voice, presumably so the camera would clearly catch what she had to say. 'Don't thank me, Riley. I told Nick you were in way over your fucking head and had to go. *Professional* documentarians observe and shoot. We *don't* become part of the show.'

'Thoroughness,' Church declared to those of us around the conference table, 'that's the difference; it's the Church difference; it's why you, Nate Dogg, are shelling out the big bucks; it's why you, E-man, hired me and haven't fired me; and it's why *you*, Riles, recommended me in the first place.'

His speech moved more rapidly than my thoughts, which sent my eyes to his coffee; only it wasn't coffee, it was water again. In fact, in the weeks since he'd arrived, I wasn't sure I'd seen him swallow a single sip of joe. He certainly hadn't opined on the minute differences in flavor and texture of his favorite roasts as he had in *The Prosecutor* – and Hawaii had some damn fine coffee. If his hand had been going anywhere near his nose, I'd have suspected speed or blow, but I'd never seen him so much as sniffle.

'So,' Church said, 'what does that mean in *this* case? It means we have the emergence of an actual defense, an itsy-bitsy foundation, which we can grow brick by brick by brick between now and trial.'

In my peripheral, I could have sworn Marissa was giving me the stink eye.

'Can we skip the prelude?' Nate said.

Nate Dogg was becoming less and less amused with Church's antics, which was making Ethan edgy too.

Church went on as if Nate had never spoken, a technique, I concede, I badly wanted to add to my own repertoire.

'. . . and from everything that Ethan's told us, and everything that Riles has said of her, and in light of the fact that Lau gave a press conference to essentially throw the victim's goodness in our faces, and since our super sleuth Jesse hasn't found so much as an unpaid parking ticket, we *know* we can't put Piper Kingsley on trial the way any decent defense attorney would hope to. We can't besmirch her, we know that, it can't be done. And what her virtue further suggests is that this young woman probably didn't have many enemies on the island, am I right, E-book?'

'None that I know of,' Ethan said quietly. Even if I hadn't known their ages, the family dynamics I'd witnessed over the weeks left no question as to who was the older brother. Ethan practically looked for Nate's approval following every answer he gave.

'*Then* . . .' Church said, 'what about those closest to her? We'll leave E-sops off the table for the moment. Who else?'

Ethan shrugged. 'She didn't have any enemies on-island, but she didn't have any close friends either. Every time she made one, they'd eventually move to Japan or the mainland or head back to Australia.'

Hawaii was a mecca for transients.

'Aye,' Church said, with an inevitable Aussie accent. 'Australia. The land Down Under. The Lucky Country. Land of Plenty. The Outback. Oz. Terra Australis Incognita, as it was first posited in antiquity.'

Nate slammed his hand down on the conference table. 'Get on with it.'

What followed was a weird, heavy silence as Church stared Nate down across the table.

Church finally broke the quiet.

'Your presence here is unnecessary, N-Dogg. Your check for this portion of the defense has already cleared. I won't need another until two weeks before trial.' Church waved his fingers as though Nate were a tray of smelly cheese he'd decided to pass on. 'Why don't you move along, so that the adults can discuss the intricacies of the criminal case that will decide your little brother's fate for the next sixty or seventy years.'

Nate rose from the table, visibly restrained himself from responding, then marched across the endless room to the door, and left.

Ethan stood.

'Sit,' Church said.

Ethan sat.

'Zane Kingsley,' Church continued. 'Piper's father. What do you know about him, Ethan?'

'Not much. Piper didn't really talk about him. They were estranged.'

Church looked at me. 'But not when you knew her a few years ago, right, Riles?'

'No, she definitely had a relationship with him back then. A good one, I thought, from the number of photos she had of him on her walls.'

'There were none when I moved in,' Ethan said.

'So something happened between then and now,' Church thought aloud. 'Riles, what did Piper tell you about her dad?'

'That he was . . .' I thought back, embarrassed I didn't remember much. 'Only that they were there for each other when her mother died. She said she and her dad didn't really have a close relationship until her mom's death.'

'How long ago did her mom die?'

'Just a few years before I met her. We met in New York not long after my own parents died. I think it was something that connected us.'

'How did she describe her father?'

'Pretty much the way we saw him on TV,' I said. 'Passionate, powerful. Rigid.'

'He has a temper,' Church suggested.

'A short fuse is what Piper called it.'

'She tell you what he did for a living?'

'Not that I remember. I just know they had a lot of money while Piper was growing up. She said she was one of those spoiled little brats she despised seeing prance around Honolulu's private schools on her way to work every day.'

Ethan said, 'She never told me what her dad did for a living either.'

'Well, that's not surprising,' Church said. 'Because Jesse

hacked into the system of the Australian Security Intelligence Organization – which is essentially the Aussie FBI. And Zane Kingsley was, at least at one time, a confidential informant in a wide-ranging investigation into the Melbourne underworld.'

In the editing room, I rewind the footage of Church's revelation about Zane Kingsley.

'. . . *a confidential informant in a wide-ranging investigation into the Melbourne underworld.*'

I have already deleted my reaction. Deleted Brody's. The only one that matters is Ethan's. And once again, from him there's no reaction at all.

'So what does this mean?' Ethan asks on film.

'It means we have some digging to do,' Church says. 'But it also means you were not the only person with a motive to murder Piper. Any enemy of Zane Kingsley is an enemy of his daughter. We find enough evidence to support Zane's ties with Australia's underworld, and we have what's known in the business as "reasonable doubt".'

'So what do we do now?' Ethan asks. 'Go to Australia?'

Church says, 'Tahoma is already there.'

I stop the footage. Fast forward through the parts where Church and Jesse give some ad nauseam analysis of the physical evidence.

The beer bottles with Ethan's prints.

A foreign footprint near the back fence.

Piper's blood in the upstairs bathroom.

And something new . . .

I play the footage.

Church says, 'A slight smear of blood on a tree roughly fifty feet behind Piper's property.'

Onscreen, my eyes shoot to Brody, but he's smart enough to disguise any reaction. He plays it cool, even as Church opens a folder and takes out a photograph of the tree in question. I, like the complete idiot I am, gasp audibly at the photograph of our perch on the night of the murder.

Onscreen, everyone is looking at me. And then they're not.

'So this tiny smear of blood may help us?' Ethan asks as he squints at the prints.

'Depends on whose blood it is,' Church says. 'But it's something.'

I pause the footage. Going through my mind at the time were two conflicting narratives. The most frightening of which was: what if law enforcement for some reason has the pit-sniffer's DNA in their database? The kinder was: what if they don't; what if the unknown blood evidence and foreign footprint combined to win Ethan an acquittal? If that were the case, I would be more than just a key player in my own movie; keeping silent would undoubtedly make me a criminal.

I play the footage, watch myself glance at my arm as though the blood were still there. With the rain, though, the blood wasn't even on my arm when I got home that night, I was sure of it. The blood on the tree in the photo was unquestionably left by yours truly. I'd even knocked into it when that mosquito flew a kamikaze mission down my throat.

Clearly exhausted, Ethan pushes himself out of his chair and paces around the table like a wounded animal.

'I think we need to adjourn,' he finally says. 'This is really taking a toll.'

Church nods. 'There's just one more piece of physical evidence I want to address before you leave this evening.'

At his seat, Ethan finally stops, sits, says, 'Before we go any further, Nick, I have to tell you that I'm uncomfortable with this angle involving Piper's dad.'

'You never even knew him,' Church says, perplexed.

'Still, it's her family, you know? Family comes first. Always.'

Church is as expressionless as I'd ever see him. 'Then you're really going to fucking *hate* what I have to say next.'

TWENTY-TWO

I'm not a big fan of monogamy. Some people say that's more a guy trait than a girl's, but those people are sexist, and I'm not a big fan of sexism either. Was I surprised that Piper hadn't been monogamous with Ethan? No, not from what I knew of her. From the few times we hung out, I knew Piper to be a free spirit, nice but a bit naughty too, a girl who liked guys and wasn't afraid to go to bed on the first date. Was I shocked by whom she was fucking? Yeah. Not because I thought highly of him, or of injury lawyers in general, for that matter. I'd dated one back in New York, for six days, seven nights. On the seventh morning, he'd nailed my then-best-friend Ally, who was visiting from Portland – in my bed – while I was sitting through a three-hour lecture on Digital Imagery and Visualization.

In the editing room early the next morning, I return to footage I've already cut. The scene now runs seamlessly, beginning to end, with dead-on shots from all four cameras. In my existential outline, this scene constitutes the midpoint of ~~my~~ our film. At the midpoint, the documentarian typically introduces something *like* dramatic conflict, which is to say, not necessarily two alpha males clawing at each other's throats. We don't need, as in fiction, to witness our hero's metaphorical death setting up a later rebirth, and this need not be the point from which 'nothing will ever be the same'. We don't need the players to go abruptly from reactive to active; we don't need anything nearly as dramatic as all that.

But if you have the footage . . .

I press PLAY.

Onscreen, there I am, standing with Brody just a few feet away in the main room, where the scene took place.

'I got rid of Nate for a reason,' Church says, with a severity not often seen from him.

'What's this about?' Ethan asks. He's weary, he's dog-tired, he's spent.

'It's about pubic hair.'

'What?'

'The correct question isn't "what?". It's "*whose*?".'

'Don't play games with me, Nick. I—'

'Your brother's,' Church spits out. 'And it was found in Piper's bedroom.'

Silence seems to suck all the air from the room.

Finally, Ethan asks, 'What are you talking about?'

But, by then, he understands. We know he understands the out-and-out gravity of Church's words from the close-ups we shot. We know he understands, because whereas a moment ago he looked like he'd just gone ten rounds with Tyson Fury, now he looks as if he's just gone another twenty. I pause the footage right there. Zoom in on Ethan's face. For the first time, I read total shock, a sucker punch straight to the gut. And something I *had* seen from him before, something easy to recognize and almost impossible to hide – I see fear.

Even though he and this moment are so far removed in time, there's a pang in my chest every time I watch this scene.

Church says, 'Jesse hacked into a private laboratory the prosecutor's office uses to reinforce their own lab findings. The DNA was close enough to yours that they tested it three times, but there's no question that it's his.'

'Wait a minute,' Ethan says, as though new life were just breathed into him. 'Jesse got this by hacking? Lau *knows* you hack into databases, you said so yourself.'

Church shakes his head. 'The laboratory would never risk that kind of collusion. They have everything to lose, nothing to gain.'

Ethan's undeterred, seemingly more convinced in the truth of his theory than where he parked his pickup this morning. 'This is a *plant*, Nick. And you fell for it; you know you did. But that's no—'

'Ethan, we have a valid copy of the test. If we were to later produce it and it was a fake: one, Naomi Lau would be disbarred, which might hurt her chances in the next gubernatorial election; two, your conviction would be overturned; and three, every defendant Lau ever prosecuted would have a strong argument for a new trial. Not to mention how the lab's poor investors would feel.'

'That's not the way it works, Nick, and you know it. Some kid they just hired takes the rap for it, and everyone else goes on their merry little way.'

'Their merry little . . .?' Church sighs deeply, and it's strange, it's sobering, it's sad to see him all-business. 'I wouldn't have told you this if I wasn't absolutely sure it was true.'

Ethan actually smiles. 'It's a head fake, Nick, I'm telling you.'

'Ethan, I know this isn't easy to accept—'

'You have unclean hands, Nick. Isn't that what they say? The prosecution *knows* you can never come forward with the fake test results.'

'Why would I not come forward if my client's life were on the line?' Church says, thoroughly perplexed.

'Your bar license.'

'My *bar* license, are you kidding me?' Church puts on his angry eyebrows. 'I've been trying to get rid of my law license since the day I left the prosecutor's office. But even if I hadn't, how can you think me so inhuman that I wouldn't sacrifice my goddamn law license *for your life*?'

Ethan shakes his head, the smile history. 'I'm leaving.'

Church grabs his arm, and for several seconds the world stops. Then: 'Get your hand off me, Nick.'

Hearing Ethan speak with that same deceptive calm he spoke with in the Breakers parking lot made my stomach twitch.

Church, perhaps recalling images from that grainy video himself, releases Ethan's arm, says, 'The tests were concluded just yesterday, and our experts will be able to test the sample themselves this coming week. The jig would be up in days, Ethan. That's not a prosecutorial strategy, that's a practical joke.'

Ethan deflates some, stares off toward the sliding glass door. 'Then this is more serious than we thought. That means the cops planted *physical evidence*.'

With a Chevy Chase double-take, for a moment our everyday Church reappears. 'Remind me, again, exactly how the police got their hands on your brother's *pubic* hair? Is there a North American Nathan Jakes Pubic Hair Reserve I don't know about?'

'Wait,' Brody says, stepping into the shot. 'How *did* they have Nate's DNA in their database?'

Ethan turns to Brody, his face burning red, a large vein in his left temple visibly throbbing. He looks like he's just been gut-punched again.

'I am on your side, Ethan,' Church says, with a vehemence usually reserved for closing arguments. 'Man, I eat, sleep and *breathe* your case. I smoke, shoot and *snort* your case. If your case was your sister, I'd be bending her over the—'

Jesse of the Speaker booms to life. 'Too far, Nick.'

'Look,' Church says, shifting gears, 'what's important is how this piece of evidence affects your case, and the fact is, it cuts both ways. On the one hand, it means Piper wasn't the picture of purity Lau would have the jury believe.' He turns to me with a palm out. 'Not because of the sex – that would be sexist – but because of whom it was with.' He turns back to Ethan. 'It also means that there are other people – plural – that we can point to at trial. It means there will be enough evidence to, at the very least, confuse the hell out of the jury.'

'And on the other hand?' I ask.

'On the other hand,' Church says grimly, 'the prosecution will argue this only gives Ethan an additional motive to kill her.'

'Do you even *hear* yourself?' Ethan erupts, his eyes suddenly wet, his hands trembling. 'My case, the evidence, the jury . . . none of that means *anything* to me compared to the accusations you're making here tonight.'

Not unkindly, Church says, 'I'm not making any accusations, Ethan. Science is.'

Ethan abruptly turns and makes for the door, his chest rising and falling like a balloon full of nitrous.

'Then fuck you, Nick,' he says, with that disquieting calmness, 'and fuck science. You're fired. First thing in the morning I'm requesting a new lawyer.'

'We need to learn everything we can about Nathan Jakes,' Church said, the moment Ethan was out the door.

Once again, Jesse's voice startled the shit out of me, this time because my mind was somewhere else entirely. 'Already on it, Nick.'

Church then turned to me and Brody. 'With Tahoma in Australia, you two are going to have to step up your game.'

'When will Tahoma be back?' Brody asked.

'Depends on what he finds,' Church said. Then added, 'And how many mornings he's still too sloshed to board an international commercial flight.'

'So what do you want us to do?'

'Go into town in the morning, find out what you can in the legal community about Nate Jakes and his law firm.'

'How do we do that exactly?' I asked.

'Strike up a conversation with lawyers – it's not rocket science, Riles.'

'Sorry, counselor, but we're *not* private investigators.'

'No, you're documentarians. It's *literally* your job to get people to talk, to extract pertinent information, is it not?'

Brody appeared uncomfortable. 'What about everything Ethan just said? What about what the client wants?'

'Fuck what the client wants,' Church said. 'It's not his reputation as a superlawyer that's on the line in this trial, it's mine.'

When we reached Waikiki late that evening, I knew I should go straight up to our apartment, smoke a bowl with Brody, maybe watch a few episodes of *You're the Worst* on Hulu. Yet I also knew, from the moment we pulled out of Ko Olina, that I wouldn't. That I wouldn't go upstairs at all, that I would instead tell Brody that I needed to go for a drive, maybe visit my friend Wendy over on the windward side of the island, see if she might be willing to perform some of our ever-increasing administrative tasks for a percentage on returns from the movie.

I knew Brody wouldn't be happy when I told him.

But I also knew he wouldn't object.

I drove up North Shore. Found Ethan on the side of the road, trudging through a steady rain toward his apartment. I tapped my horn once, twice, until he turned around. With his right forearm shielding his eyes from my headlights, he looked at the Jeep; he looked at me. Then he turned and kept walking.

Behind me, a much harsher horn sounded, causing my middle finger to instinctively leap out the window. In my rearview was a twenty-something tourist in a rented white Ford Mustang, undoubtedly drunk, with a girl nearly passed out next to him in the passenger seat.

I stuck my head out the window of the Jeep. 'This is Hawaii, asshole. *No* honk, *no* hurry.' Then added: '*Cocksucker.*' No idea why I threw that in but it seemed to work. Well, that or he might have seen Ethan standing at the passenger side of my Jeep, staring him down. We'd never know which one of us put a fright in him, but the important thing was the motherfucker backed down.

Ethan climbed into my Jeep.

We drove in silence, and without really thinking about it (probably because I'd already thought about it a lot), I steered us in the direction of Kaena Point.

When we reached the unpaved road, I put the Jeep in four-wheel drive and took us over the surface of Mars. This time, though, when the road stopped, so did I. I steered the Jeep to the right so that we faced the dark sea, and put the transmission in park.

I switched off the headlights, then the ignition, leaving us in pitch-blackness.

We continued to sit in absolute silence. Not the kind of awkward silence we'd left back at Church's suite. This was a comfortable silence, an intimate quiet, the kind of moment words can only kill. Which was why I was so disheartened when, seconds later, Ethan was the first to speak. There was beer on his breath; he'd been walking home from a bar.

'Know why Nate's DNA found its way into a law enforcement database to begin with? Because while we were at UH, we got arrested for fighting some locals – a fight I started. An ounce of shrooms I'd been carrying found their way onto the pavement during the brawl. Nate didn't even hesitate. He yelled out, "They're mine, officer. My little brother knew nothing about them."' Ethan gazed out the window at the black horizon. 'Whether they believed him or just had respect for what he did, the police cut me loose right then. Nate got booked for possession with intent.'

'He did time?' I asked.

'His lawyer pled the charges down to a misdemeanor. He ended up with a suspended sentence. But the conviction gave him all kinds of hell when it came time to pass the Character and Fitness part of his bar application. His license was delayed for months. He had to borrow money to pay another lawyer who specializes in attorney ethics cases. Had to sit through too many hearings to count. For most of those months, none of us thought he'd ever be admitted. Nate, too. He was sure he'd spent three years in law school and six months studying for the bar for nothing.' Ethan paused, added, 'Well, nothing but a quarter million dollars of student loan debt.'

'Can I be honest with you, Ethan? I think Church is right; you need to listen to your head not your heart when there's this much on the line. View this strictly through the prism of your case. You don't need to personally come to any conclusions about whether your brother slept with Piper. We just need to decide how we're going to present the evidence in a light most favorable to you.'

'Nate's my brother, Riley.'

'Nate's not on trial here. You are. And it's not for an ounce of psychedelic mushrooms. It's for your life.'

His eyes filled again. 'I feel so trapped, Riley.'

'You *are* trapped, Ethan. You're on an island and wearing an ankle bracelet. Any *more* trapped and Buffalo Bill is probably lowering a bottle of lotion to you in a bucket.'

Ethan smiled, and it was easy to envisage girls in short shorts and bikini tops swooning at one of his gigs as he crooned the lyrics to 'American Pie' or 'Brown-eyed Girl'. Fleetingly, I wondered if I'd ever have the chance to see him play live.

The rain fell harder, making beautiful music on my hard top, sounds I could listen to forever. As I listened, it suddenly occurred to me that I'd picked up an accused killer by the side of the highway and driven him to a dark, isolated spot – intentionally.

'Should we just *Thelma & Louise* it right into the ocean?' I joked.

He laughed, a real laugh, nothing like the phony mercy chuckles I received from my shrink.

He took my hands in his, gently, yet with an unmistakable power, a force I instantly identified as the capacity to decide life and death. Reflected in those big blue eyes was my fate. I just couldn't see it yet.

Then his lips were on mine, his strong hand beneath my shirt. I had thought that in this situation, if ever it arose, I would think only of Brody and Piper and how awful I was for betraying them both. But once I was out of my shorts and on top of him and he was inside me, I forgot about everything; I forgot about everyone.

For a few moments just before coming, I even forgot about my film.

In the editing room, I imagine the camera on us that night, fantasize of how we might have looked to an outside observer. I'm not tearing myself up for remembering, as I did in the days immediately following that evening, because I've finally come to the realization that you can experience both shame and excitement in the same breath. Hell, with sex, it's almost inevitable.

*   *   *

The return drive to Waikiki was bliss. But once I missed my exit, I started wondering what else I might have overlooked in my oblivious euphoria. Did I smell of him? Were there any stains I couldn't explain away? Any scratches or bite marks?

'Where were you tonight?' were the first words I heard when I stepped inside our apartment.

'I told you.' But I blanked on what I'd told him.

'Come on, Rye, I called Wendy.'

My eyes went to the television, where onscreen Marissa and I were electronically frozen on the terrace at Church's suite.

Brody raised the remote and hit PLAY.

'. . . *picked a more reasonable goal,*' I was saying, '*like maybe putting the first man on Jupiter.*'

Marissa chuckled, then her face became cold. '*What were you doing at Breakers last night?*'

Onscreen, a stupid look washed over my face, a deer between two sets of headlights.

'*Ethan told you?*'

'*Nick and I saw the surveillance footage this morning before the arraignment.*'

'*Shit.*'

She said, '*You do realize that if prosecutors can demonstrate you had a relationship with the defendant outside of attorney– client, they can call you to testify, don't you? That they can . . .*'

'I don't need to see the rest of this, Brody. I was there.'

'Just another few seconds,' he said.

'. . . *when you're called to testify, Riley? Are you going to sink Nick's client, or are you going to perjure yourself and risk prison?*'

'*I won't see him like that again.*'

Brody paused the footage.

Brody hadn't been in the habit of watching the dailies, so I hadn't given much thought to editing my conversation with Marissa, *if* the camera had captured it at all. There would be time, I thought, plenty of time. I figured Brody wouldn't view any of the footage until we were well into post.

'You're making a big deal out of nothing,' I said.

His eyes were already wet. 'Then why didn't you tell me you were there last night? Why did you lie to me about this evening?'

'Because I *knew* you'd blow this all out of proportion.'

'No, you don't get to do that, Rye. You can't say you lied because you were worried about some hypothetical reaction you dreamed up for me – that's bullshit.'

'But true.'

'Did you fuck him?'

'Are you *serious* right now?'

'Answer the question.'

'No, I didn't *touch* him. I *wouldn't*. I met him for the *movie*, Brody. *Our* movie.'

'Now it's ours, huh?'

'We know nothing about him. I was hoping, after a few beers, he'd open up a little.'

'And he was hoping *you'd* open up a little.'

I smacked his coarse left cheek, but it didn't seem to faze him.

'If I learn *who* he is,' I shouted, 'I can better direct the film. I can make certain we capture the most poignant moments – shots revealing his character that we would have otherwise missed.'

'So,' Brody said, calming, 'if it's for the film, anything goes, right?'

'That's not what I said.'

'Why did you say at the end of your conversation with Marissa that you wouldn't see him again "like that"?'

'Socially.'

'Bullshit.'

'Believe whatever the hell you want.'

I turned and stomped toward the door.

'Is our relationship permanent, Rye, or are you just in it until the movie gets made?'

I opened the door. Now my eyes were wet. 'I could find another cameraman, Brody. That's not why I'm with you.'

'Be fair to me, Rye,' he said, as I stood in the doorway. 'Is there something between you and Ethan?'

I wanted to walk out without another word, wanted to say 'asked and answered', wanted to walk back inside and take his face in my hands and assure him that he was the only man that I loved, the only man I ever *would* love.

Instead, I said, 'Sure,' as sarcastically as I could, 'because there's nothing I need more right now than another guy, with questionable talent and grandiose dreams, leeching off me.'

TWENTY-THREE

I like to come first. And in Brody's life, I do. My theory is that, without a single sane or competent parent, Brody learned to live from books, TV and movies, and men tend to treat women better in fiction than they do in real life. Sure, he has his quirks – like having to fall asleep to *Simon & Garfunkel's Greatest Hits* – but I've learned to love those oddities nearly as much as I do him. With his intellectual curiosity, his childlike fascination with all things human, his adoration of the arts, Brody challenges me in ways I never thought possible. He's my bestest buddy, the one person I want to spend every day with; it's as simple as that. Which is why I finally said yes.

'You accepted his proposal,' Dr Farrockh says with an inscrutable expression, as though I've just informed her I'd decided on pizza tonight.

I smile, a gesture I know she'll mirror regardless how she feels. 'Yeah,' I tell her, 'I'm ready, and he's everything I ever wanted. A guy who's smart, sexy, sensitive. I think I was trying to sabotage myself by waiting so long to accept.'

'Congratulations,' she says, and as sincere as she sounds, I don't trust the sentiment. 'So how have you felt since you said yes?'

'Relieved,' I say.

'Because you don't have the burden of having to make the decision anymore?'

'Happy,' I tell her. 'I've felt happy since I said yes.'

She doesn't challenge my change in answer; she never does.

'The relief,' I say, 'is more over the documentary. It's evolving faster than I ever expected. And it's even better than I anticipated after the trial.'

'How does Brody feel about the movie?'

'He loves it. He thinks we're going to field multiple offers.'

'So he's been more optimistic than usual,' she says.

'Yeah, for the first time since I met him, he seems truly content.'

'And hopeful?'

'Yeah, he talks more about the future, about *our* future, both personally and professionally. The other day he expressed how fulfilling it will be to one day hear someone say he's done well for himself, without following it up with the word "considering".'

'So he's raising the bar for himself?'

I absently lift my left shoulder and lose myself in the forest green carpet. 'Back in New York, Brody had this recurring dream where he's a pedestrian stranded on a concrete island, with cars speeding in all directions. The traffic lights are malfunctioning, so he can't go forward or back, left or right.' I pause. 'It was maddening, he said, would tear him to pieces even the next day. But he hasn't had that dream in months now, at least not since we moved to the islands.'

'So you'll be staying here in Hawaii then?'

I sigh. 'We haven't really settled on the where.'

'But he wants to remain in the islands?'

'From all indications,' I concede.

'But you think he'll go along with whatever you decide?'

'To be honest, yeah. He's my opposite in that sense. He's a go-with-the-flow kind of guy.'

'And you're the boss?'

'No, no. Not in the way my father was. My father was one of those assholes with a sign in his office that read, "Rule Number One: The boss is always right. Rule Number Two: If the boss is wrong, see Rule Number One."'

'What would your sign say? Quickly.'

'"Like it or leave it."'

'How is that so different from your father's type of authoritarianism?'

'Because I don't force anyone into anything. Brody always has a choice.'

'But his choice is either to go along with you, or to lose you. My way or the highway, isn't it?'

'No, no. I'm just not articulating this right.'

'So you and he will have an equal voice in determining where you spend the early years of your marriage?'

'I think we'll be able to reach a compromise.'

'He doesn't want to move back east, though, right?'

'Well, that's where his mother is.'

'So you've ruled out returning to New York?'

'Not necessarily. We haven't really ruled anything out.'

'You haven't ruled out Portland then?'

'No, Portland I've ruled out. I can't go back there. Not now, not ever.'

'Too complicated?'

I don't say anything but I know my lip is trembling, my eyes watering. Dr Farrockh hands me the box of Kleenex sitting ready on her desk.

Wiping my eyes, I say, 'I don't think I've ever said this aloud, but sometimes I think my parents' accident wasn't an accident at all.'

'No?'

'I think it may have been a murder–suicide,' I say, trying to rally my voice.

'You think your father killed your mother?' she says.

I slowly shake my head. 'No. I think it was the other way around.'

TWENTY-FOUR

The morning following our argument was a true test of our relationship's mettle. We rose at the usual hour, had a quiet breakfast of blueberry Eggos, then went downstairs and climbed into the Jeep. For some reason, I was sure that was when Brody would break. He'll know, I thought, he'll know I screwed Ethan in here. It might as well be written in lipstick on the rearview mirror.

But Brody turned the ignition and pulled onto Tusitala without a word. By the time we reached downtown Honolulu, I felt like we were through the worst of it.

We parked in a garage on Bishop Street and headed toward the Dillingham Transportation Building, where a lawyer named

Philip Kopec maintained a solo practice specializing in personal injury. Kopec had agreed to meet us at his office first thing but cautioned that he had to be at a deposition several blocks away by nine.

Before we left Church's suite last night, Jesse provided us a contact number 'that'll be good for forty-eight hours', should Brody and I require his assistance investigating Nate.

'Know what?' Church said. 'Why not just take him home with you?'

He grabbed the speaker box from the table and tossed it in our direction. Brody, luckily, had fast hands.

'How do we turn him on?' I asked.

Church said, 'Some cartoon porn and a pair of egg-and-cheese Hot Pockets should do the trick.'

While I had been up North Shore getting laid, Brody and Jesse had begun their research on Nathan Jakes. Although I wasn't privy to much of the evening, Brody, in an email to Church that I was generously cc'd on, summed it up thusly:

```
Performed relevant keyword search of office
and private Gmail accounts, which yielded
no   pertinent   information.   Searched
multiple  databases  of  Hawaii  State
Judiciary  and  discovered  an  open  griev-
ance  with  the  Disciplinary  Board  filed  by
Philip R. Kopec, Esq. for nonpayment of
fees  in  an  injury  lawsuit.  Contacted
Attorney  Kopec  and  arranged  meeting  at
his  office  8 a.m.  tomorrow.
```

'I went to law school with the son of a bitch,' Kopec said, pretty much as soon as we walked through the door.

My eyes went immediately to his ego wall and spotted the *juris doctorate* from University of Hawaii at Manoa, William S. Richardson School of Law. He'd graduated same year as Nate.

'Hasn't changed a single iota since then,' Kopec said. He was a round man with a headful of shaggy blond hair. 'Always looking for the easy way out, and to hell with anyone in his path.'

'Were you ever in his path back then?' I asked.

'Me? No. But plenty of my friends.' He paused, grinned. 'Well, they're my friends now, thanks to Facebook. No one ever spoke two words to me back then.'

'What did he do?'

'Well, it wasn't so much what he did, as what he didn't do. Which was to take the study of law remotely seriously. Never read the assignments, hardly ever appeared in class. Then, when exam time came around, he'd con some poor bastards into handing over their semester's work so that he wouldn't fail out. Even paid some geek to complete the take-home tests.' He shook his head in disgust. 'Derek Grasman. Some douchebag, listened to *Rocky* theme music to pump himself up before every exam – and was *proud* of it.'

'Not a fan?' I said.

He shrugged. 'I would've done the take-homes for half the price and put in twice the effort.'

'So,' I said, 'Nathan Jakes' academic dishonesty was your main beef with him then?'

'No, he also screwed around with half the girls in class, *while* he was newly married with his first kid on the way.'

'Did you know his wife?'

'I knew *of* her. She grew up one town over from me in Mililani. *Pretty* girl – Cheyenne Oh, I believe her maiden name was. Poor thing.'

'Why do you say that?'

'Nate never wanted her – not long-term anyway.'

'He told you this?'

'No, I overheard it.' He laughed. 'You pretty people think we uggos are as nonexistent as we are invisible. But we're not. We're there, we have ears, we hear things. Nate never really wanted her, never even wanted to go to law school. He knocked her up, and her family convinced him to get a graduate degree, to "make something of himself".'

'He never considered any of the alternatives?'

'I'm pretty sure he did. But something tipped the scale, and that something was her old man's money. Her father is a businessman in town, has millions, but the family has always lived modestly. They still live in central Oahu, far as I know.'

Kopec appeared winded. He checked his watch for the second time in five minutes.

'We think he's still messing around behind his wife's back,' I said.

'Wouldn't surprise me one bit. Like I said, he hasn't changed. Which is why I filed that grievance against him recently. I had this huge case against Matson, the big shipping company here. My client *literally* lost an arm and a leg in the accident. Got them trapped under one of those gigantic shipping containers. I worked the case for almost six years, through two deadlocked trials and numerous appeals. Nathan Jakes – and he's known for this, ask any injury lawyer in town – poaches my client, settles the case because he's buddy-buddy with the insurance lawyers, who undoubtedly get a cut, then wholly ignores my lien on the case and takes the entire fee for himself. Tried to settle with me for pennies on the dollar.'

'You never got paid?'

'I got paid,' he said. '*Nickels* on the dollar. I had no choice. I'd just been through a nasty divorce. He had me by the short and curlies, if you'll excuse the expression.'

'Mind sharing the client's name?' I asked.

'Not at all, it's public record now.'

'Who is he?'

'It's not a *he* at all. It's a *she*. It's *always* a she with this guy.'

In the elevator on the way downstairs, I asked Brody whether our interview with Kopec further convinced him that Nate was sleeping with Piper.

'We know he was,' he said.

'Not necessarily. Trace evidence winds up in the strangest places, for millions of different reasons. One of Nathan's pubes could have theoretically found its way into Piper's bedroom via—'

'It wasn't found in Piper's bedroom. Church just said that to lessen the blow. He was afraid Ethan would go ape shit.'

'Where in the house was it found then?'

'It wasn't found during the police search at all. It was discovered during the autopsy. While the pathologist was combing through Piper's own pubic region.'

*   *   *

That evening we sat on Church's terrace, passing a joint as the
sun dipped into the Pacific. There were five of us again tonight,
but Nathan Jakes wasn't here. To our great fortune, Marissa
Linden was with us instead. In fact, Church announced soon
after we arrived that Marissa was joining the defense team now
that we had multiple leads. (Yay!) In better news, Tahoma had
boarded a plane and was on his way back from Australia. Church
wouldn't allow Tahoma to discuss the details over an international
call, but it was clear from their conversation that Tahoma's trip
to Melbourne had been fruitful.

Upon learning the truth about the discovery of the pubic hair,
Ethan finally resigned himself to the fact that he had been
betrayed, both by Piper and his own brother, and he was prepared
to move forward.

'I'm going to hold a press conference,' Church said.

'Why now?' I asked.

'The discovery of this new evidence.'

Ethan shook his head. 'No way, that's not what I want. All of
Oahu doesn't need to know Piper cheated on me.'

'I beg to differ,' Church said. 'All of Oahu – i.e. our entire
jury pool – needs to hear this as clearly and as often as possible
over the next few months. An enlarged graphic of that pubic hair
is going on the one-sheet for the documentary. By the time this
case is over, that pube is going to be as iconic as the fingerprint
for Scott Turow's *Presumed Innocent.*'

'Let's hold off on the one-sheet for now,' I said. 'Ethan, Church
is right.'

Church scoffed. 'Why do you always refer to me by my last
name?'

'It's just easier, OK?' I turned back to Ethan. 'The public is
going to find out anyway. It's going to come out at trial regardless. Only the prosecution will introduce it early to get it out of
the way, make it seem to the jury like it's no big deal. We might
as well allow Church to maximize its impact.'

I felt Brody's eyes on me, more penetrating than any camera.
I'd just taken another step into the story. I could no longer hide
behind the guise of an objective observer. Now I was, undeniably,
one of the players on Team Ethan.

'I'm not sure introducing it now is the best strategy,' Brody said. 'First, it's too close in time to the Breakers incident. The media will tie the coverage together and dilute the hair's impact. Second, assuming we receive copies of the lab tests from the prosecution this week, waving that pubic hair around right away may make us appear desperate.'

Church bowed his head, almost humbly. 'BQ's right. We need to get it out there some other way.' He rested his elbows on his thighs and his chin on his fists. 'How do I come off as more credible?'

Marissa leaned in. 'You act more like yourself.'

'Sexy? How's that going to help?'

'I was actually going for sleazy.'

'You think I need to come off as a sleazoid?'

'You need to get into character,' she said, eying all of us now, knowing she was maybe, possibly, being brilliant in front of the cameras. 'You need to act like a lawyer.'

TWENTY-FIVE

B ack in the editing room following my appointment with Dr Farrockh, I scan my log to find Church's first press conference, which took place later that week. It's brief but impactful. I key in the time code and press PLAY.

'Good morning,' Church says onscreen. 'I know there's been some speculation about whether this press conference will be about new evidence unearthed in the case, but I'm afraid it's not. In fact, my first press conference in this case will be my *last* press conference in this case. Effective immediately, I've withdrawn from the case as Mr Jakes' attorney due to the discovery of a conflict of interest.'

'What's the conflict?' Kalani Webb calls out.

'I didn't want to go into details this morning, but I suppose it'll be made public anyway. Frankly, new evidence *has* been discovered, and it implicates the individual who was paying my client's tab.'

'How is that a conflict?' Kalani says.

'Well, aren't you a rambunctious little guy? It's a conflict of

interest because I'm interested in money, and my client doesn't
have any.'

'Isn't that a little harsh?'

'Harsh? No. Because the introduction of this evidence will
surely convince Ms Lau to drop the charges against Ethan Jakes
and to indict the proper party.'

'What if she refuses?'

'If she refuses, Ms Lau will be embarrassed at trial, because this
new evidence is so clear cut, it vindicates my former client entirely.'

I pause the video and smile. On the terrace, I had objected to
that line. I'd said, 'People aren't going to believe something just
because you say it.'

'I'm sorry,' Church had said with a theatrical frown, 'were
you not on Earth for the last presidential election?'

I hit PLAY again.

Onscreen, Church says, 'At the end of the day, it won't matter
who represents Ethan Jakes in this case. It's an open-and-shut
acquittal if ever I've seen one. Any jackass can take it to trial.
Just not this jackass.'

'What *is* the evidence?' Kalani calls out again.

'I'm sorry,' Church says, 'I didn't catch your name.'

The cameras turn on him. 'Kalani Webb, Hawaii Action News.'

'Kalani,' Church says in a condescending voice, 'have you
recently noticed hair growing on your body where there was no
hair before?'

I'd objected to this line as well, but Church insisted that 'we
need to sear this pube into people's brains; I mean *really* get it
in there'.

'For those of you in the cheap seats,' Church said loudly, even
though there were only about a dozen reporters gathered around,
the farthest maybe ten feet from him, 'I'm talking about pubic
hair. A pubic hair belonging to someone *other* than Ethan Jakes.'

I pick up the script and read along.

```
                 KALANI
     Discovered  at  the  scene?


                 CHURCH
     Discovered  on  the  body.
```

CHURCH pauses to allow the words to sink in.

                    CHURCH (CONT'D)
During the autopsy, a pubic hair
belonging to another man was
discovered on the victim's body.

                    KALANI
Where on the body?

                    CHURCH
The pubic hair was discovered by the
pathologist during a preliminary comb-
through of the victim's own pubic
region.

                    KALANI
Who does the hair belong to?

                    CHURCH
I'm sorry. That I'm not at liberty to
say at this time.

                    KALANI
Who was paying your client's legal fees
prior to this discovery?

                    CHURCH
              (with zero hesitation)
My client's brother - Nathan Jakes.

        CHURCH raises his palms.

                CHURCH (CONT'D)
That's the last question, thank you.
Before you leave, don't forget to tip
your bartenders.

Yours truly had the distinction of slipping Kalani the 500 dollars I'd offered him earlier in the week, following our strategy session on Church's deck.

Kalani didn't look happy. 'What the hell was that?'

'Church ad libs,' I tried.

Kalani tried not to smile, but his cheeks turned a familiar mauve. 'Next time he ad libs about my groin, tell him I'm going to go to work on *his* with my dad's power tools.'

I smiled back. 'I'll be sure to pass that along.'

TWENTY-SIX

I like to get paid for it. Even though it wasn't in our contract, in a rare gesture of selflessness, Church paid me and Brody for our services throughout the investigation and trial. Although the influx of cash was desperately needed, at times it felt so much like a conventional job that I feared Brody would quit just on principle. When he was a child, his mother kept him holed up in a cluttered little clothing store she owned. Paid him a full twenty-five cents an hour but forced him to buy his own food. Five hours after school would earn him a slice of pizza from the Italian joint next door. A full twelve-hour day and he could add mozzarella sticks to his order. While other children were out riding bikes and playing ball, Brody Quinlan was selling inexpensive cotton dresses to plus-sized women for basic sustenance. One night in bed after sex, I asked him why he hadn't told anybody. He said he didn't even realize at the time that child labor was wrong; in fact, he often wondered how kids whose mothers didn't own clothing stores that paid a quarter an hour *ever* ate. Besides, between the physical assaults, the emotional blackmail, the constant barrage of hateful words and unabating humiliation, twelve hours on a summer's day locked away alone in a cramped clothing store seemed almost like a vacation.

Sitting next to each other now in the editing room, I place my hand on his and kiss his clean-shaven cheek.

'I think we should go with a montage here,' he says. 'Kind

of sum up the months of tedious investigation with just the highlights and lowlights leading up to trial.'

'We can try that,' I say, 'but let's lead in with a pertinent interview – the older lady two doors down from Piper's house.'

'Yeah, but that's pertinent only in the sense that it corroborates that Nate was visiting Piper regularly. And we've already given away the store on that news with the introduction of the pubic hair. Maybe this scene should come earlier.'

'I disagree,' I say. 'If it comes earlier it lessens the impact of the pube – and the Introduction of the Pube scene is one of the most dramatic scenes until trial.'

'Chronologically, though, this interview came *before* the pubic hair, at a time before Nate was suspected of anything, and our reactions to her answers reflect that.'

'Not necessarily. And we can edit out our reactions if necessary.'

'Let's play the scene,' he says.

'I don't need to, I know it by heart. You, me and Tahoma—'

'Pre-Australia Tahoma.'

'Are you going to let me describe the scene before you start pointing out everything that's wrong with it?'

'Aren't we debating this? Isn't that why we're talking the scene through in the first place?'

I raise my palm. 'Kindly reserve all questions for after the show.'

Brody smirks.

'What?' I say.

'That was quintessential Church. Not only what you said but *how* you said it.'

'Are we really having *this* argument?'

'I think it's fair for me to point it out when you're being glaringly hypocritical. Since we started post, you've accused me of speaking like Church, acting like Church – you even accused me of stealing his *smell*.'

'His *scent*. And it *was* the same scent.'

'Because it was *complimentary* from the Four Seasons.'

'You've *never* worn cologne before, and suddenly you want to smell like a nightclub at the Jersey Shore?'

'Ugh.' He throws up his hands. 'All right, you want to know

why I used the cologne at all? Because during the trial, things were happening so fast, I didn't have time to shower for a few days.'

'Oh.'

'Is *that* vintage Church?'

'No,' I concede, defeated. 'That's vintage Brody.'

TWENTY-SEVEN

'Sometime' after the weathergirl died, Brody, Tahoma and I were back on Mount Tantalus, hitting the homes where no one answered the door first time around. Our first stop was one house down from Kalani's, two from Piper's. Kalani had been the only person I'd recognized from television thus far, but that changed when 'Neighbor' (you remember, that upper middle-age Caucasian female in the boho muumuu who appeared on the news report announcing Piper's death) opened the door.

'Good afternoon, madam,' Tahoma said after making the introductions. 'Mind if we come inside and take a few minutes of your time?'

Her name was Elanor and she'd been eying either Brody or his camera ever since she opened the door. Whichever it was, it convinced her to enthusiastically invite us inside for coffee.

As we slipped out of our sandals (a Hawaiian custom and a real blow to my self-esteem due to my aforementioned stinky feet), I quietly asked Brody if he recognized our host from the news.

He chuckled. 'Yeah, that's the woman who was on when I yelled, "Save the poem for spoken-word night, sister."'

When you live in a one-bedroom apartment and spend most of your time in a shoebox-sized editing room, most houses feel ostentatiously large, and this one was no different. Elanor Rigby (I shit you not, that is her name; crazy, but easy enough for a pair of pothead filmmakers to remember) motioned to a spacious living room appointed with island-style furniture, and told us to make ourselves at home while she put on coffee.

'None for me,' Tahoma said.

Brody and I concurred.

Elanor seemed disappointed. I suspected she hadn't had visitors in some time.

'Married?' Tahoma asked her once she was seated in an over-sized wicker chair.

'Widowed.'

'I'm sorry. Children?'

'None on the island. They've all moved away.'

She pushed back her thinning hair in a way that made me think she'd indeed been leering at the camera and not Brody. As Church would later expound: 'Everyone sees their fifteen minutes in a good murder case.'

'Did you know Piper Kingsley?' Tahoma went on.

'By sight, certainly. I didn't know her personally.' Her eyes shot to the camera. 'We ran in different circles,' she said.

'How about her boyfriend, Ethan Jakes?'

'I never saw him before, not until he was on television. Shame what he did to that poor young woman.'

I jotted a note to use that soundbite. Beneath it I wrote: *Presumption of innocence???*

Then underlined it. Twice.

'So,' Tahoma said, 'you didn't see Piper all that often, then?'

'Oh, I saw her every day.'

He smiled, a rarity but it brightened the room. 'On the evening news?'

'No, no, in the morning. Every morning, rain or shine, she jogged down Tantalus Drive and back.'

'Rain or shine, huh?'

'Rain or shine,' she repeated. 'She just wore one of those clear plastic ponchos you buy at ABC.'

Behind the camera, Brody suffered one of his infamous coughing jags (he refused to switch from joints to the vaporizer) but turned down Elanor's offer of water.

Tahoma said, 'You didn't know any of her friends, though? Didn't see anyone coming or going?'

'Well, once a car drives past my house I can't see where it goes. But I've driven by a few times.' She glanced at the camera and quickly added, 'To visit friends. I have friends up the mountain, you know.'

'Of course. So you drove by Piper's house and saw someone?'

'Not some*one*. Just a car.'

'A car?'

'A nice one, *really* nice. Not Piper's Jaguar though, something else.'

'How many times have you seen it?'

'A few times now.' She turned her head in thought. 'Maybe four or five times. Four or five times a month. For the past five or six months.'

'You drive up to see your friends pretty often, huh?'

Her face turned to ice and Tahoma immediately backed off.

'So this car in the driveway,' Tahoma said. 'What color was it?'

'White.'

'A white car in Hawaii?' Tahoma said dryly. 'Really.'

'But it was never parked in the driveway. At least never when I saw it. That's what makes it stand out in my memory – it was always parked in the garage.'

'Her garage door would usually be up?'

'I'd say at least half the time. I don't know whether she forgot it or what. Her car would always be parked right behind the white one when it was there.'

'But you never saw the guy who drove it.'

'No, never. I try to mind my own business, you know.'

'You don't like her much, do you?' Tahoma said as we drove back to Hawaii Kai.

'Elanor Rigby? Why wouldn't I like her?'

Brody was nodding off in the backseat, while I drove and Tahoma rode shotgun.

'Not her. Marissa – you don't like Marissa.'

'I didn't say that.'

'You didn't have to say it.'

'No?'

'No, I read people. That's my job, yeah? I'm an investigator.'

'I suppose you know *why* I dislike her, too?'

'You're jealous.'

'*What?*' I nearly lost control of the Jeep.

'I just don't know what you're jealous of. You got a thing for Nick?'

I scoffed. Tahoma quickly looked at Brody asleep in the backseat.

'Oops,' he said, 'sorry. I forgot he was there.' He rolled down his window and pulled out a cigarette. 'You mind?'

'Light it,' I said, 'and I'll personally burn you alive.'

I press STOP. Maybe Brody's right, maybe this scene doesn't need to be here. It's extraneous. He's outside hitting the vaporizer; I declined the invitation for the usual reason. What if I have an epiphany in the ten minutes we take for a vape sesh? But, no. It's been eight already, and nothing. I consider moving the footage to the first half of the movie, but ultimately decide it would only slow things down. Better just to show pieces of her testimony at trial, if anything at all. Same difference, right? Better here to show post-Australia Tahoma tell the defense team all he learned about Zane Kingsley in Melbourne.

While Naomi Lau may have done her homework on Nicholas Church and Piper Kingsley, she sure crapped the bed when it came to ol' Zane.

'Small-time criminal,' Tahoma said in Church's suite. 'He has a sheet – drugs, guns, assaults, even stalking. But no major violent crimes. No rape, no homicide.'

Church, who had been quietly rehired after publicly quitting the defense team, leaned forward on the table. 'You talked to the local cops?'

'Of course. They said the sheet pretty much tells the tale.'

'When was his most recent arrest?'

'Twelve, thirteen years ago.'

'For what?'

'Fraud.'

'How much?'

'A small score. Equivalent maybe to thirty grand here.'

'That doesn't make sense,' I said. 'Piper's parents were loaded.'

Tahoma shook his head. 'Piper's *mother* was loaded.'

'But they never separated, at least according to Piper.'

'Doesn't mean she didn't keep him on a short leash,' Brody threw in. 'Was there a prenuptial agreement?'

'One the size of a James Michener novel,' Tahoma said. 'I forwarded an electronic copy to Nick.'

'I went through it,' Church said. 'Zane had every incentive to stay with Piper's mom. He would've walked away with nothing in the divorce.'

'But he got it all in the will?' Marissa asked.

Tahoma shook his head. 'A chunk of it went to charity. Most went into a trust for Piper. Australian law doesn't allow you to disinherit a spouse entirely, but to the extent you can, she did.'

'What was the mother's cause of death?' Church said.

'Went down as natural causes. The local cops I spoke to said they immediately anticipated homicide and liked Zane for the murder. But the autopsy didn't support a finding of homicide.'

Church said, 'Which doesn't necessarily mean it wasn't a homicide. But, given the content of her will, he had even less incentive to kill her than to divorce her.'

'What happened to him after his wife's death?' I asked.

Tahoma said, 'Piper bought him a house, but nothing like the home he and his wife had been living in.'

Church added, 'Piper's bank statements show she was essentially paying her father an allowance, up until last year.'

'That must have been when they had the falling out,' I said.

Church folded his arms and leaned back in his seat. 'If the mother's will had left a substantial part of her estate to Piper's father, we could have fed the jury enough of this line to arouse suspicion, but without it . . .'

'What about Piper's falling out with him?'

Church shook his head. 'Not enough. It might be enough if he were on the island at the time she was killed, but he wasn't. He was in Melbourne.'

'Could have hired someone,' I said.

'True, but this doesn't have a whiff of a professional hit. It'd be too much of a stretch for the jury to buy in without linking him to the mother's death. If the will were favorable to him, we'd have something to build on, but—'

'How about the next best thing?' Tahoma said. 'Local cops said, couple of nights after his wife died, he went berserk in a pub, busted up a couple of tourists' faces. They didn't pick him up for it because his wife had just died.'

Church sat up straight in his seat, excited. 'Police had to have a better reason than that, especially if they still liked him for his wife's murder.'

Tahoma smiled for maybe the second time in the investigation. 'They did. They had him under surveillance from the day his wife died.'

'And?'

'And he went berserk at that pub because he'd just learned he wasn't the beneficiary of his wife's life insurance policy. Apparently, he and the missus had purchased a pair of policies years ago, with each other named as beneficiaries. But the wife went behind his back and changed the beneficiary from her husband to her daughter.'

'How long before she died?' Church asked.

'Three days,' Tahoma said. 'If you count the weekend.'

At home that evening, Brody and I sat on opposite ends of the couch and watched the news. Devastation in Syria, grave threats against Seoul from North Korea, Russian hacking, the past year the hottest in recorded history, again. Back on the US mainland, an NFL star was about to go on trial for murder; another committed suicide, with a gun to the chest, in order to preserve his brain for scientific study. In Georgia, a police officer had shot a black teenager carrying an air rifle that could conceivably be mistaken for a real weapon. Witnesses provided conflicting accounts. Numerous individuals had captured the aftermath on their smartphones, but the incident itself went unrecorded.

'Why would a kid raise an air rifle at police?' I said.

'We don't know that he did.' Brody fired up his bowl, blew out a tight stream of smoke. 'But *if* he did, it could be a case of suicide by cop.'

'It looks like a gun, doesn't it?'

'Somewhat,' he said. 'The question is whether it would look so much like a gun if it were being held by a pair of white hands.'

'You don't think so?'

'I don't know. And it would take one hell of a risky experiment to find out.'

*   *   *

The following morning, I met Kyle Myers for coffee. We'd been trying to hook up for some time, but, as Piper's replacement, he'd been working seven days a week until the station chose his own replacement. Which happened just yesterday.

'Piper knew she was a sugar mama,' he said, as he put his lips to the triple venti, half-sweet, non-fat caramel macchiato, which he'd already sent back twice. 'We commiserated over it often. I was a sugar mama, too, for a brief stretch of her tenure at the station. But I've since given up dating broke motherfuckers.'

His smile was devilish and I immediately felt as though I'd known him forever.

'Ethan doesn't give me that impression,' I said. 'In fact, he seems proud and super-independent.'

'That's because the individual he was dependent on is gone.'

'Did you know Ethan personally?'

'From a few station functions, and one time a bunch of us from the station went down to Waikiki to watch him perform.'

'Was he any good?'

'Not my cuppa, but I didn't have to cover my ears or anything.' He took another sip from his steaming cup. 'Crazy attractive, I'll give him that.'

'Did you ever meet his brother?'

'The Nathan from the news, yeah. As a matter of fact, he was there the night we went to Waikiki to see Ethan perform.' He leaned forward. 'Does that lawyer who announced that the whole case is over, simply because police discovered an errant pubic hair, truly believe that? Or was that strategic?'

I felt vindicated. 'Not very effective that assertion, huh?'

'Oh no, it was *extremely* effective. I mean, I wasn't swayed but you should read some of the tweets the station received, and the hundreds of Facebook comments. People only read the head-lines now. Overwhelmingly, our viewers are convinced that Ethan didn't kill Piper, and that his brother did.'

'Anyone you know personally?'

'If you're asking if I hang around idiots, my answer would be, "I only date them." Since I'm currently single and in the midst of a sexual drought, though, my answer is no, I don't know anyone personally. But we're talking about the unwashed masses here, not a Friday night crowd at Skye Bar.'

'Did you hang with Piper outside of work at all?'

'When she first arrived at the station, yes. As difficult as it was.'

'Why was it difficult?'

'She took the job I'd been dying for. But the station manager prefers vaginas, what can you do?'

'You think you got passed over because Piper slept with the station manager?'

'Think? No. Know? Yes.'

'She told you?'

'*He* told me. He was so desperate to brag about his conquest, I'm surprised he didn't produce a segment about it.'

'Mostly females at the station?'

'Well, in the good jobs, yes. There are cameramen and grips, but other than me, an anchor and the sports guy (of course), all of the on-air talent menstruates.'

'What's the station manager's name?'

'Glen. Glen Belding. B-E-L-D-I-N-G, like the high school principal on *Saved by the Bell*. Kind of looks like him too. Maybe a little thicker, a little balder.'

'Could Belding have been lying about sleeping with Piper?'

'Sure, but once it goes through the rumor mill, it becomes fact. Perception is reality. You know that – you're in television.'

'Little different scene,' I said. 'Did Piper tell you she was pregnant?'

'Actually, I asked her. She looked a little green when she came into the station one Saturday. A few minutes later she walked out of the bathroom and immediately asked me for Altoids.'

'What did she say when you asked her?'

'She said, "Great timing, too." Which I took to mean that the father was here and she was weeks away from departing for the mainland.'

'You assumed Ethan was the father?'

'Oh, I don't make assumptions like that anymore, and from the look on her face, I knew better than to ask.'

'Did she say how Ethan took the news about her moving to the mainland?'

'I know she wanted to put off telling him, and our female anchor agreed.'

'Put off telling him for how long?'

'Until she was safely on the mainland, I assume.'

I hesitate, unsure if I want the answer. 'Was she afraid of him?'

'I don't know if I'd go quite that far, but let's put it this way, she wasn't *not* afraid of him. He has a temper, as illustrated on our evening broadcast recently, with the footage from Breakers' parking lot.'

The footage of that evening replayed in my mind, as it had unremittingly since I first saw it.

After another half-hour of chatting, I said, 'You've been incredibly helpful, Kyle. I don't know how to thank you.'

'Oh, no worries. Happy to help in any way I can. Besides, I don't think I'm betraying any confidences here. I doubt I told you anything Piper didn't put in her diary.'

'Her diary?' I asked, as we both rose from our seats.

'Or journal, or whatever people are calling it these days. But yes, she was constantly jotting down her thoughts in it, and she guarded it like a rabid Rottweiler would a pound of raw meat.'

He paused, scanned my expression, then bent his carefully manicured brows inward.

'Wait,' he said, 'did the police seriously not find it?'

TWENTY-EIGHT

I like the first time. But I like the second time better. Especially when the first time is in the front passenger seat of a Jeep.

My first time with Brody was all but professionally coordinated. Third date, dinner first, back to my place, sit up in bed, ostensibly to watch a terrible movie on one of the premium channels. Watch for ten minutes, shoulders joined, pondering the logistics of it all, until finally he turns to speak, says nothing, our eyes meet, then close, lips touch, then kiss, while as smoothly as possible we attempt to get into a comfortable position for the next step in our questionable relationship. Foreplay, but not so extensive as to risk overexcitement and early release. Awkward undressing, especially the pants, especially jeans, especially tight ones. Then the sex (don't overthink it), good but brief, and understandably so; after all, he did wait for the third date, and had harbored a visible hard-on since the opening credits of the *Zoolander* sequel.

In the editing room, I've queued up our visit to the crime scene less than four weeks before trial, but the memory of that day makes my stomach twist. My second time with Ethan was the evening before that visit to Piper's home on Mount Tantalus. Since our first time at Kaena Point months earlier, I'd been lusting after Ethan in a way I'd never lusted after anyone, and all intimations were that this intense longing was reciprocated. But we knew it was too chancy to do it again. Police were likely still watching him, fingers crossed that he'd fuck up in some way and strengthen their case. I didn't know the intricacies of the attorney–client privilege, and because I was always so preoccupied with the film, never bothered to do the research. But Marissa's warning rang true, and we couldn't afford to dance in the gray areas of the law where Ethan's case was concerned.

Although the case still wasn't national news, it continued to warrant the state's full attention. Murder is uncommon in paradise; police see maybe twenty homicides a year. So Ethan, by then, was already being recognized in the streets. Some people, when they passed him, intentionally looked away, others pointed and gawked. Almost all the attention was negative, yet Ethan seemed to welcome it, strolling through town daily under the pretext of 'being unafraid'. But as much as he liked being seen, we both understood we couldn't be seen together, at least not alone.

Since spontaneity requires forethought, we arranged to meet in the one place we thought no one would look for us – the editing room, which Brody and I barely used at the time. In fact, Brody had yet to put his copy of the key on his key ring. Instead it had sat in the recesses of my underwear drawer since the day we signed the lease. Since I knew Brody wouldn't miss it, I lent the key to Ethan and told Brody I was hitting some bars with Kyle Myers, who had become somewhat of a friend. I knew Brody would have no interest in going to any of the bars I named, and that naming them would further confirm for Brody that Kyle Myers was safe.

I sat in the editing room for hours beforehand, just in case;

Ethan and I didn't want to arrive too close in time. It goes without saying that the air conditioner was on the fritz. So by ten p.m., when the key finally turned in the lock, I was more sweat than flesh. Not that it mattered to Ethan. He immediately jerked me toward him, kissed me hungrily on the lips, gripped my ass as though he'd never let go. Seconds later, my shirt fell to the floor, my hands furiously worked at his belt. Free of our clothes, we instantly melted into one another, first on the chair, then atop the expensive equipment, until finally, still inside me, he lifted me in his arms and tenderly lowered me onto a blanket I'd laid on the floor.

Sitting here now, that room seems like a place from a parallel universe, one I had no business being in to begin with. I recognize the heat and the smallness of the space. The rest, however, is alien.

I toy with the idea of skipping ahead, of editing the opening statements at trial. But that would be counterintuitive. Everything else left to be done – titles, graphics, special effects, music – falls within Brody's areas of expertise, and I wouldn't know where to begin.

Then I hear the key in the lock and know that I'm saved, at least for the time being, because Brody walks in, a sly grin on his face, an expression I only see when he either has good news or has stunk up the bathroom knowing I need to shower. Since there is no shower in the editing room, I assume the former and cross my fingers that it has to do with the movie, a treatment for which has been making the rounds in Los Angeles for just the past forty-eight hours.

'Did you just stink up our bathroom?' I ask, to be sure.

'Even better,' he says, reaching into the back of his pants and producing a small box adorned in navy velvet.

I'm not one of those girls who's been thinking of this moment since the third grade, started planning for it in the seventh. I'm not one of those girls who dreamt of what her stomach would do and whether tears would come to her eyes when presented with a box like this. I've never imagined this moment with Brody, not once, not even when I knew he was about to propose to me. But now there's a dip deep in my stomach, a steep drop rivaled only by the plunge down Splash Mountain. And when he opens the box, my eyes immediately sting, instantly well, and as I stare in amazement at the most perfect ring – not the largest, not the clearest, not the most expensive, but the most perfect ring for me from him – I do something that would piss me off if it were anyone else: I completely break down, like I've just won the Showcase Showdown on *The Price is Right.*

'Better late than never,' he says.

'Bullshit,' I tell him, as I wipe the tears from my eyes. 'You waited until I said *yes*, and I don't blame you.'

TWENTY-NINE

Inside Piper's home for the first time in years, I felt like an intruder, only worse, like an invader, a conqueror, a usurper. Standing next to Ethan, I almost felt like a cold-blooded killer, as if Piper's death was, in some strange cosmic way, my fault. As irrational as it all was, I felt as though something had crawled down my throat into my stomach and nested. That it would leave a residue I would never fully be rid of.

It didn't help that, with the exception of a few uniformed chaperones, our visit to the crime scene felt like a double date. This morning it was Ethan and me, Church and Marissa, she standing in for Brody, who'd eaten some bad sushi last night. Sadly, when I later viewed the footage, her camerawork dispelled the pleasant myth I'd created that Marissa Linden had simply gotten lucky, that anyone with a camera could have pulled off *The Prosecutor*, if only in the right time and place. But no, Marissa wasn't just a world-class director and editor, she was magic with the lens as well – a triple threat I couldn't hope to achieve in four lifetimes. It should have made me dislike her less, since I'd been telling myself her thriving on luck was what made her so unpalatable in the first place. But luck was clearly only a pretense for my hating her, because once that hypothesis was obliterated, I started hating her even more.

But, ever the consummate professional, I donned my latex gloves and polypropylene booties and surged forward into the crime scene.

First the living room, where Ethan had sat with Piper on the final night of her life, watching *Sausage Party*. A silly part of me wished I could find and replace that title with *Casablanca* or *Citizen Kane* prior to trial. I mean, what would be the difference, other than to bring a shred of dignity to the last night of Piper's existence? Don't get me wrong, I found *Sausage Party* to be a far better movie than either of the classics. It was just a matter of perception, and as I'd been told again and again by Church: 'At trial, perception is all that matters.'

Ethan, clearly uncomfortable, probably a little sick to his stomach, plodded along like the walking dead, arbitrarily pointing out fixtures and furniture and naming them like a toddler on his first tour through daycare.

'That's the couch,' he said quietly of the couch. 'That's the television, the television stand.'

Church abruptly turned to him. 'I know words, E-rotica. And what did I tell you outside?'

'Not to say anything.'

'Unless . . .'

'Unless you tell me to say something.'

Church smacked the back of Ethan's head in the way Moe would Larry and Curly. 'Pay attention, huh? Every one of the officers in this house could theoretically be called to testify. And perk up, you're on camera, for Christ's sake.'

It was as clear a demonstration as any of how drastically the power structure between these two men had changed since Nathan's departure from the case. Church was now about to try a complex murder case knowing he'd never get paid for it. It was no wonder he'd been so irritable of late.

But the uniforms kept enough distance that we could speak privately, and we did, not thirty seconds later. As Church studied the stairs leading to the second floor, he said, 'Lau won't argue she was killed upstairs. There would be bruises all over the body from the killer dragging her down. That makes the blood found in the upstairs bathroom a non-issue. For her side at least.'

'What *will* she argue?' I asked.

'Her theory will be as straightforward and comprehensible as possible, and it will align neatly with every provable fact.'

In the center of the colossal living room, Church said, 'Riles, come here. Marissa, move back for a wide shot. E-moji, you need to be out of the shot altogether.'

When Church positioned me in the center of the room, the knot in my stomach grew three sizes. Of all the things I'd dreaded about today, I never imagined I'd be standing in for Piper herself, certainly never fathomed I'd be reenacting her murder.

As he talked us through Lau's probable theory of the case, Church gently manipulated my body to demonstrate. 'The defendant,' he said, 'about to lose his meal ticket, snaps. An argument, likely over her leaving the islands, escalates into a physical encounter. During which the defendant grabs the victim by the throat and applies pressure.'

As he said it, Church placed his hands around my throat without touching it, as though I were protected by some invisible forcefield that Piper wasn't lucky enough to have that night. Then he let go.

'She loses consciousness,' he continued. 'It happens quickly, in the first fifteen, twenty seconds. Her body goes limp; he thinks she's dead. He begins to look for a way to stage the scene, maybe runs upstairs and takes a spare shower curtain from the linen closet.'

I lay on the floor and closed my eyes.

'But when he returns,' Church continued, 'she suddenly gasps for air. She's alive, terrified now because this has turned violent. The phone is not enough, she needs the fastest way out of the house. She scrambles to her feet, heads toward the sliding glass door.'

I went through the motions, hoping I wouldn't throw up. Church stopped me at the sliding glass door, had me yank it open with as much strength as I could.

He said, 'Seeing her run puts the fear into the defendant. If she goes out that door, he knows he'll never see her again, not after what he's done, not after nearly choking the life out of her. Desperate, he pursues, but not before grabbing an empty beer bottle standing on one of these pieces of furniture.'

He edged me forward out the sliding glass door.

'He catches her,' he said, slipping his arm around my waist and nudging me forward from behind. 'Smashes her head with the beer bottle. She's stunned, maybe even loses consciousness again. He runs inside and grabs the shower curtain he was about to wrap her body in.'

I stood in a daze, my eyes glued to the pool, now eerily empty of all but a thin layer of muck at the bottom. The patio table around which I'd once downed a dozen mai tais appeared as though it had been abandoned for years.

Church came up behind me. 'The victim is back on her feet. The defendant wraps the plastic around her face. She struggles, hence the cuts on her feet. But he's too powerful. This time it takes a full two minutes for her to lose consciousness. But this time, when she does lose consciousness, he doesn't stop. This time he makes damn sure she's dead.'

From behind the camera, Marissa said, 'This is one of the prosecution's biggest obstacles, Nick. What did he put over her face to suffocate her? What happened to the murder weapon, where did it go?'

Church drew a deep breath. 'Lau will say the murder weapon went wherever the victim's clothes went. And that their location is something known only by the defendant.'

THIRTY

I n the editing room, Brody slips the ring on my finger. It's slightly too large, but he assures me we can have it resized in an hour at a place just down the street.

'That's an hour I'll have to be without it,' I say, my eyes still moist. 'I'd rather give them my finger and have them make it a little bigger to fit the ring.'

He smiles. 'The swelling alone should do the trick.'

I place my arms around him. When he lifts me up, I wrap my legs around him, until my weight forces him into my chair.

Gazing deep into his eyes, I say, 'When are we going to do it?'

'I was thinking right after we finish the movie. There's a little nondenominational chapel right in Ko Olina near the Four Seasons. I thought maybe we could tie the knot here on Oahu, then hit Maui or Kauai for our honeymoon. Your choice.'

I smile, excited because I am, but stifle a question I'm not sure I want the answer to. What are we going to do once the honeymoon's over? Where are we going to begin the rest of our lives?

Ethan and I took advantage of Brody's bout with bad sushi, only this time we barely even hid. Instead, we stole a cushion from a cabana at the Hilton Hawaiian Village and made love on the lip of the ocean, following a long moonlit walk along Waikiki Beach.

Afterward, we lay side by side, under a sky as dark as death, both of us wearing long shirts, no pants, as though we wanted those curious enough not only to notice us, but to take pictures.

'How are you going to show all those experts we hired without putting your audience to sleep?' Ethan asked me.

'Is that really what we're going to talk about until you're ready to go again?'

He chuckled. 'If that's what we talk about, I'll *never* be ready to go again.'

'They were pretty awful, though, weren't they? I mean, brilliant but boring. That could be a concern during trial. We don't want the jury sleeping through the science. At least not the science that helps us.'

'I asked Church about that right after our visit to Piper's house. Only not as eloquently, of course.'

'What did he say?' I asked, gazing up at the stars.

'He told me that if he thinks the answers aren't interesting enough to keep the jury's attention, he'll make sure that the questions are.'

In the dark, I smiled.

Following a few seconds of contented silence, I turned my body to face his. 'How did you learn to fight like that? The way you did in Breakers' parking lot.'

'Nate and I grew up in a pretty tough neighborhood. A place where people didn't necessarily like *haoles*. Especially *haoles* of the asshole variety, like Nathan and myself.'

'You have scars?' I asked.

'Some.'

'Can I see them?'

'Can you see *me*?'

'Can I feel them, then?'

He took my hand and ran it up the inside of his shirt. A long, jagged scar ran down the left side of his ribcage. On his stomach, something circular, something that felt more like a burn than a cut.

'It just occurred to me,' I said. 'We've known each other for months, and we live in Hawaii, yet this is our first time on a beach together.'

'Well, if I'd known it was going to be this much fun . . .'

I fake-punched him in the chest. I don't know why, and I felt stupid immediately afterward.

'There was the night at Kaena Point,' I said. 'The night I came face to face with a Hawaiian monk seal for the first, hopefully last, time. We were sort of on a beach then.'

'Well, let's hope this night ends up better than that one.'

We giggled until our giggle turned into a kiss, maybe the most perfect kiss of my life. Easily the most memorable.

'I let you feel my scars,' he said in his sexy, gravelly voice. 'Can I feel your tattoos?'

'The ones covering practically every inch of my body?' I laughed, but considered suggesting he do so with his tongue.

'Why is all your ink abstract?' he asked.

'So that the images exist on me alone. I make sure the artist burns the design right afterward.'

'You regret any of those tats?'

'Not one. Each of those tattoos reflects in some way who I was on that particular day of my life.'

Following a brief gap in conversation, Ethan's tone became more serious. 'Did you see that our case made it onto *Judge Jacqueline* last night?'

I tried to keep things light. 'What's with this *our* case shit, huh? *I'm* only facing bad reviews.'

He laughed, but it was more like one of Dr Farrockh's pity laughs than the Ethan Supreme.

'After watching that show,' he said, 'I never wanted heroin so badly in my life.'

Curiosity got the best of me. 'What's it like, heroin? It's, like, the only drug I never tried because I know so many people who OD'd on it.'

'It's like having someone gently remove the top of your skull and place a warm compress directly on your brain.'

'That sounds extraordinary.'

'It is,' he said. 'There are so many human experiences that are extraordinary – right up until the moment they kill you.'

When I walked into the apartment just after midnight, Brody was finishing up a conversation on the phone.

'That was Marissa,' he said.

Bizarrely enough under the circumstances, I felt a stab of jealousy. Unlike myself, Brody and Marissa had been getting along fabulously from the start. The other day he said he'd learned more from Marissa in a few months than he'd learned in two years in film school.

'There's a problem,' he said. 'Marissa wouldn't get into it over the phone.'

'Let me guess.' I headed straight for the bedroom, wanting nothing more than to curl up in the sheets and sleep for a week. 'She wants us at Church's suite first thing in the morning.'

Brody shook his head. 'She says it's urgent. We need to get over there now.'

THIRTY-ONE

I prefer women. My shrink, my gynecologist, primary care physician, even my dentist; all women. I can't articulate precisely why, though I've ruled out various reasons. Obviously it's not that I don't like being alone with men, or having men touch me. It's not a sexual thing. It's not a matter of trust because I trust men just as much as I trust women, which is to say, not much at all. It's not that I think women are smarter or somehow superior in the field of medical science. Maybe I simply feel like, when I step into a female doctor's office, I have for at least an hour or so, a female friend.

'You didn't have many female friends growing up?' Dr Yasmin Farrockh says.

'I was a bit of a tomboy. At least at school. At home, around my father, I had to be all girl. Until it came to sports. Sports he liked. He fantasized daily about what his life would be like had I been a son.'

'How did that make you feel?'

'Sad, at least when I was very young. In middle school, I couldn't begrudge him for it, because by then I was fantasizing what my life would be like had I been born to a different father.'

'How would your life have been different then?'

'I think I would have been able to express myself more, maybe make friends with similar interests. Instead, I was always the weirdo in a group I didn't belong in.'

'How would your life be different *now*?'

I play with the ring around my finger as I've caught myself doing whenever I get nervous over the past few days.

I say, 'I think I'd be a few years farther along in my career. I think I would have gone to UCLA and majored in film, never taken a job with Big Pharma.' I chuckle. 'I'd probably be spending less time in your office.'

She smiles. 'Why is that?'

'I don't think I'd second guess every decision I make.'

'Which decisions are you second-guessing?'

'None in particular.' As I say it – as if the psychiatry gods themselves have it in for me – my engagement ring slips from my finger and rolls under Dr Farrockh's desk.

She bends over, scoops it up, and hands it back to me.

'Very pretty,' she says.

'Thanks.' I shake my head to get back on-topic. 'I just don't trust my judgment.'

'Is that true? You seem to trust your judgment when it comes to making a documentary.'

'I feel like that's something I can get right. Everyday life, that's another story. I don't make good day-to-day decisions outside of the editing room.'

'You had a good teacher in the editing room. Not so much in the real world. How *could* you trust your own judgment, Riley, when during the most crucial years in your brain's development, that judgment was constantly criticized by your father and supplanted with his own?'

'I've been out of that house for almost as long as I was in it now.'

'You bring up *time* again?' She says it smiling. I only amuse my therapist accidentally. 'You seem to believe the cliché that time heals all wounds.'

'Doesn't it?'

'Not all wounds simply heal with time. Some, unless they're treated, become infected, some fester. Others, unless you apply a tourniquet, will cause you to bleed out. The wounds your parents cause, they're severe wounds. Not papercuts or scrapes on the elbows and knees. Depending on the parent, they can be more like gunshots. Often, we survive them; sometimes, they're fatal.'

'I thought children were resilient.'

'They are. They can be downright stoic in the face of terrible things. But their adult selves often pay the price for that stoicism.'

'Mental illness?'

'Sometimes.'

I try my best to grin. 'Am I mentally ill?'

'I don't know, are you?'

I exhale. 'Nicholas Church says we're all mentally ill. Some of us just more than others.'

As soon as we stepped inside, I could feel it – an indescribable force like a bitter cold or an oppressive heat permeating the entire suite. In the wee hours of the morning, the $17K-a-night penthouse felt like a cramped, dank basement that might or might not contain human corpses.

'Thanks for coming,' Marissa didn't say.

Instead: 'He's in the bedroom, but you can't see him just yet. We need to talk first.'

'Is Ethan here?' I asked.

Marissa shook her head. 'That's the last person in the world Nick needs to see tonight.'

Brody and I followed Marissa to a sectional that probably cost more than my Jeep.

'Our digital forensics expert faxed us his report a couple of hours ago,' she said, once Brody had set up the camera and sat. 'Ethan lied.'

'About what?' I asked.

'About everything.'

Brody and I shared a look. Onscreen, I knew it would appear as though we were perfectly in sync, as if the same thought bubble had materialized over our heads at the same time. Yet I was a hundred percent certain that he and I were thinking very different thoughts in that moment.

'Additional emails were discovered,' Marissa said, 'ones Ethan apparently attempted to delete. He knew Piper was leaving Hawaii.'

'When did she tell him?'

'She didn't. He learned it some other way. But that's not important right now. What's important is that he knew. He knew about the pregnancy, too. And the prosecution can prove it.'

If Ethan lied about these things, I thought, he not only lied to Church, he lied to the police. He lied to me.

'But that's not the worst of it,' Marissa said.

Heart, meet throat.

'The Craigslist ad for "roofing tar",' she went on quietly, 'and the email address Ethan received the instructions from – they both originated from Piper's desktop at home. Both within forty-eight hours prior to the murder.'

My jaw fell, my eyes froze in shock. As something vile rose and swelled inside me, a dense fog appeared at the edges of my vision.

Marissa said, 'Forget about murder two or voluntary manslaughter. Forget about any affirmative defenses. Forget about professional hits and unknown intruders. This is clear evidence of premeditation by someone with access to her computer.'

Marissa's lips continued moving but I could hear only white noise. In my anarchic head, I tried to separate my feelings for Ethan with the impact this evidence would have on his case. Meanwhile, another part of my brain, a part not known for its patient silence, shamelessly considered what this meant for my movie. Would this film die with a plea bargain after all? Would Lau even make an offer with this material evidence now on the table? A plea could help Ethan avoid decades in prison. But if he pled guilty, the sound of the gavel at sentencing would be the death knell for my film.

'So what's Nick's plan?' Brody asked.

'That's the even bigger problem,' Marissa said.

'Is Nick in the bottle again?'

'No,' she said. 'Well, yes. But that's not the problem. If it were, it would only take a few days, maybe a week, to dry him out. What's going on with him now, that usually takes a hell of a lot longer to turn around.'

I'd been catching bits and pieces but only now were things beginning to register. 'What are you saying?' I asked.

She took such a deep breath, I briefly feared we were in competition for the oxygen left in the room. She said, 'Remember in *The Prosecutor*, Nick is always either carrying around a thermos of coffee, or drinking from a steaming cup, offering his opinions on various roasts?' She paused. 'Well, Nick hates coffee. Hasn't touched a drop since college. In fact, he doesn't consume any caffeine at all, not even the occasional soft drink, not even mixed with liquor.'

'I don't get it,' I said. 'Why would he *make believe* he's a coffee connoisseur?'

The enveloping silence made me feel like an idiot, even though I knew my brain just desperately needed sleep.

'To conceal something else,' Brody finally said, so quietly I barely heard him.

Before I could ask Brody what he meant, he and Marissa were up and headed toward Church's bedroom. Marissa wouldn't allow us to bring the camera, and once we stepped inside, I understood why. Even in the dim light, the enormous room was a sty. Not like a bachelor pad, not even like a fraternity house. This was tornado damage. This was earthquake devastation. This was post-apocalyptic. There were pants covering the windows, curtains being used as table cloths. One corner of the room looked as though it had been on fire.

Church himself, naked but for a washed-out pair of yellow boxer shorts, lay sprawled across the king-sized bed, which was now diagonal in the center of the room. Brody and I approached him. His eyes were bloodshot, the flesh around them red and swollen. His breath smelled like a blend of cheap cigars and expensive bourbon. He somehow appeared as though he hadn't shaved or showered in a week, even though I'd seen him only a few hours earlier.

'Your stomach feeling better, BQ?' Church asked, in a voice usually preserved for Vito Corleone impressions and last words.

'Yeah, Nick. Thanks.'

'So it *is* booze,' I said.

Marissa shook her head, condescendingly. 'It's not that simple. The drinking is just a symptom.'

'What are we talking about here?'

She ran a hand across her forehead. 'This is just the culmination of what's been happening over the past few weeks. He's cycling.'

'I have no clue—'

'The coffee,' Brody said softly, making me feel like Daphne from *Scooby Doo*, 'it wasn't to mask his drinking. It was so people would think he was constantly overcaffeinated.'

Marissa nodded.

I still didn't get it.

Brody, recognizing the WTF look on my face, said, 'It's mania.'

'He's manic?' I asked, still perplexed.

Marissa shook her head, said, 'Not anymore. Now the pendulum has swung in the opposite direction.'

THIRTY-TWO

In the editing room, I wrestle with how to execute this final turning point before Act III, this unmitigated disaster on what's commonly (if not accurately) called the eve of trial. At the time, I knew virtually nothing about Church's illness. Maybe I'd read a paragraph or two about bipolar in my Intro to Psych class first year of college. Other than that, the word itself conjured only varied images of the conventional comedy and tragedy theatrical masks. Those, and maybe a loony bin. If viewers shared my ignorance, a significant aspect of the movie would be grossly distorted.

I can almost hear Professor Leary in my ear: '*Show* the story with images; don't *tell* it with interviews.' I don't want to use a single scene even *resembling* an interview. But I can't simply *show* the illness. That would do both the illness and Church a tremendous injustice. Because a few cutaways to his manic behavior and devastating depression cannot tell the whole story. Only Church himself can tell it.

'Want to know how I really decide whether to take on a homicide case?' Church says.

Onscreen, dawn arrives, the sun more distant than I've ever seen it. Church, in his hoity-toity Four Seasons bathrobe, and I sit alone on his terrace, staring off into the Pacific, while a camera standing on a tripod a few feet away captures us as clearly as any footage we've shot. I'm reminded now how lucky we were that morning. Church initially refused to discuss his illness on camera but, in a woeful turn of irony, his depression ultimately drained him of his wherewithal to object.

He says, 'I don't need to know, after studying the evidence, that the prospective client is innocent.' He paused, finally turned to look at me. 'I just can't *know* that he's guilty. *I* need to have a reasonable doubt.'

'Hasn't this ever happened to you before? New evidence is discovered in cases all the time.'

'Nothing close to this. I thought I knew exactly what was on those computers. Ethan seemed intelligent enough to know better than to lie to me. I explained to him, the earlier I know the evidence against you, the more I can do to suppress, undermine or discredit it.'

'This is what triggered the depression?'

He shrugs, speaks so much slower than usual, it's like I'm sitting with another lawyer altogether. 'Probably a combination of factors. Stress of the upcoming trial. Marissa, most likely; she's usually to blame, even when she isn't.'

Still processing it all, I ask, 'How did you get away with it so long?'

'Get away with what? My illness? I dropped the whole coffee charade years ago. I was ready to take the stigma head-on. Hell, when I'm good and grandiose, I still fancy myself becoming the Martin Luther King Jr. of the mentally ill.'

'But no journalist ever asked you about it?'

'*The Prosecutor* put the idea into people's heads of an eccentric, overcaffeinated Church. Once something's in people's heads . . .'

'So it's not going to affect your ability to try the case?'

'I didn't say that.' He pauses, makes a visible effort to find his next words. 'Ever have one of those days where you just want to drink yourself into the ground?'

'Once or twice.'

'Well, for me, once I've cycled into depression, that's a good day. At least drinking myself into the ground is a meaningful objective.'

'But when you're manic . . .'

'Barely controlled chaos that gives the illusion of brilliance.'

'Aren't there medications?'

'A few. I've tried them all. Some my body rejected, others my head. The drugs affect different people in different ways. Lithium turns *me* into a zombie on ketamine, watching a Ken Burns documentary, while listening to Adele sing a lullaby.'

'I never thought for a second . . .'

He manages a half-grin. 'The signs are there, Riles. C'mon. I fell in love with the woman who fired a guided missile at my legal career. My best and only friend is a speaker box from the seventies. I occasionally demonstrate complete breaks from reality.'

'What caused it?'

He lifts a shoulder. 'Genetics are part of it. Life events trigger the actual illness. Abuse and neglect in childhood, toxic marriages, bad break-ups, too many Woody Allen movies.'

'Which was it for you?'

He puts a glass of iced water to his lips. 'It took Marissa six years of hate-fucking me before I told her, so don't hold your breath.'

'When did it start?'

'I can't pinpoint it. I've always been reckless. Impulsive. Always abused substances. I figured I was just a really fun guy.'

'When did you realize you were ill?'

'First year of law school. Professor Kara O'Hara's criminal law class. She was smart, beautiful, and I genuinely liked the subject. Hell, I *loved* it, even planned on making a career of it. Yet I couldn't sit there. I couldn't sit in *any* class. I had people sign my name to attendance sheets, I had to cram a semester's worth of information into a couple of weeks right before final exams. Frankly, that I got through law school, passed the bar exam *and* was licensed to practice law made me lose every *scintilla* of confidence I had left in American jurisprudence.'

'That's why you've been held in contempt so much? Why you're under investigation by ethics committees in six states?'

Scratching the stubble on the right side of his cheek, he says, 'Yeah, well, that sounds as good an excuse as any.'

'So this has cost you a lot.'

'Me? I've gotten away easy so far. With this illness, you're lucky if you get away with croaking of natural causes. Lifetime risk of suicide is one out of five. You have better odds playing Russian roulette.'

Onscreen, there's a visible lump in my throat. 'Have you ever . . . tried?'

He looks at me with those sad, terrified, bloodshot eyes, suddenly glistening in the orange hue of the sunrise.

'Just about every night.'

PART III
Objectionable Material

THIRTY-THREE

like playing dirty. Always have. So much so that by trial, my anticipation that Church would employ some of the filthiest tactics in the history of American criminal justice had ballooned to such an extent that I half-expected to float away before opening statements. One week before jury selection, however, Church burst that bubble with the sobering news that, although he was in no way above tampering with a jury or otherwise obstructing justice, he wouldn't be utilizing any such measures in this case.

'These days,' he says, 'the risk far outweighs the reward. One of the greatest casualties of the modern world is honor among thieves.'

Onscreen, Church and I sit alone on his deck, heavy trade winds playing havoc with the audio, to say nothing of our hair. 'Thirty years ago,' he says, 'a lawyer offers a juror a bribe, the juror either takes the money or goes straight to the judge. At the millennium, a lawyer offers a bribe, the juror either takes it or haggles for more. Today, the juror immediately demands more, takes the money, then comes back and extorts you because she recorded the entire transaction on her phone.'

In the editing room, I attempt to decipher how to illustrate scenes I never even imagined we'd be shooting until later that day when Church sat us (*sans* Ethan) down in his suite and declared that cases are won or lost in jury selection.

From every courtroom drama and true crime documentary I'd ever watched, from every litigator I'd ever spoken to, I had been thoroughly convinced that jury selection was bullshit, that the first twelve were as good or as bad as any other twelve. Some criminal lawyers I knew from past projects regularly waived jury selection altogether. Others swore by tired stereotypes related to race, ethnicity, gender, age, education and social class. Still others insisted the only two purposes of jury selection were to educate the pool on your theory of the case, and to persuade as many people as possible to *like* you. Many lawyers even professed to relying solely on their gut instincts.

'Going with your gut makes about as much sense as going with your asshole,' Church says, standing before a whiteboard onscreen. 'Trying to get the jurors to *like* you, attempting to convince them that your theory of the crime is the correct one – a complete waste of time. Trial lawyers think a comfortable *voire dire* is a successful *voire dire*. My rule is, if at least one prospective juror doesn't leave the courtroom in tears, I haven't done my job.'

From the speaker box in the center of the table: 'That's hyperbole.'

Church frowns. 'If you're not careful, Jesse, we're going to cut you out of the film altogether.'

'*Good!*' Jesse cries.

'*Or*, we just might play Kenny G in the background every time you speak, so that viewers think he's who you're jamming to in your mom's basement.'

There are still flashes of the Church I knew, the Church from *The Prosecutor*, the Church who led this investigation for nearly six months, but it's clear even on film that he's now merely a melancholic man playing a role, a mediocre comedian doing an impression of a dynamic man he once saw perform.

Church says, 'Most judges are so cynical, they strictly limit the time allotted for *voire dire*. If defense counsel complains, they remind everyone that jury selection is meaningless and accuse counsel of trying to indoctrinate the jury.'

'Not enough defense lawyers even complain,' Marissa says. 'Some lawyers ask the same goddamn questions to every juror. That's how Roderick Blunt's attorneys did it. Routine questions, reliance on stereotypes and gut instincts – the lead attorney even boasted about it on camera during deliberations. Then they were shocked when an all-black jury returned a first-degree murder conviction against their client.'

Church says, 'Most criminal attorneys use the same set of questions for every *case*, never mind each individual juror. Which is why so many incompetent prosecutors have such high conviction rates.'

'So how *do* you select a jury?' Brody asks.

Turning over the whiteboard, Church says, 'Jury selection has nothing to do with selecting a jury, BQ. It has everything to do with getting the individuals who will *hurt* our client the hell out of the courtroom as fast as humanly possible.'

When Church moves to the right, he reveals his drawings on the whiteboard. Stick figures, and crude ones at that. Four dozen of them. Some male, some female, some blue-faced, others blank.

'That's got to be racist,' I say.

'It's not racist,' Church says. 'Racist would have been if I'd given half of them slanty eyes.'

I throw up my arms. '*That's* racist.'

'It's not racism when you're making fun *of* racism. Christ, Riles, have you never heard of satire?'

I turn to Brody for backup. 'Is this conversation satirical?'

'Now it is, yeah.'

'Minorities,' Church says, 'are represented here only to illustrate that falling back on stereotypes puts your client in peril.'

'Actually,' Brody says, 'Hawaii's the only state in the US where Caucasians are a minority.'

'Good,' Church says, 'because I have plenty of honkey and cracker jokes.'

Marissa nods. 'Nick's an equal opportunity asshole.'

'Our objective in jury selection,' Church says, 'is to determine which jurors will *not* be receptive to our theory of the case. And we can't learn that by asking *yes or no* questions. Leading questions only lead to aspirational answers – responses that jurors think you and/or the judge want to hear. So we ask open-ended questions designed to expose preconceived notions that will hurt us. Once we figure out who possesses these preconceived notions, our job is to immediately dispatch them, *not* to try to change their minds.'

I say, 'The questions you pose will be hypotheticals, right?'

'*Not* hypotheticals,' Church says. 'Again, the juror will try to provide the "right answer". The best indicator of what a juror will do in deliberations is what they've done *before* they stepped into that courtroom. We want to know as much as we can about each juror's life, and any life experiences that might color that juror's perspective in one way or another.'

'Remember,' Marissa says, 'jurors don't only answer with

dialogue. They answer with body language. Sometimes the *way* they reply to questions tells us more than their words.'

Church says, 'Be particularly cognizant of how each juror regards Ethan. If they have difficulty making eye contact, if they cringe when they see him, if they suddenly light up their fuck-me eyes, I need to know about it.'

Marissa says, 'Also – and I can't stress this enough – watch how each juror looks at *Nick*.'

Church nods with a mirthless grin. 'Especially when my back is turned.'

Marissa says, 'Since we can't film jurors outside either, we're going to need every pair of eyes at this table the morning jury selection begins. As potential jurors walk up those courthouse steps, you're going to surreptitiously observe them.'

'How do we know who's a juror?' I ask.

'They're the ones who look like they're entering Disneyland,' Church says. 'Remember their faces. Eavesdrop. Identify what they're carrying: a newspaper, a Grisham novel, marital aids. Read their T-shirts. If someone's T-shirt reads "I'm with stupid", note who's standing next to them.'

Marissa says, 'Also keep an eye out for jurors who make friends. One, it indicates they're extroverts who may have the potential to take charge in the jury room. Two, if Nick wants one of them on his jury, he'll be sure not to make the other one cry.'

'So there's no specific personality we're looking for,' Brody says.

'As defense counsel,' Church says, 'I'd personally love to have in the box twelve Type-A jurors, each with the courage to hold out, even when the count is eleven-one against them. Remember, only one is needed for a hung jury.'

'But we want an acquittal,' I say, perhaps with too much vigor.

'And Marissa would rather be dating Hugh Jackman,' Church counters. 'We do the best we can with what we're given.'

Unlike the shark that circled us so many times over the past half-year, this Church moves tenuously, as though guarding an injury. His typically clean-shaven face is all stubble, his modest island attire in stark contrast with his usual pricey garb.

At the board, Church says, 'The lawyers should do the least amount of speaking in the room. In *voire dire*, we want the *jurors* to talk, we want them to say as much as possible, to divulge as many secrets as possible. Most lawyers are afraid a biased juror will taint the jury. Bullshit. A biased juror may expose other biased jurors, but *no one* is coming out of that courtroom a different person than when they went in.'

He picks up his glass and gulps some iced water. 'Not only do we not want to silence a biased juror, we want to do everything we can to fatten that bias, to exploit it. We want to convince the judge to discharge that juror for cause so we can preserve our peremptory challenges – our golden tickets to toss jurors without needing a reason.'

Jesse says, 'In Hawaii, in a criminal case where someone's charged with an offense punishable by life imprisonment, each side gets twelve.'

Marissa says to Church, 'Since we ultimately want to toss the jurors we think will be unreceptive to our theory of the case, don't we need to *know* our theory of the case?'

Church sags in frustration. Says, 'I told E-surance he needed to make a final decision today.'

In a move he's clearly been dreading, Church digs his Android from his pocket, scrolls through his contacts, drops his phone onto the table, stabs at a number and places the call on speaker.

It rings five, six times, then finally Ethan's voice. 'Nick?'

Ethan had admitted to his lies of omission about Piper's leaving for the mainland and her pregnancy, but swore that he had nothing to do with creating the Craigslist ad or email account. Someone else, Ethan insisted, must have had access to Piper's computer.

Without preamble, Church says, 'We've arrived at the point of no return. I need to start picking my jury, which means I need to know *now* whether our trial strategy is to attempt to pin this murder on some hypothetical thugs from another continent who may be out to do Piper harm because of the sins of her petty criminal father, or—'

'Or we pin it on my brother,' Ethan says glumly.

'*Or* – I was about to say – we use the set of facts and physical evidence available to us to create in the minds of the jury a reasonable doubt that you, *Ethan* Jakes, murdered your soon-to-be-ex-girlfriend in your soon-to-be-ex-home on Mount Tantalus.

I've prepped my team for either scenario, so what's it going to be, E-wok?'

The night before jury selection formally began, I vomited in the guest toilet in Church's suite – an infraction that would have gotten me tossed from the penthouse on nearly any other occasion. But tonight, I was needed. That morning we'd received completed questionnaires with basic information for the forty-eight jurors who would comprise the pool in *State of Hawaii vs Ethan Jakes*. We knew names, addresses, ages, marital statuses, occupations. We knew their education, whether they owned or rented their home. We knew their hobbies, their political and religious leanings, the names of their favorite television shows. Whether – and how often – they drank alcohol.

'Roughly *two thirds* of most panels are unsympathetic to the defendant,' Church said. 'A *quarter* of the people think the police would never arrest someone for murder unless they were absolutely sure that person was guilty. *One third* wrongly believes the defense has the burden of proof in a criminal case.'

'How do you overcome such staggering ignorance?' I asked, admittedly more for the camera than anything.

'Preparation. The first step is creating a profile. What type of juror are we looking for, given *this* set of facts? No wrong answers here,' Church assured us. 'Just use common sense.'

'A misogynist,' I said. 'Someone who thinks Piper had it coming.'

Church scribbled on the whiteboard. 'Lifetime members of the He-Man Woman Haters Club, good. *But* not ones with daughters between the ages of twelve to, say, twenty-nine.'

'People with imagination,' Brody said. 'With the ability to think in abstractions. People who will accept that the simplest answer isn't always the right one.'

Church nodded. 'Artists, good. Musicians, actors, writers. Who else?'

The gist of the exercise was first to select jurors who could best empathize with the defendant: the young, the broke, the dreamers, the hopeless romantics. Next, we lined up the most likely witnesses for both the prosecution and the defense, making note of each witness's nationality and other known characteristics. For instance, the lead detective, Lance Fukumoto, was an older, openly gay

Japanese man, so we most likely wanted to avoid other older, openly gay Japanese men. With respect to our own witnesses, the strongest was currently Cheyenne Oh, a now-separated Korean mother of two, whose husband had cheated on her with the victim. Women scorned might well sympathize with her, though not those who had personally known victims of domestic violence. The factors to be considered seemed endless.

As did the night.

For hours, we plumbed the bowels of the internet, studying the social media accounts of the four dozen most boring mammals ever to walk the planet. At first, hey, it sounded like fun, delving into the lives of forty-eight strangers, determining who they loved, what they loathed, crafting narratives about their existence. But after the first few searches, I was already sick of navigating through timelines, tweets, throwback Thursdays and #FridayReads.

Right, I recalled, this is why I abandoned social media in the first place.

At three a.m., Brody and I finally began packing away our cameras. Court started precisely at nine. I once again envied Marissa, who had gone to bed more than an hour ago.

'Don't drive,' Church said. 'Let me call Ollie, get you guys a room downstairs.'

As he moved toward the phone, I made a show of gazing around the ginormous penthouse suite that could comfortably sleep ten people, at least.

'Not an option,' Church said as he dialed. 'Night before jury selection, I can't even *think* of sleep. As soon as you leave, I intend to wake Marissa. And I plan on things getting as weird as they do loud.'

THIRTY-FOUR

In the editing room, I replay the shaky footage of Church escorting us to our own room overlooking the night ocean. As we enter, he turns to the right, checks the light switch twice then slowly moves on to the lamps.

'What is this?' I say. 'Some sort of OCD thing?'

'Not at all,' he says, as a three-way goes the distance twice. 'It's habit. Let's just say that, occasionally, my "disorganization" makes visits from the hotel staff unworkable.'

'So you need to make sure none of the bulbs are burned out?'

'Not just that,' he says. 'Light affects my mood so much, I need to know that no bulbs are on their *way* out.'

I follow him to the rear of the room. 'So you make sure none are dim?'

He switches the lights in the bathroom on and off twice, then turns to look at me, sweat beading the flesh on his forehead and upper lip, despite the cool temperatures both outside and inside the room.

He says, 'You'd think so, right? But no.' He steps past me and opens the hall closet. 'For some reason, it's always the brightest bulbs that are the first to flame out.'

The next morning, Naomi Lau and Nicholas Church stood side by side before the first twelve jurors, eying them like they were selecting the ripest cantaloupe in the produce aisle. I half-expected Lau to reach out and start squeezing cheeks.

'Please, share with us the worst thing you or someone you know has done to their brother or sister,' Church asked of a middle-aged female juror with three siblings. We knew little else about this woman, other than that she was a private elementary school teacher and 'Other Pacific Islander'.

Instantly closing herself up like a flower in reverse bloom, she was so transparent the blind could have read her body language. 'I suppose it would have to do with a will.'

'A parent's Last Will and Testament?'

'Yes.'

'What did one sibling do to the other?'

'She fed our mother secrets and lies during the final years of her life and had everyone but herself removed from our mother's will.'

'She exerted undue influence?'

'That's just what happened. That's what we argued in court, but our case got dismissed, probably because she went to bed with the judge.'

Hightower spoke. 'For the record, I did not preside over that probate matter.'

He soaked up what few chuckles wafted over from the gallery. Hightower looked like a different man from the one we'd first met at Ethan's arraignment. According to Church, the judge had had his stomach stapled in order to appear trim for the cameras.

Church said, 'Is there anything you think your sister *isn't* capable of?'

'Absolutely nothing.'

Church turned to the camera and mouthed the words, 'She'll do.'

Unfortunately, Lau, after trying and failing to have the juror dismissed for cause, used one of her peremptory challenges. But that was OK, Church assured us. 'Every peremptory challenge she uses, it's one less she has to kick the perfect juror out of the courtroom. Running out of peremptory challenges early is like having your star point guard foul out in the first quarter of Game Seven of the NBA Finals.'

To another juror, Church said, 'Just a reminder. Some of my questions might be about sensitive topics. If you prefer to answer in private or at the bench, you may.'

The juror, a young Asian woman, with long black hair cascading over her shoulders like a painted waterfall, nodded her head.

Church said, 'Describe for us the most serious time you or someone you know was cheated on.'

'That's easy,' she said. 'I was cheated on by my last boyfriend.'

Church encouraged her to keep talking.

'He was a few years older but, you know, he liked me because he said I was so mature, even more mature than women his own age, so we start going out more and more, only we'd always grab a quick sandwich at Subway and bring it back to my place and eat while watching TV, so I just thought, you know, that he was a cheapskate, and I've dated cheapskates before, sometimes they're better than the splurgers, right? But then I find out this ass— Sorry, but then I find out he is seeing like four other girls behind my . . .'

She continued while Church walked back to the defense table and drank from his mug. 'I'll tell you,' he whispered to me, 'this stuff tastes like shit but it gets the job done.'

Church walked back to the rail, thanked the woman mid-sentence, and said, 'Moving on . . .'

An hour later, Church was *voire dire*-ing an upper-middle-aged blue-collar man, who we knew had been divorced three times. 'Describe for us the most serious mistake you or someone you know has ever made due to jumping to a snap conclusion.'

The man seemed to think about it, but I suspected he was thinking more about *how* to phrase what he had to say, rather than *what* he had to say.

'My second wife,' the man said, 'she was the one. My soulmate. I had it in my head that she was cheating on me with my best friend. I accused her. She denied it. My best friend denied it. I couldn't let it go. It became a tremendous source of tension between us. And eventually she left me because of it.'

'She left you because you wrongly accused her of sleeping with your best friend?'

'That's right.'

'And you regret losing her?'

'Not one bit. Turned out she *was* cheating on me. Just not with my buddy but a complete stranger. What keeps me awake at night isn't losing her, it's losing my best friend.'

'Riles? BQ? You two wear the same clothes so often you could be cartoon characters.'

That was how Church invited us to go shopping at Ala Moana Center later that day, a breathtaking open-air shopping mall with stores so ostentatious half of them have their own dress code.

'Wardrobe isn't exactly in our budget,' I said.

'Well, it's in mine, and if you two are going to sit next to my client during trial, we're going to dress you up in something that once bore a security tag.'

'Great!' I told him.

Brody appeared less effused. 'Should we pick up Marissa?'

'No-o-o-o-o,' Church said. 'Marissa doesn't understand how the economy works.'

I was about to ask Church what he meant by that, when I became distracted, daydreaming about buying a dress that wouldn't ride a conveyer and be crammed into a plastic bag with my toothpaste and tampons.

'Should we take my Jeep?' I asked.

'No-o-o-o-o,' he said. 'We're taking a limo.'

THIRTY-FIVE

In the editing room, I consider whether to show the footage we shot at Ala Moana or jump straight to the aftermath. The Ala Moana footage is shaky and shrunken to phone-mode, like those clips outside LA nightclubs you see on TMZ. Because Brody and I hadn't anticipated wanting to record our picking out, trying on and purchasing of new clothes. But then, Nicholas Church made even the most mundane events unpredictable. And, OK, yeah, more than a little fun.

Although I had my sights set on Neiman Marcus, Church insisted we first visit the fourth floor of the mall. Squarely in its center sat a large bar and grill, where physically fortunate young women in matching tight summer dresses delivered cocktails and dishes to a largely male crowd watching UH women's volleyball on the flatscreens overhead.

'Hungry?' Church said.

Brody's gaze followed a tray carried by a chick who could have easily stepped off the cover of the *Sports Illustrated* swimsuit issue. He said, 'I could eat.'

With the slip of some cash, we bypassed the lengthy line of people waiting for a table, which made me feel a bit pompous and elegant at the same time. As we entered, I apologized to the people in line who paid us no mind, and turned my nose up at the wretched peasants with the audacity to give us the stink-eye.

Once we sat, we ordered food, and lots of it, as usual. Church also insisted we order mai tais, which were as tall and as strong as any I'd had outside of the Royal Hawaiian. Raising toasts to each of the forty-eight prospective jurors, we were on our fifth round before I realized I was in danger of tipping over and falling out of my armless chair.

What happened following our hours at Mai Tai Bar is as blurry in my head as it is on film. Recording on his phone, Brody first follows Church to a kiosk where Church purchases a $600 Panama hat without trying it on. Next, Cartier watches for the three of us. 'We're a team,' Church said, 'we need to be synchronized.'

Then on to Mont Blanc where Church purchases four pens for roughly 2,000 dollars. Then into Long's Drugs where he picks up two dozen Bic pens for two dollars because, 'This is the only shit I'll use.' Then back upstairs for shots of bourbon. Then back down to buy out the inventory at Victoria's Secret, because 'Marissa looks incredible in lingerie'. Then back upstairs to Mai Tai Bar because last time we were there, Church left the bag with the pens behind. 'The Bic *and* the Mont Blanc,' he slurred.

Onscreen, Church finally leads us through the Store that Shall Remain Nameless (because they won't, to this day, sign a location release), randomly grabbing big-ticket dresses off racks and tossing them at me.

'I don't need all these,' I protest.

'It's a week-long trial, at least.'

'None of these are even my size,' I say.

A concerned saleswoman impedes Church's progress in the center of the store as I eye the exorbitant prices on the clothes Church has thrown at me.

'May I help you, sir?'

'Not unless you're on my jury,' he says, studying her. '*Are* you on my jury?'

She glances at me, baffled. I shrug my shoulders because I don't know what else to do. Church steps past her.

'Riles,' he calls over his shoulder, 'we need shoes. And not those Crocs or whatever you've been wearing.'

'I've never worn Crocs in my life,' I say, loud enough so that everyone who heard Church hears me as well.

Church spins around. 'BQ, what are you doing?'

'Grabbing some footage.'

Church pulls out his wallet. 'BQ, here's a fifty. Shut off the camera and go grab yourself a Supercuts while I pick out a few dresses for Riles and Marissa.'

'Sir—' the woman starts again, at which point Church removes an Amex Black card from his wallet and frisbees it in the general direction of the cash register.

'Ring up as much damage as you think I can do to this store,'

Church says. 'If you come within a thousand dollars, I'll take you out for drinks tonight.'

The saleswoman gracefully picks up the card but says thanks but no thanks to the drinks.

I don't know how much Church spent that night. I don't want to know. Because I feel terrible for it. I should've declined to go with him, should've stopped him after the second or third mai tai, should have *at least* stopped him after the second or third store. But I'd had a few too many too, as had Brody. Add to that our stealing away to vape a few grams of OG Kush, and I'm surprised I remember anything from that evening. But I do remember some things – I remember more than I'd like.

Back at Church's suite, we continued drinking and performed some bastardized version of a blind taste test to determine whether we could tell the difference between sentences written in Bic from those in Mont Blanc. (To Church's great chagrin, we could.)

To display our new duds, we then held an hour-long fashion show, which could easily be edited into a hilarious three-minute montage in and of itself. Once we had run out of shoes, suits and dresses, and arrived at the lingerie, Church stood and announced that he was going to wake Marissa. But when he turned around, he found her standing menacingly in the doorway to their bedroom.

'You do realize you have court first thing in the morning?' she scolded.

'We'll hydrate him right now,' I said, leaping off the couch and nearly losing my footing.

'It's not Nick I'm concerned about,' Marissa said. 'He's a seasoned alcoholic. This is rather tame for the night before opening statements. He'll be fine in the morning. I don't know the same will be true of the two of you. Like it or not, since Nick and I are both participating, this film is going to be forever linked with *The Prosecutor*. So every one of us here has skin in this game.'

In that moment, I wanted to hug Marissa, because she *had* been extremely helpful over the past several months, despite my inexplicable coolness toward her.

'We'll be OK,' I tried to assure her. 'I promise. We'll drink plenty of water. And I had my molars out a couple of months ago, so if we *are* a bit hungover in the morning, we can just pop a few Vicodin.'

Marissa's eyes immediately welled over. Baring her teeth, she looked as though she could rip my tongue from my mouth. Instead, she spun and quickly retreated into the bedroom.

Church went after her.

'What the hell just happened?' I asked Brody.

'About a year ago, Marissa's son died of an opiate overdose.'

'She had a son?'

'Seventeen years old.'

'I didn't know. How was I supposed to know?'

Brody turned away from me. Muttered, 'It's on her Wikipedia page, for Christ's sake.'

THIRTY-SIX

'I like being the dominant one.'

Dr Farrockh crosses one leg over the other and asks, 'Is that good or bad?'

'I don't know anymore. I don't want to be my father. I don't want to dominate my husband in the way he dominated my mom.'

'Then don't.'

'Problem is, I'm not sure where the line is anymore. I don't know whether Brody is doing something he *wants* to do, or doing something just to please me.'

'Are these two things necessarily mutually exclusive?'

I lean back on the camel-colored couch and exhale. Some days with Yasmin Farrockh, I feel like I'm in the middle of that maze in *The Shining*, and she just keeps growing hedges taller and taller.

'Why not ask him?' she adds.

'Brody will just tell me what I want to hear. He'll say it's for him, no matter what it is.'

'He'll lie?'

'No.'

'He'll tell you the truth, then?'

'No.'

'Well . . .'

'I get it,' I tell her. 'If he lies about this, he'll lie about other things.'

'That's not at all what I'm suggesting. From everything you've told me about Brody, his integrity is not an issue. Except—'

'Except he'll lie to please me? By denying he's doing something *to* please me?'

Dr Farrockh sighs. 'You said Brody will go wherever you want to go, and that he won't resent you for it. So why haven't you spoken about this with him yet?'

'I haven't made a decision yet.'

'So you want to make the decision on your own and then tell him what it is?'

'No, that doesn't sound right.'

She smiles (one of those fake ones), says, 'Is it possible that you've already made a decision – even if it's just returning to the mainland – and you're afraid of presenting that decision to him?'

I bow my head. 'That sounds more like it.'

'He's made it clear he wants to stay in the islands?'

'Abundantly. But as much as I love it here, this isn't the best place for my career – it's *so*, so remote.'

'You're afraid he'll take that as, "I'm more concerned about my career than about your feelings."'

'Yeah.'

'Then the reverse is true, too, isn't it? Brody needs to decide if he wants to live here permanently or marry you.'

'It's just . . .' I don't want to say it aloud; it feels tantamount to an admission that I care only about myself. 'I know this place is best for him. He needs to live at a slower pace. I see the difference in him here from the time we were in New York. He can't fully articulate it, but he says this island's the only place that's ever felt like home.'

'You need to discuss this with him, Riley. That's the only fair thing to do. And know beforehand what you're going to say and, more importantly, what you're genuinely *willing* to do.'

'Can Brody and I hash it out in here?' I joke.

'Of course,' she says. Of course.

'You've never met Brody, yet sometimes you seem to understand him better than I ever will.'

'I think you understand him just fine, Riley. Now you need to understand yourself *in relation* to him.'

THIRTY-SEVEN

'Ladies and gentlemen of the jury,' Lau said to begin opening statements, 'I'm loath to use the word *simple* to describe any homicide case. But the one upon which you will be deliberating at the end of this trial cannot be described in any other way. Over the next few days, the State will prove to you beyond any reasonable doubt, that on February twenty-second of this year, the defendant Ethan Parker Jakes murdered his girlfriend Piper Kingsley, in her home, and then made some grievous errors in his attempt to cover it up.'

Lau looked spectacular, and – ever the consummate public servant – she accomplished it in an inexpensive pants suit I'd seen at Ross.

'The following facts,' she continued, 'are not in dispute. By the defendant's own admission, we *know* he was in Piper's home at nine p.m. that evening. We *know* the defendant called nine-one-one to report "an accident" at nine thirty-one p.m. We *know* the defendant was home during that half-hour because he attempted so sloppily to create an ali—'

Church was out of his seat. 'Objection, Your Honor. Ms Lau is making argument.'

Hightower gazed down at Lau from his perch. 'Ms Lau, you know better.'

Lau turned back to the jury but paused before she spoke. 'We will *prove* to you that the defendant was home during that half-hour by introducing *evidence* that he attempted to create an alibi for himself using Piper's computer.'

Having observed Lau become rattled by his first objection,

having seen her need to push aside her annoyance before continuing her opening, Church rose from his seat with objections nearly every sixty seconds for the next twelve minutes. Although each objection was overruled, with each interruption Lau's level of irritability seemed to rise. But just when it appeared she'd be derailed at any moment, she adapted, deftly dismissing Church's objections until the jurors themselves grew tired of them.

Lau said, 'From emails he attempted to delete, we know that the defendant *knew* that Piper Kingsley – his girlfriend and meal ticket – had accepted a job on the mainland, which was to begin soon. We know the defendant *knew* that Piper was pregnant, in all likelihood with his child. We know the dire financial position the defendant would have been in once Piper left him. We know the defendant considered himself a resident in Piper's home, we know that his name is on a lease with four other men for significantly downgraded digs in Waialua, *and* we know that he was two months – plus late fees – behind in rent at the time of the murder. Piper Kingsley's leaving Oahu would have been *devastating* for the defendant. Not only would he be without his closest companion for the previous eight months, he would have become one of Hawaii's unfortunates – the defendant was destined to join Oahu's ever-growing homeless population.'

At this, Ethan's chin fell to his chest, his eyes watered, his neck burned bright red.

'With respect to *physical* evidence,' Lau said, as she strutted in front of the jury with a confidence I could only dream of, 'we have no shortage of that either. We have the defendant's fingerprints on a beer bottle that the defendant used to *smash* Piper over the head. We have enough DNA evidence at Piper's home of Ethan's presence that the defense has stipulated to *all* of it. What's more, we have zero, zip, zilch evidence of anyone else being inside Piper's home at the time of the murder. Not a hair, not a fiber, not so much as a print belonging to anyone *but* the defendant and his victim.'

I glanced at Church, who had, since ceasing his objections, remained stoic.

Lau stepped up to the jury rail. 'So why are we even here, you're no doubt asking yourselves. We're here because it is the defendant's right as a citizen of the United States to confront all witnesses who will testify against him. We're here because the Constitution guarantees *every* criminal defendant – no matter how heinous the crime or how much evidence the State has against him – the right to a fair and honest trial. And we are here, the defense will no doubt argue, because of a single pubic hair discovered on the victim's body.'

Without doing either, Lau somehow communicated both an eyeroll and a smirk, before adding, 'Unfortunately, for the defense in general, and the defendant in particular, that pubic hair only *strengthens* the defendant's motive. That single hair, I submit to you, proves only that the defendant had even *greater* reason to kill her.'

Once the trial was underway, the media swarmed. While most major outlets continued covering the chaos in Washington, others needed a break from the nation's capital. And this case was just the thing. It promised it all – drugs, sex, violence, quasi-celebrity, sibling rivalry – and where better to report from than Honolulu, Hawaii?

Because of the crowd outside the courthouse, security suggested we eat lunch in the lawyers' room downstairs. But Church refused to eat anything from the cafeteria. Security then suggested he sneak out by himself in a hat and sunglasses. But Church refused both eating alone and messing up his hair with a hat. Security finally suggested we *at least* go out the back door where HPD could better keep the mob away. But Church again refused, this time in a flurry of expletives about defense lawyers being treated like second-class citizens.

We went out the front. And walked straight into an ambush. Led by Kalani Webb.

'Mr Church, do you remain confident in your client's innocence?'

Church stopped. The mob stopped with him.

'I hadn't planned on issuing a statement today,' he lied. 'But since there's tremendous interest in this case, and understandably so, I'll take a few questions. Starting with Mr Webb's. Yes, my client had nothing to do with his girlfriend's murder. Ethan's only sin was having an older brother.'

A female reporter stepped forward. 'Nathan Jakes has repeatedly threatened to sue you over past comments made to the press. How do you respond?'

'Nathan Jakes should concern himself with one case and one case only – his own forthcoming indictment for the murder of Piper Kingsley.'

After lunch, Church smiled at his jury. 'Prosecutor Lau turns a fine tale, doesn't she? The yarn she's spun fits neatly in with so many of the facts of this case. But there are problems with her story, "plot holes" as novelists like His Honor might call them.'

Hightower beamed from the bench.

'Ms Lau attempted to bury these plot holes in her opening statement. She dismissed them as mere inconveniences. She's even trying to turn one of those massive plot holes into a positive for her case. She's trying to say it points to motive. But it doesn't. It points to the real killer. It points, sadly enough, to Ethan's brother, Nathan Jakes.'

Nathan wasn't in the courtroom because he would be testifying for the prosecution during their case-in-chief.

'A pubic hair, ladies and gentlemen. A pubic hair belonging to Nathan Jakes was discovered *on* the victim's body, in her pubic region. Which tells us, indisputably, that Nathan Jakes was with her that day, *and* that they had sexual relations. Pull on this pubic hair, I say to you, and the state's entire case fast begins to unravel.

'Just as Ms Lau did with Ethan, we'd have to speculate about Nate's true motive. Did Piper tell Nate that day that she had to break things off with him? Did she tell Nate that she had accepted a new job and was moving to the mainland? Did she tell him she was pregnant, and that he might well be the father? Only Nathan Jakes knows the answers.

'Ms Lau also insinuated that Ethan set up the bogus Craigslist ad and email address from Piper's computer as an alibi. She then told you that the murder occurred inside the house, even though there is *absolutely zero* physical evidence to support this. But for argument's sake, let's say the killer did murder Piper inside the house. If that is true, he left no trace, which our experts – *and* the prosecution's experts – will tell you is perfectly common. Someone, anyone, can enter a house, commit a murder, and escape without leaving a trace. It doesn't take a Houdini.

'Why, you're probably asking yourselves, did the police choose one brother over the other? I'll explain. See, it really wasn't a choice so much as a mistake. A mistake made by one man who was not used to making mistakes. One man who, until this point, until this night, had a long and illustrious career. But he *may* – and I don't want to be ageist here, but an innocent man's life is on the line – he may have stayed on past his time.'

I glanced at the jury. It suddenly made sense why Church had used challenges on seniors who seemed to me to be perfectly clearheaded and openminded.

'Detective Lance Fukumoto, who Ms Lau promised as your star witness, *snapped to conclusions* the night of February twenty-second. During his testimony you're going to learn that Detective Fukumoto *hadn't even gotten to the scene* when he decided who he liked for the murder. This may seem comical – and I'm not above cracking a joke or two – but this is dead serious. *On the way* to the scene of the crime the detective googled Ethan Jakes. He then downloaded one of his songs. Why? So he could manipu-late the man he *knew* – just from hearing the nine-one-one call – was guilty of this crime.

'Could he really be so proud, you're probably asking your-selves, that he'd allow an innocent man to go to prison for the rest of his natural life, rather than admit a mistake? This man with thirty-six years on the force, this man of impeccable integ-rity? No.' Church shook his head to emphasize it. 'No, I'm *not* for the wholesale degradation of the police. I don't see in this case some elaborate conspiracy. I see a man, a good man, a man with seventy years on this earth, nearly forty with the HPD, who, in this particular case, made a mistake and then, as police are sometimes wont to do, developed *tunnel vision*.

'Tunnel vision,' Church repeated, and I jotted it on my pad as a possible title for the movie.

'Tunnel vision,' he said again. 'That's what this case is about.

'But wait, you're saying to yourselves, what about the pros-ecutor? What *about* the prosecutor? Now, as I said earlier, I am not for the wholesale degradation of the police. I *am*, on the other hand, all for the wholesale degradation of lawyers.'

This earned a chuckle that spread like the flu through the courtroom.

'Ms Lau is busy,' Church said, 'Ms Lau is impatient, Ms Lau is preparing to campaign for govern—'

'*Objection!*' Lau was on her feet so fast I wondered whether she'd been an athlete in college. 'Counsel is making a personal attack on—'

'Withdrawn,' Church said, his hands parallel to his head in the you-got-me pose. He turned back to the jury. 'Ms Lau is busy, Ms Lau is impatient—'

'*Objection!*'

I wasn't sure Lau had even had time to sit down.

'Sustained,' Hightower said in his best tenor. 'Mr Church . . .'

'Your Honor, I swear, I thought Ms Lau's objection was strictly about her upcoming campaign for governor.'

'*Your Honor!*'

'Mr Church,' Hightower commanded, 'this is your *final* warning. Go down this road again—'

'Your Honor,' Church said, 'may we approach?'

In the editing room, I read from the transcript of the first of many sidebars during trial.

```
CHURCH:     Your   Honor,   with   all   due
            respect, this is our theory of
            the   case.   That   Detective
            Fukumoto   rushed   to   judgment,
            which he did, and that Ms Lau
            wholly ignored that fact, not
            because   she   is   a   terrible
            person,   but   because   she   is
            busy, impatient—
LAU:        Judge!
CHURCH:     See what I mean, Your Honor?
            She won't even allow me to
            finish my thought.
JUDGE:      Ms Lau, you'll get your turn.
            Mr Church?
CHURCH:     Ms Lau's political ambitions
            clearly   interfered   with   her
```

```
                    judgment in this case. Quite
                    frankly, Judge, with such a
                    conflict of interest, I can
                    hardly believe she didn't
                    recuse herself.
   LAU:              This is outrageous.
   CHURCH:           My sentiments exactly, Your
                    Honor.
```

'Tunnel vision,' Church says onscreen, without missing a beat following the sidebar. 'Detective Fukumoto had it. Other people, who shall remain nameless, had it.' As he says this, he lifts his brows and subtly nods in the direction of the prosecutor.

Lau starts to rise, but catches sight of the jury, who are (sadly again, offscreen) falling in love with Nicholas Church.

'In defense of Detective Fukumoto,' Church continues, 'let me say this. Although he jumped to the wrong conclusion, it wasn't a ridiculous jump to make. After all, Detective Fukumoto wasn't aware of all the facts that first night. Or even before he charged the defendant. He didn't know that Ethan's brother Nate was sleeping with Piper Kingsley. He didn't know, as Piper's neighbor Elanor Rigby knew, that a white BMW was parked in Piper's garage some nights, on dates which we'll show you correspond with Ethan's performances in town. He didn't know, for example, as Nate's ex-wife Cheyenne Oh will testify, that Nate had pined for Ethan's lifestyle every waking moment of his marriage and fatherhood. When Detective Fukumoto first snapped to his conclusion – when he first developed tunnel vision – he didn't know that Nate had been struggling at his law firm, losing cases he should have won, clearly because of preoccupation.

'Preoccupied with what? I'll let you decide during the presentation of the evidence.

'Ladies and gentlemen, I get no joy out of telling you this tragic story. But when I took on Ethan as a client, we agreed that we would seek the Truth together, that we would go wherever the evidence took us. Ethan certainly gets no joy out of this. But my defense team and I, we went where the evidence led.' He turns his gaze to Lau, says, '*Someone* in this case needed to.'

*   *   *

Once opening statements concluded, the judge adjourned the proceedings.

'Until tomorrow,' Hightower said, 'when the prosecution will put on its first witness.'

He reminded the jury not to speak about the case, not to watch television or read newspaper articles about the trial. Church assured me, however, that jurors *never* listen to this instruction. 'It's only human,' he said. 'People get excited. For eleven of those twelve people, this is probably the most exciting thing happening in their lives.'

Which was why Church again refused to use the back door to exit the courthouse. Instead we proceeded out the front door, where we were once again swamped by media.

Mercifully, Church would say only, 'I think my opening statement speaks for itself.'

The moment we departed courthouse property, our uniformed escorts stopped holding back foot traffic, and we were suddenly swarmed. For an instant I lost sight of Church. Lost sight of Brody.

As I searched for them, I saw only one person I recognized. Not the full person exactly, just the clean-shaven head bulleting toward us.

I turned and found Church just as Zane Kingsley confronted him.

'Talk about my lil' girl like that, will ya. You fucking gutful of piss.'

Church's eyes widened at this.

'That's right,' Zane said, 'I know you. I know you *and* your lot.'

Zane Kingsley made as if he was going to strike Church, but Church didn't flinch.

Just when I expected Zane to produce a weapon, he was tackled by a trio from the HPD.

'What the hell's a gutful of piss?' Brody asked, as Zane was escorted out of sight in handcuffs.

Church looked at Brody, and for a moment I was sure he was about to grace us with that obnoxious Aussie accent. But he didn't. He simply shrugged his shoulders as though they were suddenly fifty-pound weights.

'He called me a drunk,' he said.

* * *

'I don't think they're safe,' I told Brody on the drive back to Waikiki.

'Who? Nick and Marissa? The Four Seasons is probably the safest place on the island, and the penthouse suite the safest place in the hotel. Only you and they have keys.'

'He's been getting death threats, you know.'

'I know. I filmed him receiving one in the mail.'

Brody searched my eyes as I tried to maintain focus on the road.

'Come on. Chin up, Rye. Opening statements were dramatic. That confrontation with Zane Kingsley will make great footage. This is exactly the movie you envisioned before we came out here.'

I felt sick to my stomach and feared I might have a panic attack on H-1.

'George Leary was right all along,' he added. 'You have a great eye, Rye. You better be ready for it – this film may well lead to fortune and fame.'

THIRTY-EIGHT

*L*ove ain't nothing but sex misspelled. That's what Harlan Ellison said. If Riley Vasher's words are ever worth anything, I'd say sex is merely a catalyst. If lust sparks the ignition, love is the engine that either sputters and dies early, or leaves you stranded down the road. Seldom does it go the distance. With Ethan, I think I mistook lust for love. Think I saw a man as sensitive as Brody but without all the baggage and jumped on him. Think the lust was so intense that I figured, *to hell with the invisible wall*, and let the fucking thing topple all around me.

In the editing room, I decide to cut all the tedious science, to eliminate the ho-hum explication of digital forensics, DNA, and trace evidence such as hair and fibers. Leave all that to the writers of *CSI*. I prefer to slice straight to the conclusions through visual evidence of late-night strategy sessions, Church's cross of key witnesses, and both sides' closing arguments. I'm determined not to lose sight of what this movie is meant to be: a lurid account of the events surrounding the death of local weathergirl Piper Kingsley, and the subsequent murder trial of her sexy live-in musician Ethan Jakes.

Onscreen, I sit next to Church on a park bench not far from the courthouse, eating lunch. As was the norm, Brody had declined the lawyer's invitation in favor of the cafeteria, and Ethan professed to having no appetite.

'The visual evidence we present *should be* salacious,' I tell Church. '*Should* appeal to the audience's prurient interests and earn our film a hard R. The FCC *should* slap us with a TV-MA and require viewers to use discretion.'

'If viewers had any discretion,' he says, 'you'd have to find another line of work.'

'Yet you credit Marissa's movie with turning your life around.'

'Don't get me wrong,' he says, this time with a mouthful of Italian sub, 'I'm a *product* of tabloid journalism.' He scans the area, presumably for jurors, then swallows and follows it with a full bottle of FIJI. 'But,' he adds, 'just because I am a product of tabloid journalism, doesn't mean that I need to *like* the mockery the media has made of our legal system, or our political system for that matter. These, however, are the present rules of the game. I can either ignore them on principle or use them to my client's advantage. I choose to do the latter.'

'You've fully embraced the fame, though.'

Church grins. 'Everyone desires fame, Riles. It's just the famous who are willing to admit it.'

'You're suggesting fame is the ultimate achievement?'

'Hardly,' he says. 'In the era of Chewbacca Mom, *anyone* can become famous.'

I nod. 'We're not living in the best of times, are we?'

He glances at the outrageously expensive watch he purchased a few days ago at Ala Moana, and shrugs. 'Popular culture reflects who we are. This is the direction of the species. Like it or not, watching TV is like gazing into a mirror. That's us, that's who we are. People whose jaws drop in disgust at reality TV are just disgusted that this is our reality. Because *we're* the worst of reality TV, *we're* the worst of social media, *we're* the fucked-up

narcissistic Frankenmonster stomping blindly over our own
fragile existence.'

'Holy cynicism, Batman.'

He smiles, then leans in as if to share a deep secret. 'Riles,
you and I both know that the world has become absurd. We either
accept the new reality or go insane trying to convince everyone
else of the world's absurdity.'

Next, I pull up footage of Brody with Church. I haven't decided
how much of this relationship I want to show. Side by side, they
look like the ultimate odd couple, yet they've bonded in a way
few hetero males do. What makes the friendship even more peculiar
is that they don't seem to share very much in common. Then again,
Church refuses to speak about his life prior to law school, so there
are numerous pieces of the puzzle I'm missing. I've repeatedly
asked Church about his parents, about his childhood, about the
onset of his illness, but the closest I've come to a positive response
was during jury deliberations, when he winked at me and said,
'We have to save *something* for the sequel.'

Still, I think Church is my answer to developing Brody as more
than just a background character. So much of Brody's experience
during principal photography was behind the camera, and the rest
consisted mostly of offscreen technical talk with Marissa Linden.
There are a few profound conversations between Brody and Church,
but most of those contain personal content that Brody wouldn't
want aired. Brody sees our arrival in Hawaii as an unequivocal
fresh start. A rebirth, a rewind, an incontrovertible kickoff that
erases all things past. But without his past, Brody is an incomplete
player. Without his past, Brody isn't Brody.

Yet, how would I introduce Brody's abuse and neglect? How,
short of reenactments, would I show a mother deliberately with-
holding from her child the basics for survival? How would
I show her locking food in the trunk of her car? How would I
show her holding a blow dryer to the boy's scalp in ninety-degree
heat as punishment for sweating while playing outside? How
would I show the physical attacks? How would the audience
experience the child's isolation? How would they hear his mother's screams, her taunts, her constant wishing aloud that Brody
had never been born?

How would viewers bear witness to the public humiliation of

having a mother with a mixed salad of untreated mental illnesses? How would they hear the boy's futile pleas for his mother to seek help for herself?

I lean back in my chair. Even if I could somehow show the horrors of Brody's childhood, I'd only be knocking down another invisible wall and making the cameraman the most sympathetic character in the movie. No, this film cannot be about Brody. This film cannot be about me. This film cannot be about Church.

This film needs to be about Ethan.

THIRTY-NINE

On the first day of testimony, Naomi Lau walked Detective Fukumoto through the investigation in its entirety. From the initial call, through the collection of evidence, to his conclusion that Ethan Jakes had murdered Piper Kingsley, the detective carefully explained his motive behind every move, the thought process behind every decision he made. To preempt Church's own inquiry, Lau and Fukumoto even ushered the jury through Fukumoto's few minor mistakes. The prosecution had such a good morning that by lunch I felt sick to my stomach.

But I had scheduled lunch with Kalani Webb at a café down the street from the courthouse.

'So what do you think?' he said, after we ordered.

'I think it was a difficult morning for the defense.'

'Have you been online this morning?'

'Not yet, why?'

'Your guy seems to have caught whatever Jodi Arias had.'

It took me a moment to remember the Jodi Arias case. 'She was convicted of shooting, stabbing and slitting her boyfriend's throat, right?'

'She also took to Twitter during her trial and seemed to enjoy all the attention.'

'Are you shitting me? Ethan's on social media today?'

'He tweeted that Fukumoto is a senile old bastard who should have been put out to pasture years ago.'

'Christ. The *jury* will see that.'

'Even if they're trying to obey the judge's instructions – which I don't think happens too often – it'll be pretty hard to miss it. The *Star-Ad* is following the case as closely as any trial in the state's history. People are obsessed.'

'I see you've been writing every feature. How'd you land that sweet gig?'

'It didn't go unnoticed by the editor-in-chief that I live one house away from the crime scene.'

'I'm sure it didn't hurt receiving scoops from *us* every week.'

'Don't think for a second I don't appreciate it,' he said with a charming smile. 'This is *old school* journalism. One hand washes the other, yeah?'

'Church has been sufficiently entertained by the coverage so far.'

'This case is kind of making a name for me, but print's not my future. My real goal is still to make it in television.'

I reflected for a moment. 'The first time I noticed you on TV was the morning after Piper died.'

'Yeah, that was my first real report. I'm still hoping it opens some doors. What did you think?'

'Is this one of those times you want an honest opinion? Or just a pat on the back?'

'An honest opinion, though it sounds like I may regret asking.'

'You have a terrific presence onscreen. I've seen it in our own footage at pressers and outside the courthouse as well. But I thought that initial report was a little dry.'

'Shit. I haven't even watched it – I've been too afraid.'

'Did you know Piper well?' I asked him.

'I talked to her a few times. When I finished school I went to her for advice, but she kind of brushed me off. I auditioned at her station but never got the call back.'

'It's a tough industry to break into.'

'That's what makes me want in so bad I can taste it.'

Following lunch, Lau abruptly tendered the witness, no doubt in the hopes of swaying Church even slightly off course. On the witness stand, the seventy-year-old lead detective showed no signs of tiring.

'He looks like he can go another twelve hours,' I whispered.

'Give me five minutes with him,' Church said as he rose from his seat. 'Then make another assessment.'

The previous night, during our strategy session, Church had been more animated than we'd seen him in the past couple of weeks. How much of that exhilaration could be attributed to adrenaline, and how much to the contents of his oversized LAWYERS DO IT IN THEIR BRIEFS mug, we didn't know. But it felt damn good having that electricity back in the room.

'There are no rules to cross-examination,' he explained as he paced before the whiteboard. 'It's not something you can pick up overnight. You hone your skills over years so that your judgment, your ability to execute and adapt in a split second becomes instinctive. Cross-examination is psychology, it's staring someone down to elicit a desired response. And how do you get desired responses? Preparation. You need to know the evidence inside and out, and you need to know the subjects you'll be touching on. If you're crossing a cop, for instance, you'd damn well better know how police are *supposed* to conduct a criminal investigation.'

CHURCH: Is it not standard procedure in the investigation of a homicide for the lead detective to use all available resources to canvass the surrounding area?

FUKUMOTO: It is.

CHURCH: Did you instruct any of your officers on the night of the murder to canvass the area surrounding the crime scene?

FUKUMOTO: I did not.

CHURCH: Did you not have the resources available to go door to door along Tantalus Drive?

FUKUMOTO: I had the resources.

CHURCH: Yet you skipped this critical step in the process. Tell us,

Detective. Was the reason you didn't canvass the neighbor-hood that evening because you had already determined that Ethan Jakes had murdered this young woman, yes or no?

FUKUMOTO: No, it was because—

CHURCH: You've answered my question, Detective. Did it in any way enter into your think—

LAU: Objection. The witness should have a reasonable opportunity to provide his answer.

CHURCH: It was a yes or no question. He'd provided his answer.

LAU: You cut him off mid-sentence. The question was framed in such a way the witness should be able to provide a brief explanation.

JUDGE: Counselors, you will address the Court, not each other. The objection is sustained. Detective, if you need time to continue your answer, you may do so now.

FUKUMOTO: I have nothing further to add.

CHURCH: Well, now I'd like to hear it as well, Detective.

FUKUMOTO: I did not order a canvass of the neighborhood because this was a late-night crime scene. Standard procedure for late-night is to only interview significant witnesses or eyewitnesses.

CHURCH: I'm sorry, remind us what time you arrived on-scene.

FUKUMOTO: 9:36 p.m.

CHURCH: So 9:36 was past business hours? When are your operating hours, Detective, so we can note them for future reference?

FUKUMOTO: I use my discretion.

CHURCH: OK, so your discretion told you that 9:36 was too late-night to canvass the neighborhood in the wake of the murder of a young woman. Would it have made a difference if you'd arrived at 9:29?

FUKUMOTO: No.

CHURCH: How about 8:45?

FUKUMOTO: Unlikely.

CHURCH: Did you have any objective criteria at all to determine when to canvass the area and when not to?

FUKUMOTO: I used common sense.

CHURCH: Which told you that 9:36 p.m. was too late for a canvass?

FUKUMOTO: In that neighborhood, yes.

CHURCH: In that neighborhood? What does that mean, Detective?

FUKUMOTO: In that area, people tend to go to bed earlier.

CHURCH: Because they're older? Maybe even well into their seventies?

FUKUMOTO: No, that's not the reason at all.

CHURCH: Then how do you know this, Detective?

FUKUMOTO: When I drive by at that time of night, everyone's lights are out.

'Don't ask one question too many,' Church had said the previous night. 'Once you have what you want, move on. A smart witness will use the opportunity to hurt you, if not with something substantive, then by endearing himself to the jurors.'

```
CHURCH:     Do you drive up Mount Tantalus
            around   that   time   often,
            Detective?
FUKUMOTO:   I do. My husband and I bring
            our seven-year-old nephew up
            to the park at least once a
            week to set up our telescope
            and study the stars.
```

In the editing room, interspersing footage of Church's cross with footage of the previous night's strategy session, I glance at the watch Church bought me and decide to keep going.

Onscreen, Church writes the word *Plan* on the whiteboard. Says, 'We need a plan that's consistent with our theory of the case, which is that *Nathan* Jakes committed this murder. An unfortunate consequence of that theory is that it undermines what little physical evidence we had going for us. The foreign footprint? Too small. Not Nathan's. The blood on the tree behind the victim's house? Not Nathan's. We're left with very little. So, on cross-examination, we need to collect as much favorable material for our summation as possible.'

```
CHURCH:     Detective,   when   you   first
            learned that a pubic hair
            belonging to Nathan Jakes was
            discovered   in   the   victim's
            pubic region, did you request
            a search warrant for Nathan
            Jakes' vehicles, yes or no?
FUKUMOTO:   The first thing I did—
CHURCH:     My question wasn't about the
            first thing you did, Detective.
            Please catch up.
LAU:        Objection!
```

```
CHURCH:     Withdrawn. Detective, do you
            need the question repeated
            back to you?
FUKUMOTO:   No, I did not request a search
            warrant for Nathan Jakes'
            vehicles.
CHURCH:     When you learned of the pubic
            hair, did you request a search
            warrant for Nathan Jakes'
            house, yes or no?
FUKUMOTO:   No.
CHURCH:     When you learned of the pubic
            hair, did you request a search
            warrant for Nathan Jakes' law
            office, yes or no?
FUKUMOTO:   No.
```

Onscreen, standing before the whiteboard, Church says, 'Witnesses wiggle like earthworms. It's our job to pin them down. Once they're inextricably linked to their responses, we exploit any inconsistencies from past statements, any testimony contrary to physical evidence, and any testimony that contradicts other witness testimony. But we need to gauge each witness. We need to know, if we push this witness will he backpedal? Will he cave? Or will he push back in a way that strengthens his unfavorable testimony. We need to know *when* to go in for the kill, and when not to.'

```
CHURCH:     Just so we're clear, Detective.
            Is it your testimony that, as
            you sit here today, you still
            have not recovered the clothes
            the victim was last seen in?
FUKUMOTO:   We don't know that they are
            missing. We don't know that
            such clothes even exist.
CHURCH:     Really? So you didn't search
            for the UH T-shirt and shorts
            that an eyewitness - namely
```

```
                  my client  -  told  you  the
                  victim was last seen wearing?
FUKUMOTO:         We  searched  for  them.
CHURCH:           Where  did  you  specifically
                  search  for  these  items  of
                  clothing, Detective?  In  the
                  victim's  house?
FUKUMOTO:         Yes.
CHURCH:           Around      the      victim's
                  property?
FUKUMOTO:         Yes.
CHURCH:           In  the  victim's  vehicle?
FUKUMOTO:         Yes.
CHURCH:           In  my  client's  vehicle?
FUKUMOTO:         Yes.
CHURCH:           In  my  client's  apartment  up
                  North  Shore?
FUKUMOTO:         Yes.
CHURCH:           In   the   woods   behind   the
                  victim's  house?
FUKUMOTO:         Yes.
CHURCH:           In   the   drainage  pipes  and
                  storm  sewers  in  that  area?
FUKUMOTO:         Yes.
CHURCH:           Well,  Detective,  I'm  almost
                  out  of  breath,  but  it  sounds
                  to  me  like  you  did  an  awful
                  lot  of  searching  for  clothes
                  you  don't  think  exist.
```

'We need to maintain control of our witness at all times. We *do not* want to give the witness a chance to "explain" a yes or no answer.'

```
CHURCH:           As   you   sit   here   today,
                  Detective,  have  you  ever
                  recovered  a  weapon  that  may
                  have  been  used  to  kill  Piper
                  Kingsley,  yes  or  no.
```

```
FUKUMOTO:   No, but—
CHURCH:     No further questions for this
            witness, Your Honor.
```

'And we don't need to concern ourselves with trying to elicit favorable conclusions – *we* will make the conclusions ourselves during summation.'

'Do we know who's testifying tomorrow?' Brody asks, onscreen, in Church's suite.

'The chief medical examiner, Sheila Rutley.' As Church paces, he gulps from his mug. 'Just as with jury selection, our technique on cross changes from case to case, witness to witness. It's like surgery; we need a different tool for every part of the operation.'

'What do we know about Dr Rutley?' I ask the speakerphone, which by now, I'm used to, maybe even enjoying a bit.

Jesse says, 'Straight shooter, as far as I can tell. Apolitical. Has clashed with past prosecutors who pushed her to give more than she was willing to give.'

'Does the local defense bar like her?' Church asks.

'Right up until the point her straight-shooting is aimed at them.'

'We *are* a fickle bunch, aren't we?'

```
CHURCH:     So, as chief medical examiner,
            you cannot tell this jury, to
            a reasonable degree of medical
            certainty, whether the victim
            died from suffocation?
RUTLEY:     No, I cannot.
CHURCH:     You cannot tell this jury
            whether the victim died from
            strangulation?
RUTLEY:     No, I cannot.
CHURCH:     You cannot tell this jury
            whether the victim died from
            drowning?
RUTLEY:     No, I cannot.
```

'Finally, we can't be afraid to say, "No cross-examination, Your Honor." We don't want to go fishing. We don't want the witness repeating damaging information elicited on direct, and we *never* want to ask a question we don't know the answer to.'

He abruptly ceased pacing. 'I *cannot* understate the dangers of cross. Too many defense lawyers inadvertently fill in the gaps of the prosecutor's case on cross. If we don't think we can improve our case, we walk away. Last thing we want is to elicit statements prejudicial to our client. Declining to cross a witness, if done properly, gives jurors the impression that the witness's testimony wasn't all that important. Better that than hurting ourselves.'

```
JUDGE:    Mr Church, you may cross-
          examine Mr Zane Kingsley?
CHURCH:   No desire for cross, Your
          Honor. The defense is sympa-
          thetic to the witness, but as
          Ms Lau just so deftly demon-
          strated on direct, Mr Kingsley
          has no firsthand knowledge of
          any facts or evidence relevant
          to this case.
```

FORTY

'I never cybered, I never sexted. Never got the point, really. Sex should be intimate, it should be sweaty. I don't like what technology has done for sex over the past twenty years. People are losing the distinction between distance and closeness.'

Dr Farrockh says, 'I don't disagree. If they asked me two decades ago, what's needed to improve sex, I'd have told them it's good as is.'

I smile. 'They always want to fuck with the formula.'

'Everyone's so desperate for discovery. People are afraid to learn this is all there is. Nowadays, you can travel the world as a young adult, you can conquer an industry by the time you are thirty. What do you do with the remaining half-century?'

'I'll be thirty when my film is released. Marissa Linden was only twenty-eight.'

'Life is not a competition, Riley.'

'Tell that to society.'

'I'm telling *you*. You have very lofty goals, and that's wonderful. You have the talent and ability to achieve them, and that's even better. But your timelines could use some revisions.'

'They're not *my* timelines, they're the film industry's. It's not just actors, you know. It's writers, it's directors, it's cinematographers, musicians. If you don't get in while you're young, you don't get in. And I feel like I wasted two precious years of my life schlepping for Big Pharma.'

'You constantly obsess over those two years, and some of the decisions you made and a few that were made for you. But have you thought about the fact that if you had gone to UCLA's film school, you may have never gone to New York, you may have never met Brody, you may have never met Professor Leary? You wouldn't likely have been here in Hawaii when your friend was murdered, and you likely wouldn't have had the money to make the film, even if you were.'

'You're right, it all comes back to the movie. This is my opportunity.'

'This is *an* opportunity, Riley. Remember that. Be better to yourself.'

I sigh, settle deeper into the sofa. 'Next week, before she and Church head off to Maui, Marissa is going to come down to the editing room to review the present cut and give me notes.'

'That's kind of her, right?'

'If making me feel sick to my stomach with nerves is kind, then yeah.'

'You're nervous because you respect her opinion.'

'I don't like her.'

'You don't have to like her to respect her opinion, Riley. Those are two very different things. And, I should point out, you still never put your finger on *why* you don't like her.' She pauses.

'Why don't you like her? First words that pop into your head, fast.'

'I don't like the way Brody looks at her.'

'He's still attracted to her?'

'Yeah, but that's not it. I think he's also attracted to Nate's ex-wife, Cheyenne, and that doesn't bother me. It's more his *fascination* with Marissa.'

'Is she fascinating?'

'Yeah.'

'As are you.'

'Not yet. Maybe once this movie is in the bucket—'

'No, Riley, no. "Once the movie is made, once the movie is sold, once the movie is distributed, once it premieres, once it wins an award, once I begin my second film . . ." There will always be *something* you want more. There will always be a more significant achievement. Victories are brief, and we're never more than a broken rung from falling off the ladder. Work hard, but don't *wait* for something great to happen to love yourself. Today is as important as the day your movie comes out.'

'I'm terrified of failing.'

'I was terrified too once. When I first came to the United States as a small child, from Iran of all places, I was sure I would never make a friend.'

'Let me guess. You met someone the first day, and you're still friends with her.'

She shook her head. On her face was a deep and painful sadness. 'No,' she says, 'the first friend I made was in my junior year of high school. And she was military, so she moved away after one semester. I didn't make another real friend until medical school.'

'How did you get through all that time?'

'I kept in mind something my father told me when I told him I feared I was a failure at making friends and always would be. He said in his thick Middle Eastern accent, "Keep trying, Yasmin, try every day. And if you keep trying, if you try every day, if you try right up until the moment you die, you'll never even know that you failed."'

To say we did not know what to expect from Nate's testimony would have been a monumental understatement. The brothers had not spoken since their blowup, and the strategy employed by the defense over the course of this trial was not going to mend any fraternal fences anytime soon. Church intended to persuade the twelve men and women in the jury box that Nathan Jakes, not Ethan, had murdered Piper Kingsley on February 22 of this year.

Church wasn't necessarily placing Nathan in legal jeopardy, not directly anyway. It was highly unlikely, absent significant new evidence, that the prosecution would pursue Nathan Jakes if Ethan was acquitted. No, the damage Church inflicted on Nathan Jakes was already done. We'd witnessed the death blow at Church's 'First/Last Press Conference' months ago, when Church revealed to the world that Nathan Jakes had had sexual relations with the victim on the day she was murdered.

Since that day, Nate's life had been in a downward spiral. After losing Piper and the love of his only brother, he lost Cheyenne and the kids. Because Cheyenne could prove infidelity, she would have swept the floor with Nate in divorce court. Nate chose instead to settle quietly, but he paid dearly for that silence. Then, not long after the divorce settlement was finalized, the other shoe dropped. Because of his toxicity and the overwhelming media scrutiny (to say nothing of his continued poor performance), Nathan Jakes lost his partnership at the firm.

Church had Tahoma tailing Nate ever since. After moving out of the family home, Nate rented a small studio apartment in Waikiki. He went out nightly, got drunk, hit on tourists. He was tossed out of three different bars on Kalakaua alone, two for the night, one for life. The cops on the beat didn't like him either. They watched him closely, hoping he'd piss in public, purchase an eight ball, maybe sock one of the locals in the eye, so they could slap on the cuffs. Police did, however, look the other way when Nate took hookers to his room, but only as a courtesy to the hookers.

The night before Nate's testimony, Church told us to prepare for the worst. Ethan, who had been regularly skipping strategy sessions in recent weeks, had been summoned to this one. For the first half-hour, as Church discussed Nate's likely direct testimony, Ethan remained silent. He was inexorably torn. Personally, I didn't know Nate well enough to decide whether he'd hurt his own brother with the stakes this high. But then I also felt that if Nate intended to help Ethan in any way, he would have at least contacted the defense team to discuss. But no, he'd even declined Tahoma's request for a witness interview. The best we could hope for, I was sure, was neutral testimony.

'Before we discuss anything else,' Church said, circling the table, 'we're going to address the two-hundred-pound jackass in the room. Anyone want to take a shot at pinning the tail? I'll give you a hint – he's fucking trending on Twitter.'

We all remained silent.

Finally, Ethan said, 'Most of it's been positive. People want to be supportive.'

'Let's see,' Church said, pulling out his phone. 'Ah, this is positive. Cumbubble83 says you look "tall, dark and killy".' Church scrolled. 'Ah, here. Barebackit871 says, "Look at the size of those hands. Wouldn't mind havin' em around MY throat. Hashtag: RestrictMyO2". Oh, wait, this one's supportive. WhitePowerHour40 says, "His asshole's gonna be the size of a lamppost by Day 2, and that's only if he don't drop no soap on Day 1". Grammatical errors are your fans', Ethan, not mine.'

'I won't post anymore,' Ethan said quietly.

'Are you sure, Ethan? There are no swimsuit pics you'd like to throw out there for PussyInBoots32? Maybe pull out your Anthony Weiner and post a few dick pics? That'll increase your number of followers, I'm sure.'

'I *said* I won't post anything else. Let it go.'

'Unless you're a Disney princess, I don't accept those three words, Ethan. I will *not* let this go. Not until you understand how cosmically *stupid* it is for anyone on trial for murder to tweet a single fucking character. Hell, it's stupid enough when you're *not* on trial for murder.'

'I understand, Nick. It won't happen again. I'll delete my account.'

'Jesse deleted your account the moment we found out about your online antics. In fact, Jesse deleted all your social media accounts. Not just deactivated them, he *deleted* them. It's as if they never existed. If you open a new account, if you post so much as one fucking word, one syllable, on social media again, I will throw this fucking trial, do you understand?'

Ethan, every bit as calm as he was just before going berserk in Breakers' parking lot, assured Church he did.

We moved the meeting to the deck just as the sun began to set over the Pacific. In the orange light, Nicholas Church, dressed meticulously in one of the uber-expensive suits he'd purchased at Ala Moana, paced the planks as he peered down at his phone.

Finally, he said, 'Wow, I think Bustmynut84 just broke this case wide open. He says, "She hot. Bet he went necro on dat shit. Dude looks like American psycho".'

'*Enough!*' Ethan shouted, as he shot out of his deckchair.

Church, still scrolling through tweets, never saw him coming.

In the editing room, I rewatch the footage in slow-mo. As Ethan lifts Church over his head with little exertion, I think about Church's words back at the crime scene, about how Piper Kingsley could not have been killed in the upstairs bathroom because of the physical strength it would have taken for someone to pick up her body and carry it downstairs without badly bruising it on the stairs along the way.

By the end of the incident, as Church is pulling himself out of the infinity pool with Brody's help, I consider how to depict the events that took place over the following days. It all happened so fast, the story reads like a blur in my brain.

I fast-forward. As I watch Brody and myself onscreen, cleaning up (Ethan had left hours earlier), and finally walking toward the door to leave Church's suite, I feel a pang of guilt.

'Won't whatever Kyle Myers shared with us tonight be rejected as hearsay?' I ask Church on camera.

'Trust me, Riles. We won't need his testimony. I intend to get everything we need from Nathan on cross.'

Onscreen, Nate walks calmly to the witness stand, head held high in the air, no doubt intended for its effect on the jury.

Everything is, Church assured me.

The previous day, Nathan Jakes had been battery-mates with Naomi Lau, who'd guided him gently through direct. The reason she'd put Nate on the stand became clear right from the start of Lau's questioning. Her objective was to blunt any evidence expected to be presented by the defense – his lies, the affair, his having no alibi for the night of the murder – by dismissively getting it out of the way. Church, of course, had anticipated this and disrupted Lau at every turn, adding the relish Church felt any particular testimony deserved.

On direct, Nate testified that he first met Piper Kingsley about six months before she was murdered. His brother Ethan had introduced them at a bar in Waikiki, where Ethan was performing. He didn't recall whether Ethan introduced Piper as his girlfriend. From their behavior, though, it was clear that Ethan and Piper were together. Nate only learned later that Piper and Ethan had been in a romantic relationship for two months.

Ethan didn't tell Nate about Piper before that evening, Nate explained, because in the event the relationship went sideways, all of Ethan's future girlfriends would be compared to her.

'What did you take that to mean?' Lau asked Nate.

'That Piper was beautiful, smart and successful.'

'That it would be extremely difficult to do better?'

'Something like that, yeah.'

'Did there come a time when you became attracted to Piper Kingsley?'

'I was attracted to her the moment I met her. I'm sure most men were.'

'Were you close to your brother when you first met Piper?'

'I would characterize our relationship then as close, yes.'

'Did there come a time when you had sexual relations with Piper Kingsley?'

'Yes.'

'When was the first time?'

'A few nights after we met.'

'But *after* Ethan told you they were together.'

'Yes.'

'What were the circumstances that led you to sleep with Piper?'

Nate testified that not long after first meeting Piper, he 'accidentally' ran into her outside the station where she worked. He invited her for coffee so that he could 'talk up my brother', and she agreed. From the coffee shop, they went to a bar. There, Piper confessed that she didn't think she would remain with Ethan forever, because 'his life just isn't going anywhere'. (Ethan teared up at the defense table on hearing this.) Piper had grown up well-off and enjoyed 'a certain lifestyle', Nate said.

Meanwhile, Nate confessed to Piper that he hadn't been happy in his own marriage for years and had planned on filing for divorce 'as soon as it became practical'. Following drinks at the bar, they got a room at the Pink Palace. They were 'hooked on each other' after that.

'Did you consider your brother Ethan at the time you took Piper to the Pink Palace?' Lau asked him.

'In the moment, I was not thinking of Ethan.'

'How about afterward?'

'Afterward, it pained me very deeply.'

'Yet you continued the affair.'

'As much as it pained me, I continued the affair, nonetheless.'

On cross, Church took Nate back to the beginning, to college, when Ethan and Nate performed together as The Two Jakes. He established the brothers had made a pact that they'd stick with their music no matter what it took, even if they had to get by on bartending gigs. Sometime after college, however, Nathan Jakes met and fell in love with Cheyenne Oh.

Cheyenne, who was very close with her family, loved Nate too, but made clear she needed more security than a struggling musician could provide. So, with the financial help of Cheyenne's parents, Nate sat for the LSAT, did well and applied only to UH's law school. After being waitlisted for two months, he was accepted.

Once Nate left The Two Jakes, his relationship with his brother admittedly cooled. They stopped calling each other, stopped visiting. Nate involved himself with his studies, then his law practice; Ethan with his music and the odd jobs he picked up just to survive.

'Yet you were envious of Ethan, weren't you?' Church said.

'Not envious.'

'You questioned your own decisions about leaving the group and going to law school.'

'Somewhat, maybe.'

'You weren't satisfied with the law.'

'Not really, no.'

Church delved more deeply into Nate's relationship with Ethan following the dissolution of The Two Jakes. Nate categorized the relationship as lukewarm.

'Did you still love your brother?'

'Of course.'

'Let's return to your relationship with the victim,' Church said. 'When was the first time you saw Piper Kingsley?'

'As I testified on direct, it was—'

'No, the question isn't about the first time you met her. It's about the first time you *saw* her.'

Nate's gaze fixed on some spot deep in the gallery, but he didn't appear to be rooting through his brain for the answer to Church's question – he was rooting through his brain trying to figure out how Church obtained the information, and thereby, how much Church knew.

He was thinking Cheyenne was the source.

'On television. Maybe a few years ago.'

'Did you watch her on a regular basis after that?'

'I watched the news, if that's what—'

'No, you know damn well what I'm talking about.'

I glanced at Lau, who seemed to be too riveted to object.

'Yes,' Nate said. 'I watched the weather pretty regularly.'

'And did there come a time when Piper Kingsley became less of your local weathergirl and more of a private obsession?'

'No, absolutely not.'

'No? Before you met Piper Kingsley, had you ever downloaded photos of her?'

Nate hesitated, probably considering his computer at the firm.

'Yes, I did.'

'Before you met Piper Kingsley, had you ever emailed her at the station?'

At this moment, I dug into Church's briefcase as if searching for crucial documents. When I looked up, Nate's eyes were directly on me.

'Yes, I did.'

'More than once?'

'Yes.'

'More than *five* times?'

'Yes.'

'More than *ten* times?'

'Yes.'

'More than *fifteen* times?'

'Probably.'

'What was the nature of these emails, Mr Jakes?'

Nate sunk lower into the witness stand. 'Fan mail,' he said. 'I think I asked for a date in a few of the emails.'

'Did you propose marriage?'

'Jocularly, maybe.'

I glanced at the jury and wondered how many of the twelve knew what the word *jocularly* meant.

'Now tell me when you *really* learned about Ethan's relationship with Piper.'

'Objection,' Lau said. 'Asked and answered.'

'Overruled. Mr Jakes may answer.'

'I'd heard . . . a *rumor*, if that's what you're referring to.'

'That your brother was dating the local weather reporter, Piper Kingsley?'

'Yes.'

'Who told you that rumor?'

'My wife. She'd run into Ethan in town.'

'So it was more than a rumor, right? Unless your wife is given to telling tall tales.'

'I believed the information.'

'Did your wife Cheyenne share any other "rumors" with you that day?'

'She told me Ethan might be closing a record deal in the near future.'

'That didn't come to fruition. But at the time, the double blows must have been painful, weren't they?'

'I was happy for Ethan.'

'So happy that you called him *that* day to celebrate?'

'It was around that time, yeah.'

'But you didn't congratulate Ethan, did you? You asked Ethan to set up a night out. You asked him to bring Piper along, didn't you?'

Nate shifted in his seat. 'I told him to bring Piper and have Piper bring her friends.'

'And did she bring friends?'

'Yes.'

'Do you remember their names?'

'She brought just one. The weekend weather guy, Kyle Myers.'

'That must have been a disappointment for you.'

'Nice enough guy, but no, he wasn't my type.'

'What was the condition of your marriage at the time?'

'Awful.'

'The night you, your brother, Piper, and her friend Kyle Myers went out – do you remember that night well?'

'Well enough.'

Church went in for the kill. 'Mr Jakes, isn't it true that you *lied* earlier on the stand about when you first had sexual relations with Ms Kingsley?'

Nathan said nothing.

'Let's go back to the night you first met Piper Kingsley in Waikiki. Was it really *days later* that you first had sexual relations with her?'

Nathan didn't respond.

'Mr Jakes, isn't it true that you had sexual relations with Ms Kingsley on *that* night? The very night you met her, the night your little brother introduced you to her as his date?'

Quietly, Nate said, 'Yes.'

In the gallery, a few gasps were quickly extinguished with Hightower's gavel.

'So you lied about the night you met her.'

'Yes.'

'You lied to the *police* about that night.'

'Yes.'

'You lied to this *jury* about that night.'

'Yes.'

'You lied to your *wife* about that night.'

'Yes.'

'And you lied to your *brother* about that night.'

'No.'

'No?' Church took a slight step back, an inscrutable look slowly washing over his face.

'No,' Nate said from the stand. 'Ethan knew Piper and I had sex. He was there too.'

FORTY-ONE

The next day's tabloids predictably squawked: THE *TWO JAKES?*

From the moment the words left Nate's lips on the stand, Church and I each blamed ourselves.

'It's on me,' he said, as soon as we were out of earshot outside the courthouse. 'I went one question too far.'

'How were you supposed to know,' I said, 'when I gave you the wrong information?' I frantically scrolled through my cell phone contacts as we walked.

'Put that away,' Church said.

'No, that little bastard lied to me and—'

'Kyle Myers didn't lie. All he implied was that Piper slept with Nate that first night they met for drinks in Waikiki.'

'That sure as shit wasn't the whole truth, was it?'

'It was the whole truth as far as he knew it.'

'What do you mean?'

'I mean, life's like college, right? If you know you're talking to the campus gossip, you don't reveal the whole story, do you? You say, sure, I went out last night, got hammered on Mad Dog and passed out naked at the edge of the lake. But you leave out the fact that you chugged half that Mad Dog out of the crack of another guy's ass, just because some townie with nine fingers and even fewer teeth dared you to do so. It's common sense.'

'You think she told Kyle that she slept with Nate, but left Ethan out of the story.'

'I do. But in this case, I don't think she lied because she was afraid of "looking bad". From everything you've told me, she wasn't ashamed of her own sexuality.'

'She didn't want to make Ethan look bad?' I said.

'The dive bar musician? C'mon, Riles. Piper didn't even tell Kyle that Ethan was living with her; she was already embarrassed of him. She didn't want to make *Nathan* look bad. Because Nathan is the only brother she was ever serious about.'

Over the next forty-eight hours, the late Piper Kingsley was vigorously slut-shamed online.

The Two Jakes became heroes among (most) men, and killers among (most) women.

'A debate,' said an anchor on one of the twenty-four-hour cable news networks, 'is brewing over *which* of The Two Jakes murdered Piper Kingsley. Are you on Team Nate, or are you on Team Ethan? Let us know by going to our website's Pulse Live question of the day!'

How all this would affect Ethan's case was anyone's guess.

'I'll request a mistrial,' Church said, as we stepped into the courthouse. 'Hightower will deny it, but at least we'll have a basis for appeal.'

'What about the jury?'

Church stabbed at the elevator button.

'Luckily, because I purged the pool of seniors, we have a fairly forward-looking twenty-first-century jury. I don't think unconventional sex will hurt our client much.'

'This case went from local to national pretty fucking fast,' I said, as the elevator doors opened and a wave of people rushed out. 'People are now saying The Two Jakes "broke the internet". Whatever the fuck that means.'

'Which side are people falling on?' Church asked matter-of-factly. 'Team Nate or Team Ethan?'

'So far, most people are on Team Ethan,' I told him as we stepped onto the elevator. 'The consensus seems to be that Nate is the only brother with the sophistication to pull off the creation of an online alibi like he did.'

'Interesting. That's something I'll use in closing.'

'Do you feel confident?'

As a family with a handicapped child attempted to board, Church raised his hand, palm out, and said, 'Sorry, my assistant just passed gas in here. You're going to want to take the next one.'

As the doors closed, he turned to me and said, 'Confident enough. You?'

* * *

In the editing room, I've come to The Footage. The footage which
– as much as I will it – refuses to spontaneously combust. Once
at 60 Centre Street in Manhattan, I made the mistake of telling
Brody that courtrooms are an aphrodisiac for me, that I'm drawn
to them like others are to expensive restaurants and megachurches.
He took me a little too literally.

I can't even watch. I read along with the script and play only
the audio.

```
INT. COURTROOM - DAY
The gallery finally comes to order as
Hightower raps his gavel.

                 HIGHTOWER
     Before we bring the jury in
     this morning, I believe Mr
     Brody Quinlan would like to
     put a statement on the record.

Brody tugs Riley by the arm out from
behind the defense table and stands her
before it. He drops to one knee as a
horrified expression washes over her
face.

                   BRODY
     Rye, you're my love, you're my
     light, you're my everything.
     Will you marry me?

Riley nods in the hopes of ending this
spectacle. In the moment most women
dream of, she looks as though she could
shoot her boyfriend in the face.

                 HIGHTOWER
                 (smiling)
     I'm sorry, Ms Vasher, but we're going
     to need you to provide a verbal
```

```
       response  so  the  court  reporter  can
       take  it  down  for  the  record.

       Riley's  cheeks  burn  a  shade  of  crimson
       they'll  never  fully  recover  from.

                          RILEY
                   (through  clenched  teeth)
            Yes.

       The  gallery  politely  applauds.

       CUT  TO:

       Church  standing  next  to  Ethan  behind
       the  defense  table,  gawking.

                          CHURCH
            Did  BQ  really  just  get  down  on  one  knee
            and  propose  in  front  of  a  packed
            courtroom  without  a  fucking  ring?
```

'About a year ago,' Church says, to open his closing, 'I was at a funeral for a seventeen-year-old boy, who I'd known well, almost the span of his entire life. He was not my son, but he very much felt like one. I heard his first word, I helped him take his first steps. I took him to his first day of school. I played catch with him. I taught him to ride a bike. I taught him how to play video games.' He pauses. 'OK, I got him *addicted* to video games.' Some laughter floats above the courtroom. 'He was, in all likelihood, the closest thing I'll ever have to a son.

'I wish I could tell you that he died for some cause. Wish I could tell you that he jumped on a landmine to save half his platoon, or that his organs saved the life of another young person who would have otherwise died, but they didn't. His death, in fact, was as *pointless* as it possibly could have been. He died of an opiate overdose.' He paused in an effort to control the emotion in his voice. 'Now, I recognize that it's an epidemic. But the fact that it's happened to so many other families doesn't make it any easier on the people I consider mine. All that matters is him. All that matters is Daniel.

'I consoled his mother as best I could, but I might as well have set out to cure cancer. I never felt more useless, more helpless than I did when I held his mother in my arms that night and every night after for months and months.

'Although so little of the time after Danny died is unstained by tears, a few memories *do* exist. One is from the day of Daniel's funeral, when a guy who I never before met walked up to me and casually said, "Shit, this is a sad occasion, ain't it?"

'I could only stare at him; he'd struck me speechless. Now I realize he didn't know that Daniel was practically my own son. He thought I was just another mourner, another old acquaintance of Daniel's mother, maybe, which is what he turned out to be. But after his "Shit, this is a sad occasion, ain't it?", he asked me, "You have any kids?" I shook my head. He said, "Losing one of my children is my greatest fear. Probably everyone's. What is it for people who don't have kids? What's yours, chum?"

'The situation was so surreal I thought it needed to play out, so I thought about it. I thought about it a lot. So much, in fact, that this nut I never met before told me to take my time. It happened that *too many* things jumped into my mind. The threat of nuclear war, terrorism, climate change, my own mortality if I was going to be honest with this stranger, and I had decided I was. But more than anything else that frightened me, one thing led in a landslide. "The conviction of an innocent man," I told him. "The conviction of an innocent man."

'Now, you may think I've told that story to a dozen juries, but I haven't. Trial transcripts are public record, you can check them if you'd like. But those of you who *do* know who I am, from the papers or television or *The Prosecutor*, must know that truer words were never spoken. Because there is one case, one trial, one execution, one *name* that will be forever melded with my own – the case of *North Carolina v Roderick J. Blunt.*'

Lau stands. 'I am sorry, Your Honor, but I have to object.'

'On what grounds?' Hightower says.

'Relevance.'

'Your Honor,' Church says, 'I am only telling this story to this jury to impress upon them the gravity of their decision, and the fact that if they erroneously convict an innocent man, it is almost *impossible* to ever correct that error.'

'I'll allow it,' Hightower says.

Church continues. 'In prosecuting the *Blunt* case, I opened pretty much how Prosecutor Lau opened this trial. I told my jury that, though I'm loath to call any case simple, this is a simple case. The defendant, I told them, *truthfully*, has a history of domestic violence. He has a motive – the victim, who was his ex-wife, had threatened to have him arrested for unpaid child support. The gun – a cheap one – was owned by the defendant. His prints alone were on it. There was no forced entry, I told the jury, so the killer had to be someone who either had a key, or someone the victim knew well. The defendant had no alibi. He was alone and drunk in a dark park not two blocks away. The case *was* simple, wasn't it? Open and shut, as we lawyers like to call them.

'I told my jury that the victim was calling us from the grave, telling us to open our eyes, that the obvious is what transpired here.' He paused. 'But she wasn't calling from the grave. No murder victim does, as much as prosecutors like to use that turn of phrase in their statements to the jury. In my case, if the victim could have spoken, she would have told us that she hadn't seen her ex-husband that day. And she would have told me something no one else knew – that she had been seeing a man named Lenny Coyne. She would have told me that Coyne, too, had a history of domestic violence, though his was much more severe. He'd previously been charged with the attempted murder of an ex-girlfriend.

'I alone am not to blame – though, I admit, it feels that way most days – for Roderick Blunt's execution by the State of North Carolina. The lead detective – someone I held in high esteem – had made numerous mistakes at the scene. One of which was his failure to canvass the area the night of the murder. From nothing more than a preliminary verbal report from the responding officer, my lead detective zeroed in on one man and one man only, and when he handed off the baton to the prosecutor's office, we never looked anyplace else. Why?' He waits a few beats. 'Because we were too damn busy. Because the district attorney was about to launch a political campaign for Attorney General. Because we had developed . . .'

Half the jurors say it with him. 'Tunnel vision.'

As he neared the conclusion of his statement, Church walked over to the defense table for a final gulp from his mug, then returned to the rail. 'You may have noticed that I refer to juries past and present as "my juries". There's good reason for that. Although I don't claim to know the prosecutor's motive in choosing you twelve, I *do* know my own, and I'm going to share it with you. I chose *you* to judge my client because I believed *you* when you told me that you would presume my client innocent unless and until the prosecution proved their case beyond a reasonable doubt. And I am holding you to that promise.

'I'm holding you to your promise not to consider evidence not presented here in this courtroom. I'm holding you to your promise to hold the prosecution to their burden of proof. I'm holding you to your promise not to consider my client's silence an admission of guilt. And I'm holding you to your promise that if, as here, the prosecution fails to prove my client guilty beyond a reasonable doubt, you will vote for an acquittal.

'Prosecutor Lau argued that my client committed this act because he was afraid of the victim abandoning him. Yet from what we learned at trial, this motive applies to Nathan Jakes as much as it does to Ethan, *only more so*. Prosecutor Lau argued that Ethan's knowledge of the pregnancy gave him a reason to kill the victim, but I ask you to think hard about whose motive was stronger. Ethan's? Who in the prosecutor's next breath she will tell you is desperate and broke? Or Nathan's? Who had everything in the world to lose – from his wife and children to his partnership at the firm – if his paternity were to be discovered?

'Ask yourselves, which one of these brothers knows the *law* well enough to think he can get away with something like this? Which one of these brothers has the *sophistication* to attempt to pull this off? But above all, ask yourselves, which brother *has already demonstrated* his willingness to hurt the other over a period of more than six months?

'Nathan Jakes is a *liar*. He lied to Piper, telling her that he was going to leave his wife Cheyenne for her. He concealed the entire affair from the brother he supposedly loved. Then he lied to police about the genesis of their relationship. He lied to Ms Lau on direct. He lied to you, the jury. *Under oath.* What does this tell you about the man's character?

'Sex and money, Prosecutor Lau told us in her closing, are the classic motives. Regardless of what each of us might think about his sex life, Ethan had a clean conscience so far as sex went. Nathan did not. Nathan was cheating on his wife, whom he feared would find out about the relationship, especially in light of Piper's pregnancy. If he was the father, there would be child support. Lots of it. Because Nathan does very well for himself. Ethan, not so much, right? So Nathan, not Ethan, has the *only* monetary motive in this case.' He paused, said, 'Sex and money. I ask you to consider: which brother couldn't care less about either? And which brother is obsessed with both?'

He paced the rail a final time, then stopped and said, 'As you head into deliberations, I would be remiss not to remind you that trials are had to protect the *rights of the accused*, not the state.' He looked each juror in the eye. 'Contrary to what Prosecutor Lau said in her closing statement, the twelve of you are *not* here to see justice done. You are here to protect my client, Ethan Jakes, from a great *injustice* that cannot be undone.'

The case went to the jury at one p.m. Certain we wouldn't have a verdict by five, Church and Brody elected to spend the rest of the day at the Mai Tai Bar at Ala Moana Center.

'Besides,' Church added, 'a fast verdict is usually good news for the prosecution. I don't want to be both present *and* sober for that.'

Ethan and I decided to stick around the courthouse instead. We went downstairs to the lawyers' room, which was mercifully empty today.

'It was you?' Ethan said as soon as we sat. 'You told Church about Nate?'

'I'm sorry. I couldn't take the chance you wouldn't let Church use it. But I had no idea you were involved in . . . it.'

Ethan sighed. 'We destroyed his life and sullied her name, and for what?'

'You did nothing wrong – you were three consenting adults. Society's sexual hang-ups aren't your problem. The wrongdoing was Nate's continuing to see Piper behind your back.'

'With all that out there, even if I'm acquitted, what the hell am I going to be able to do with my life if my music career fails?'

'Porn?'

Ethan smiled. 'Well, I guess that's one way to commit to your art.'

'What's that?' I asked.

'Make sure no other profession would have you.'

We sat, talking like that, for the next ninety minutes.

Then Brody walked in and informed us that the jury had reached a verdict.

'Not good news for me,' Ethan said.

'You don't know that,' I told him. 'The O.J. verdict took only four hours.'

FORTY-TWO

I like happy endings. *Love* them, in fact. There are just so few in real life.

The moment the foreperson finished reading the verdict, Ethan instantly crumpled to the floor, triggering a collective gasp that seemed to suck the courtroom walls inward.

Only then did I remember that night at Breakers when Ethan told me about the cyanide pill.

The chaos in the courtroom lasted several minutes as court officers formed a perimeter around Ethan that kept even the most panicked of us away. I tried like hell to squeeze through but there was no chance; the court officers were simply too large, too strong, too determined not to let us through.

I looked for Church to take control, but spotted him standing alone on the inside of the perimeter with his jaw at his chest, his fingers clutching his hair, his eyes bulging out of his head. Brody, meanwhile, was climbing benches to higher ground to capture the entire spectacle on film.

At the instruction of the judge, the court officers finally permitted one person through. She ran as hard as she could and slid on her knees beside Ethan's still form. Certain Marissa Linden was about to put her lips to Ethan's lips, some sick part of me felt jealous, and another much sicker part tried to keep me from cautioning her that Ethan had a mouthful of cyanide. Nevertheless, I shouted, '*Don't give him mouth to mouth!*' – words which were instantly drowned out by the rabble.

I watched in horror. But instead of placing her lips on Ethan's, Marissa cracked open an ammonia inhalant directly under his nose. A microsecond later, Ethan's eyes shot open and his entire body tensed on the floor.

The collective sigh of relief that followed was not nearly as enthusiastic as the collective gasp at his collapse, and failed to swell the courtroom walls back to size.

I dropped to my knees, tears filling my eyes. I glared at Ethan, willing him to turn his head and look back at me, but he never once did.

After court officers managed to get Ethan to his feet, Judge Hightower swiftly brought the courtroom to order, revoked Ethan's bail, and set a date for sentencing.

Finally, the court officers slapped the handcuffs on Ethan and led him through the door he had passed through wearing a tangerine jumpsuit on the morning of his arraignment.

Less than forty-eight hours after the verdict, Detective Fukumoto received an anonymous tip that led to a search warrant for Nathan Jakes' apartment in Waikiki.

There, police discovered Piper's missing UH clothes, as well as what police now believe to be the murder weapon: a plastic poncho purchased from an ABC Store, presumably the same poncho Piper was seen wearing by Elanor Rigby during her morning jogs.

'Rain or shine,' Elanor had said. 'Rain or shine.' And yet no one from either the prosecution or the defense had thought to check the inventory from Piper's home for the poncho. Terrifyingly enough, it's these little things upon which justice so often hinges. If football is a game of inches, litigation is a game of minutia.

Despite receiving the verdict she wanted, Naomi Lau's theory of the case underwent a drastic transformation following news of Nathan Jakes' arrest for murder and conspiracy to commit murder.

At an afternoon press conference before a substantial number of reporters from both local and national news outlets, Lau explained to the public that The Two Jakes had, in fact, acted in concert to kill Piper Kingsley.

This sordid and tragic story, Lau said for the cameras, ended like it started – with the three of them, the victim and her two lovers. A triangle at war with itself.

FORTY-THREE

'So,' Dr Farrockh says, 'have you discussed things with Brody since we last met?'

'I'm going to tell him tonight. We're having dinner at Duke's to celebrate the completion of the film.'

She glances at her watch, which is annoying enough when you're having drinks with someone, but downright devastating in the middle of a therapy session.

'He doesn't know yet?' she says.

'No, he still thinks we're heading back to the mainland at the end of the month. I wanted to be sure before I told him. We won't need the editing room after this week, but I was able to extend our apartment lease for six months. That should afford us enough time to find a more permanent place on Oahu.'

'Good for you.'

'Yeah, I decided I'm willing to live in paradise with the guy that I love. How brave of me.'

She smiles. 'Has Marissa Linden looked at your film yet?'

'This evening, actually. I'm meeting her at the editing room at six-thirty.'

She glances at her watch again. 'So you're getting married soon?'

'I reserved the nondenominational chapel in Ko Olina for this weekend. That's the other surprise I'm going to unveil tonight.

Brody thinks we're putting it off until we get settled on the mainland.'

'That's wonderful.'

'Yeah, I'm having it filmed – I'm hoping parts will make it onto the director's cut of our movie. Marissa's offered to be my maid of honor, and I'm pretty sure Church will offer to be Brody's best man.'

'Great.'

I can't help myself. 'You never believed this relationship would work, did you?'

She tilts her head to the side. 'I just wanted you to be sure there was going to be room enough in your relationship for your own problems.'

She glances at her watch again. 'Do you mind if we stop a little early today? My daughter has a dance recital in Kailua this evening.'

'Not at all,' I say, wishing she'd told me that in the first place.

'Mind if I walk you to your car?' she asks.

'Not as long as you write me a fresh script for Klonopin. I seem to be burning through my tranqs much faster these days.'

Dr Farrockh's office is located in a cute little plaza with a tropical fountain at its center. A setting that's extremely tranquil, and one of the reasons I drive all the way out to east Oahu to see my psychiatrist.

When we reach the parking lot, I catch the scent of the steakhouse to our left and am suddenly starving. But I'm meeting Marissa at the editing room at six-thirty. It's a quarter to six now and I still have one more stop to make. My appetite is going to have to remain on hold until Duke's tonight.

Dr Farrockh halts in front of a late-model forest green Buick LaCrosse.

'I'm right here too,' I tell her, 'parked right next to you.'

Yasmin Farrockh freezes and stares at the Jeep, which I parked somewhat crookedly.

'Everything OK?' I say.

'Yeah, everything's fine. I was just trying to remember if I forgot something back at the office. It can keep until Monday.'

Dr Farrockh gets into her vehicle and starts the engine just as

I put the key in the ignition. Although she's in a hurry, she waits for me to pull away before backing out of her space.

My next stop is on Tantalus Drive to meet with Kalani. He's agreed to help me get interviews with some of the major players, who don't necessarily care much for the defense team. Among the interviewees I'd like for the film are Naomi Lau and Lance Fukumoto. Professor Leary was strongly opposed to interviews, but I feel a few gaps need filling in, especially in light of everything that occurred after the verdict. I'll also do an interview with Kyle Myers, who assures me he's ready for his close-up.

I park across the street from Kalani's home. Before I can get out of the Jeep, Kalani is out of his house and walking toward me.

'Hey, Riley. I'm so sorry, but we're going to have to reschedule, yeah? I just got called down to meet with the station manager to talk about a possible audition at KHNL.'

'Awesome,' I say. 'Yeah, no problem.' My gaze falls on the locked-up fence at the side of Kalani's house. 'You keep gold bars back there or something?'

He steals a glance at it. 'Nah, the night Piper was murdered, after the cops came, someone set off our backyard security light. Dad was at the window, got a pretty good look at the kid – just some scrawny teenage boy with light hair and a red tank-top.'

'Oh,' I say, swallowing hard.

'Dad says he saw someone going back there much earlier in the evening, too, but I don't think the police believed him because Dad's a heavy day drinker. He once reported seeing a chupacabra on Tantalus. Never regained his credibility with police after that.'

I drive downtown, park in our usual garage, and hoof it over to the editing room to meet with Marissa. Although I'm several minutes late, she isn't here, and as unfair as it may be, my mind shoots straight to the day I was supposed to pick her up at the airport.

I try her cell, but my call goes straight to voicemail. I try Church with the same result.

Shit, she forgot.

Worse, maybe she's intentionally standing me up.

The Four Seasons has a viewing room, doesn't it? Do I drive
up to Ko Olina? Traffic should be thinning out now, but it's still
a hell of a hike just to discover she's not there either. I try Brody
to see whether he wants to come with, but his phone, too, goes
straight to voicemail.

I sit in the chair in which I spent so many hours and wait. As
cramped, as smelly, as sweltering as this room is, I know that
I'll miss it the moment I hand back the keys. Nostalgia is peculiar
that way. *Although*, this may well be the room where I edited
my masterpiece. I have already had conversations with a reputable
Hollywood agent who's excited to see the finished product before
we begin shopping it. She's confident the final Two Jakes twist
will be enough to make studios want to take a look, and that the
brilliant execution will make the sale. I can hardly believe we've
reached this point; it feels surreal.

Surprisingly, so many times over the past couple of weeks, I
flashed on the idea of calling my mom to share with her everything that's going on. Only now do I truly feel the permanence
of her absence. I've done a lot of crying recently. No one ever
tells us we'll cry *more* as adults than we did as children – or
that most of that crying will be alone. Unsurprisingly, I think
Professor Leary said it best over fortune cookies: 'Life is nothing
but tears, Riley, with a few smiles snuck in between.'

As tears threaten to well yet again, I chuckle at my earlier
concern that a quarter century of true crime has somehow desensitized me. Hey, *if only*.

I glance at my Cartier watch (I switch between this and my
Swatch) and lean back in my chair, ready to fall asleep. Closing
my eyes, I play parts of the film on the inside of my lids. The
crime scene, the Great Stall, the arraignment, the defense meet-
ings, the Introduction of the Pube, jury selection, trial, sentencing.
Life without parole.

I keep myself from crying this time.

Where the shit is Marissa?

In my head, I play the scenes where Church is at his kindest,
his most vulnerable. I think of the way he wept after Ethan's
sentencing, his thousand-yard stare the following day, Marissa
cautioning us that he couldn't be left alone for the near future.
I think about the night Marissa and he let us in on his illness,

how his bedroom appeared as though a monsoon had hit it. I think of what he said about manic-depressives being dealt worse odds than you get in a game of Russian Roulette – and I suddenly feel sick to my stomach with an uncertain dread.

'*Have you ever . . . tried?*' I asked in that scene on the deck.

'*Just about every night,*' he said.

I push myself out of my chair and lock up. Drop a few dollars to our homeless friend on the return walk to the garage. I try Marissa and Church once again. Then I get in the Jeep and pull onto H-1 heading west toward Ko Olina.

FORTY-FOUR

B y the time I arrive at the Four Seasons, it's full dark, and though I still haven't gotten hold of either Marissa or Church, I'm already overwhelmed with the feeling that I've overreacted. There were times during the investigation when I couldn't get hold of Church for three or four days in a row. Sometimes due to excessive drinking, other times because he'd simply decided to stop answering his phone.

In the elevator, I pull out my key, which is going to be difficult to give up next week, particularly in light of Church's standing invitation for us to crash and order room service any time we'd like.

As I reach the seventeenth floor, I wonder whether I'll ever be in a penthouse suite like this one again. Maybe if Brody and I stay in touch with Church and Marissa. Maybe if our movie's a hit. Maybe if it wins awards. But then, maybe that's not what matters anyhow. Some of my happiest moments were spent in a dank NYU cafeteria, away from everyone else, eating Chinese food with Professor Leary.

I step off the elevator, stop at the door and knock loud enough to worry the guys in the meth lab up the street. When no one answers, I put the key in the door, cover my eyes with my forearm so that I don't see anything I can't un-see, then turn the lock to enter.

When I open my eyes, I'm immediately shook. The dark suite is a shipwreck, not so unlike Church's bedroom the night we learned about his illness. Some furniture is turned over, the floor peppered with broken glass. All the windows are covered, allowing in only slivers of moonlight. I turn and hit the light switch – once, twice – but nothing happens.

Then I see blood, slick and ink-black in the darkness. Bile instantly rises in my throat.

With my eyes, I follow the narrow trail of blood to a blind spot behind the sectional. Slowly, I step alongside it, a growing unease in my chest.

When I finally peer around the sectional, I find Marissa Linden facedown on the floor.

Without thinking, I rush to her side. Gently but firmly turn her body over. She's breathing, she's alive. She has two black eyes, probably a broken nose, and there's blood dripping steadily from her lips. *Fresh* blood.

Oh my god, he's still here.

As quietly as possible, I rise to my feet and say softly, 'Sheena, call Jesse.'

When I hear the bedroom door open behind me, I freeze and wait for Church's voice.

'Rye?'

But when I turn, my eyes instantly lock on Brody's.

'What the shit's going on?' I say. 'Why the *fuck* are you dressed like that?'

He's wearing a Tyvek white paper body suit, nitrile gloves, hospital moccasins, a hair net. There's blood on the suit, blood on his gloves.

He pulls down his surgical mask, streaking that with blood as well. His bottom lip is trembling as though he could break into a cry at any second. 'You have to understand, Rye,' he says, trying to steady his voice, 'that I did all this for you.'

'Where's Church?' I shout.

'In the bedroom. Sleeping it off.'

'Sleeping *what* off?'

'The Klonopin.'

My Klonopin.

'Brody, you're scaring me. What did you do to Marissa?'

'Nothing,' he says, with a slight tremor in his voice. 'Church did it.' He spreads his arms out. 'Don't you see, Rye. It's the perfect story. Sixteen years ago, Marissa obliterated his prosecutorial career. He's been a mental and emotional wreck ever since. Today he finally snaps and kills her. And we're here to cover the trial. We don't have to leave paradise. We don't have to leave *home*.'

Only now do I fully grasp everything's he's done and why.

'Piper,' I manage to spit out.

'Rye, all that time you thought I was wasting at the beach and in bars, all that time you thought I was *slacking* during preproduction, I was actually prepping things for our movie. I was setting it all up. It's like Leary always said: spontaneity requires forethought, right? And I put *a lot* of forethought into this, Rye. I chose the best story for us, the best story for our film.'

'What the hell are you talking about?' I squeak.

'At first, it was going to be Yasmin Farrockh. I even followed her for a couple of weeks, internalized her routine—'

'That's why she recognized my Jeep today,' I say, in a voice little more than a whisper.

'*Our* Jeep, Rye, OK?' There's anger in his voice now. 'I think I deserve at least that.' Slowly he moves between me and the door. 'I almost chose the shrink, *wanted* to. I knew she was planting ideas in your head, pushing you to get rid of me. I knew our lives would be better with her gone. But no, instead I chose the best *story*.'

'Story?'

'The psychiatrist had just turned forty. A woman murdered at thirty-nine, *maybe* a story. At forty, not even close, even as attractive as Yasmin is. Plus, she's Iranian, dark-skinned. It would've presented serious problems for any studio hoping to market it in flyover country.'

'But why *anyone*, Brod—'

'*Why?* Rye, don't you *get it*? You can *sense* when someone's falling out of love with you. Those first three weeks in Hawaii were the best of my life. But I *saw* you getting restless. You were still upset over Leary, the move out here cost more than we'd expected. I knew I could lose *everything* in a blink.'

'What made you think that—'

He holds up a hand. 'Don't, Rye, just don't. I'm sorry but once I started suspecting something was up, I started reading your emails.' A lump forms in his throat. 'And I was right. You *were* unhappy, you felt isolated. The money wasn't going to last us. You still loved me, I realize that, but you also thought you needed to go back to the mainland – don't deny it. I *knew* you'd go, with or without me. And I couldn't fucking go back.'

'We could have *talked.*'

'I couldn't risk *losing* you, Rye. I couldn't risk that talk devolving into a fight and driving you away from me for good. *You* make real life seem like there's something to look forward to. Like there's a future on the other side of university walls.

'I was terrified of losing you, Rye, of losing this life. Then one night while we were watching the evening news, it comes to me – a way to save my life in paradise *and* make your dreams come true. The weathergirl. She'd make a dynamite hook for our film. So I start watching her, like I did the shrink.

'But she didn't have many players in her life. Her only constants were her co-workers. And out of them, her only real friend was Kyle Myers. To be honest, I started losing interest in the film. But then I began watching *Ethan* too. I followed him one afternoon to Kakaako Beach Park, where he made a hand-to-hand, and that put my mind into motion again. I started seeing how events could come together. I started to see our film.

'Then, just as I'm about to wrap surveillance, something wildly interesting occurs. Ethan leaves for a gig, and not ten minutes later, a white Beamer crawls up the mountain and pulls into Piper's garage. Stays for over an hour. When I run the plate through Net Detective the next day, I'm sure I made some mistake, but no. It's Ethan's own fucking *brother's* car.

'So I watch Ethan's heroin dealer, Guy, for a few days, and find out how people find him. Make an anonymous nine-one-one call, and cops discover enough H in his pad to put Guy away till he turns gray. Maybe till he turns dead.'

As Brody speaks, his excitement builds. 'Piper downloads a GIF from a spoofed email address and – *voila* – full remote access and control of her computer to place my own ad on Craigslist. I stay ready for a couple of days, then sure enough, Ethan emails looking to score.'

He snaps his fingers. 'I'd already timed the walk to the top, sliced the pay phone wire, and snatched a pair of Budweiser bottles from Piper's recycling bin. I'd followed Nate. Knew there was one night a week when he drives aimlessly, stops at random beaches, and sits for an hour or two before heading home. With neither brother having an alibi, I *knew* it'd make an incredible whodunit, Rye.'

I'm trembling all over, chicken skin climbing up my arms and legs. 'You're sick, Brody.'

'Rye, don't say that. *Please* don't say that.'

'Who *are* you, Brody? You *deplored* violence.'

'I still do, Rye. But *you*, you *love* it. And I love you.' Before I can object, he says, 'Don't tell me you're not desensitized, Rye. I was there when you learned Piper was pregnant. That pregnancy tore me up inside, but it didn't even stir you.'

'Maybe because I wasn't suffering the guilt of fucking having *killed* her.'

'Do you think any of this was easy for me, Rye? It *wasn't*. But our money was running out.'

The words are out of my mouth before I think them. '*My* money.'

'*Cut the shit*, Rye.' His shout echoes through the suite. 'I deserved that money every bit as much as you did.'

'How can you say that?'

He sighs heavily as though he has a decision to make.

Finally, he says, 'Because George Leary might have lived another ten or twenty years if not for me.'

The silence in the room grows thick enough to smother me. I think I'm about to faint.

His tone softens. 'He didn't suffer, Rye, I promise. I placed a pillow over his face in his sleep.' He steps toward me as if to comfort me. 'I'm sorry. But you were spending so much goddamn *time* with him. Then you started talking about staying in New York, so that Leary could help with the film. I couldn't stay, Rye. I *couldn't*, you know that.'

Tears stream freely down my cheeks. My voice shakes. 'Two people are dead, and two men are in prison for what you did.'

'I had an *out* for Ethan. I was going to prevent him from being convicted at the last minute and make Church into a fucking superhero. That's why I left the shoeprint in the yard. I'd planned to give the shoes and Piper's poncho and clothes to Roy down the street from our apartment.'

'You were going to frame the *homeless* guy! The one you made friends with? The one you brought up to our apartment to shower?'

'I put him on a bus that day so he'd be seen in the area. For *you*, Rye. I did it for you, for *us*.' He clutches the back of his neck, the way he does when he's stressed. 'But then you . . .'

'I *what*?'

'You *fell* for him. Even after Breakers, I was willing to let him off the hook. But then you meet him in our editing room, fucked him on Waikiki Beach . . . Why the hell would I then do him the favor of *getting him off*?'

'But George Leary? Piper? How *could* you?'

He hesitates, the anger over Ethan falling away from his face, replaced by a look of worried confusion. Then, in little more than a whisper, he says, 'I looked at them and saw her, Rye. I looked at them and saw my mother.'

He steps toward me, clearing tears from his eyes, his tone suddenly sharp and efficient. 'Let me finish Marissa and stage the scene, all right? Then we'll get out of here, you and me. No one will check on them till room service tomorrow morning, right around the time Nick Church will be waking from his Klonopin nap.'

I don't know what to do. Now that I know what he's capable of, I'm petrified. I can't play along until we get outside, because it'll be too late for Marissa. I can't believe how much I want to save her fucking life right now.

Surreptitiously, I scan the room for something, anything, I can use as a weapon. But it's dark and my head is swimming, and I feel like I'm going to throw up.

Finally, I spot what I need. And it's within grabbing distance.

'Do what you have to do,' I tell him in as firm a voice as I can muster.

He studies my facial expression, as he's done so many times before. I soften my features, tilt my head, part my lips, look him warmly in the eyes.

'It's brilliant,' I say, fully committing myself to the role and taking a step toward him. 'How can I fault you for this, Brody? How? You're giving me everything I ever wanted.'

He nods his head, a new hope visible in his eyes. He sniffles, exhales in relief, then wipes his nose with the side of his arm. A look of excitement slowly spreads across his face.

'This one's going to be even bloodier, baby, even sexier.'

Oh no. Heart pounding, I'm suddenly drenched in sweat. My hands are trembling. I'm lightheaded, short of breath. I push back a threatening nausea and steady myself. Tell my body over and over again: *Not now. Not now. Not now.*

'Stand back,' he says, covering his mouth with the mask. 'You don't want to get any of this on you.'

He pulls a large kitchen knife from his body suit and moves deliberately toward Marissa. As soon as he steps past me, I go for the seventies speaker box in the middle of the dining room table. I heft it over my head and with both hands bring it down on the back of Brody's skull with every ounce of strength that I have. We both go crashing to the floor.

The knife skids in one direction.

In the other, a gun I've never seen before.

We both go for the latter, only I don't get to it in time.

Rising to his feet, he holds the gun on me.

I think it's a .38, but it's too dark to be certain.

With his free hand, he rubs the back of his head, flinches, then stares at his palm, which is now crimson. In the darkness, tar-black.

'How could you hurt me, Rye?' he asks with genuine sincerity. 'How could you hurt someone you promised to unconditionally love? How could you aban—'

Suddenly, sirens sound in the distance.

Startled, Brody stops dead, says, 'Did you . . .?'

I shake my head.

'*I* did.'

Jesse's familiar voice emanates from the seventies speaker box lying broken on the floor at Brody's feet.

Brody stares down at it with a look of amused disbelief.

Sobbing, then, as hard as I've ever seen him sob, he raises the gun, levels it at my head. He says, 'I told you, Rye. If we're not meant to be together, then we're not meant to be.'

I close my eyes, as warm pee dribbles down my inner thighs. I cry silently and wait for the bullet because it's all I can do.

He'll shoot me, I assume, then Marissa and Church. Then he'll shoot himself. His own tidy Shakespearean tragedy. His own *Game of Thrones.*

But instead of diving headfirst into oblivion, I hear Brody's footsteps retreating toward the door.

And when I open my eyes, he's gone.

I think of the gun and wonder.

And listen. To the sirens closing in, to the screaming of brakes in the lot.

It was too dark to see the gun.

Thirty seconds later, I hear four, maybe five rapid shots.

And I think of our conversation about the boy with the air rifle.

In my head, I hear Brody use the ghastly three words: suicide by cop.

EPILOGUE

At the end of Ethan's set, he steps past his dozen or so new groupies and takes the seat I've been saving for him at the bar.

'What did you think?' he says.

'I like the original stuff best.'

'Of course you do.'

The bartender asks him what he's having.

'Another mai tai for her. I'll have a bottled water.'

'Staying off the sauce?' I ask him.

He smiles and goes all Bruce Banner on me. 'Don't make me drink. You wouldn't like me when I drink.'

I like him just fine when he drinks, but I won't say so.

'What's next for you?' he asks.

'Still tinkering with the movie. I'm going to stick around the island until Marissa's up on her feet again.'

'That's sweet of you.'

'Well, she promised me notes on my film, and damned if I'm not going to get them.'

He laughs.

I fucking love his laugh. It's a shame that everything Ethan's been through – the death of a girlfriend, the heinous accusations and legal jeopardy, the betrayal by his brother – has propelled him straight out of my league.

'Did you and Nate bury the hatchet?' I ask.

'I don't know about that, but we did speak. He finally told me the story behind his elopement to Vegas. Nate had gotten a call from some two-bit lawyer out there, who said he needed money for our father's defense. Our dad had gotten in with the wrong crowd – well, *his* crowd, I guess – and got pinched trying to pull off a smash-and-grab at a pawnshop. Nate knew I wanted nothing to do with our dad, which is why he didn't tell me. He and Cheyenne tried to make the trip a positive by getting hitched.'

'You knew about Zane Kingsley's criminal past too, didn't you?'

He bows his head. 'It was one of the many connections I felt to Piper – we both had shit dads.' He grins mirthlessly. 'Probably one of Nate's connections to her too.' He shrugs it off. 'Anyway, around the time I met her, Piper found out her dad had returned to that life, and she immediately wrote him off for good.'

I'm about to scrounge up another inane question when Ethan abruptly turns to another female demanding his attention.

Yeah, so, like, I'm single now. Back amongst the pit-sniffers of the world.

Did I forget deodorant tonight?

As inconspicuously as possible, I sniff my pits one at a time – a move that one underwear company publicly designated a 'smelfie'. Thanks for calling attention, guys! What's next? Shoes that emit tiny pastel stink lines whenever you have foot odor?

Another mai tai lands in front of me, and I go for the straw with my lips. Which means I'm at the 'Hey! Look ma, no hands' stage of drunkenness. Good to know.

My iPhone buzzes in my back pocket. I excuse myself (though unnecessarily) and head outside.

'Where are you?' Kyle Myers says with a seriousness that's rare for him.

'Lulu's, watching Ethan play. Why don't you come down for a drink?'

'I'm at the station.'

My stomach drops. 'The police station?'

'No, the television station.'

'What the shit for?'

'Remember Piper's diary? The one I told you about but the police never found?'

'Yeah.'

'Well, I *found* it.'

'What? *Where?*'

'Remember the station manager I told you about? Hefty guy, losing his hair?'

'Principal Belding.'

'Well, Glen Belding, but close enough. Piper's diary was in *his* desk. I accidentally found it while fishing for a cheat sheet to give my weekend replacement. The pervert must have snatched it as soon as he heard about Piper's death.'

'Tell me you haven't gone through it,' I say.

Eight, nine, maybe ten seconds pass in silence.

'I could *tell* you I haven't gone through it.'

As I take it all in, Ethan comes up behind me and kisses my head. Like you might a poodle before leaving to buy groceries at Safeway.

'About to start the next set,' he says. 'Coming?'

Not tonight, I'm not.

'Sorry,' I tell Ethan, 'I've got to run. But call me sometime.' I make the universal phone signal with my thumb and pinky, even though I'm holding a *real* phone in the other hand.

Fortunately, Ethan thinks it's a shaka and throws one back at me. 'I will, Riley. I will definitely call you.'

I turn swiftly and start up the street.

'You there?' I say into my phone. 'I need to see it.'

'Hire an Uber. I'll meet you here at the station. The *television* station, not police headquarters.'

Three days later I'm in the cafeteria at the Pali Momi Medical Center in Aiea. Church sits across from me, nothing in front of him but a tall can of Monster Energy Drink, which he no longer needs to conceal in a mug. I, on the other hand, have a plateful of roast pork with snow peas. Church appears offended by what I'm eating, by what everyone in the cafeteria is eating. He also looks as though he hasn't slept since he woke from the dozen Klonopin with which Brody spiked his bourbon.

'How is she?' I ask.

'Stable, with a fair prognosis.'

At the hands of Brody Quinlan, Marissa Linden suffered a skull fracture, a broken nose, three cracked ribs, and various internal injuries which Church refused to enumerate for me when I first met him at the hospital following the incident.

'For what it's worth,' I say, 'Piper had intended to stay in Hawaii to raise the child with Ethan. She planned on breaking things off with Nate when she met him on the day she was killed. Instead they wound up in bed together.' I shrug. 'Been there. It does happen.'

'She was going to ditch Nate even before she knew for certain who the father was?'

I nod. 'Ethan didn't know about Nate, and Piper never planned on telling him. She figured Nate had his own reasons to remain silent.' I shovel a spoonful of peas into my mouth. 'Anyway, after all the lies Nate told her, she didn't trust him anymore. In the end, she realized the good brother was the broke musician, not the wealthy scumbag attorney.'

He raises an eyebrow. 'Whose idea was the threesome?'

'According to Piper's diary, Captain Morgan is to blame for that. Piper wrote that it was understood by all parties to be a one-time thing, but after that night, Nate continued pursuing her. She initially resisted, but then Nate convinced her to go out for coffee. One thing led to another . . . You know the rest.'

'Who did she love?' Church asks.

'For a half-year, she genuinely loved them both.'

He nods. It's maybe the first thing about this case that makes perfect sense.

'So you read the whole thing?' he says.

'Every page.'

'You're just the worst kind of person.'

'I know.'

Although I realize that it was an unforgivable invasion of her privacy, I don't regret reading Piper's diary. Those pages filled in so much of the background of the one player I knew so little about. Turns out, for instance, Piper did not sleep with Glen Belding to get her job at the station. In fact, much of the prose in her diary was devoted to making a record of Belding's sexual harassment over the years. Whether Belding stole the diary because he feared what was inside it, or – as Kyle insists – for some sort of creepy sexual gratification, we'll never know. But Kyle *did* anonymously send copies of the relevant pages to Belding's higher-ups – and, yes, got the big, bald perv shit-canned from the station. Hashtag MeToo.

Church leans back and sighs deeply.

I say, 'How are you holding up?'

He tries a smile but it doesn't fit.

I say, 'Please don't tell me you intend to quit the law.'

He shakes his head. 'Nah, what else would I do with myself?

I'm too fucking crazy for any other profession. Just the right amount of crazy for this one. I'm not leaving the law until I die, or some ethics committee kicks me out of it. Whichever comes last. Because fuck them.'

I grin. 'So you're going to wait for that next "big case"?'

Church scans the cafeteria, says quietly, 'Truth is, Riles, I only handle one major case at a time because, emotionally, it's all I *can* handle.'

I smile, say, 'Maybe it's for the best. Because I can only film one documentary at a time.'

I've decided to play the audio of Brody's confession (as recorded by Jesse) over the footage captured by a handful of tourists and a pair of police body cams outside the Four Seasons. It's so damn difficult to watch; there are moments when I just want to scrap the whole project. Maybe film a documentary about Hawaii's endangered wildlife (like the monk seals) or modern-day Pearl Harbor.

Funny, early in post, I thought referring to Piper as the 'weathergirl' would help distance me from my friend's murder. Although I may not have realized it at the time, I wanted her, *needed* her, to be only a player. Maybe my two and a half decades of watching true crime granted me the ability to do that for as long as I needed to complete this film. But what's clear from the tears I shed over the past several days – over Brody, over Ethan, over Piper – is that true crime hasn't completely desensitized me. Not in the way a surgeon becomes accustomed to blood, or a cop to corpses. Like Church and his 'crazy', true crime has fucked me up just enough to allow me to do my job. I finally *feel* like a documentarian.

Since this film is about Piper more than anyone else, about the life cut short and the selfish, despicable reasons for it – and since Piper always loved the title and who am I to argue? – my movie is now called *The Weathergirl*.

'How *sexy* is that job title,' Piper once said over tequila shots. 'And in the end, no matter what else we do on this earth, don't we all just really want to be remembered as sexy? If that's possible, of course; if not, you find something else.' She laughed at that, fired back another shot, then added somberly, 'Maybe that's why so many beautiful people in this world die young.'

'By the way,' Church says, 'I was very sorry to hear about your professor.'

Smothering leaves no marks on its victim unless the victim puts up a struggle. Which is the real reason Brody killed Professor Leary in his sleep, not out of compassion. Because of the professor's age and the fact that there were no external bruises or other signs of a struggle, there was no autopsy. But now that there's a confession, there's no question: Professor Leary was killed by a coward while he slept.

But I'm not going to let this past year make me jaded. At least not any more jaded than I already am. And I'm not going to veer from the damaged and vulnerable of this world. Because it's so often not their fault – and because they need us the most.

'You OK?' Church asks me.

'Yeah, I was just thinking of how this all came to be so bizarre, and how that will affect viewership and/or ticket sales.'

He purses his lips. 'I suppose the more bizarre the world becomes, the more bizarre our stories should be.'

'But will people watch?'

'People will watch,' he says with his usual confidence.

'I like when people watch.'